DARKNESS AT DAWN

By the same author

Perestroika Christi

DARKNESS AT DAWN

John Hands

HarperCollins*Publishers*

HarperCollins*Publishers*
77–85 Fulham Palace Road,
Hammersmith, London W6 8JB

Published by HarperCollins*Publishers* 1993

1 3 5 7 9 8 6 4 2

A catalogue record for this book is
available from the British Library

ISBN 0 00 223958 2

Set in Linotron Futura and Sabon

Printed in Great Britain by
HarperCollinsManufacturing Glasgow

For Eddie Bell

ACKNOWLEDGEMENTS

I wish to thank the following, listed by location, who helped in the preparation of this novel.

Moscow
Sir Rodric Braithwaite KCMG, then British Ambassador in Moscow, and Lady Braithwaite; Geoffrey Murrell, Minister/Counsellor at the British Embassy; Dr Andrei Kokoshin, Deputy Director of the US-Canada Institute; Colonel Vitaly Shlykov, Deputy Chairman of the Russian State Committee on Defence; two serving officers of the successor organization of the KGB who gave their names as Lieutenant Colonel Andrianov and Major Alexandrov; two serving officers of the GRU (the military intelligence service) who gave their names as Koval and Petrov; Ilya Danilov of ASEET; and John Kampfner, Moscow correspondent of the *Daily Telegraph*.

Kiev
Colonel Mikhail Vertushkov, Lieutenant Colonel Yuri Galimonov, and Captain Alexander Krylov of the Kiev Military District; the commander of an offensive regiment (the first Soviet regiment into Afghanistan), the name of which is classified; a serving major of the Strategic Rocket Forces who wished to give no name; Major General Valkyv of the Ukrainian National Guard; the staff and troops of the Vyshgorod Training Centre; Lieutenant Colonel Valery Zakharovich Olynyk of the Ukrainian National Security Service (successor of the Ukrainian KGB); Lieutenant General Vasyl Durdynets, Chairman of the Parliamentary Commission on Defence; Stepan Khmara and Serhei Kolisynk,

members of the Ukrainian Parliament; Ivan Drach, President of Rukh; Volodymyr Muljava, head of the Rukh Coordinating Committee, Deputy Chairman of the Union of Ukrainian Officers, and adviser to the Ukrainian Ministry of Defence; Bohdana Kostiuk of the External Affairs Division of Rukh; Anatoli Rusnachenko, Secretary of the Rukh Collegium; Dmytro Korchynsky, member of the Republican Headquarters of the Ukrainian People's Self-Defence Force, and Viktor Melnyk, head of the Executive Committee of the Ukrainian Nationalistic Union; Susan Viets, Ukrainian correspondent for the *Independent*; Chrystia Freeland, Ukrainian correspondent for the *Financial Times*; John and Carol Cockburn, then of Ernst & Young; Vladimir Bogoslovsky, Leonora Chrystiakova, and Valeria Bogoslovskaya.

USA

Bruce G. Blair, Senior Fellow in Foreign Policy Studies at the Brookings Institute in Washington DC, adviser to the US Congress on Soviet nuclear missiles, and a former Minuteman missile launch officer of the US Strategic Air Command.

UK

Professor John Erickson, Centre for Defence Studies, University of Edinburgh; Elaine Holoboff, Centre for Defence Studies, King's College, University of London; Ustina Markus, London School of Economics; Christopher Bluth, Department of Government, University of Essex; Philip Mitchell and Ken Petrie of the International Institute for Strategic Studies; Dr Alasdair Dow, Senior Registrar in Anaesthetics, Bristol, and formerly Attending Anaesthesiologist, Baltimore Shock Trauma Center, Baltimore, Maryland, USA; Professor Rab Mollan, Professor of Orthopaedic Surgery, Queen's University, Belfast; Bill McGookin, Royal Ulster Constabulary; Godfrey Hodgson, Foreign Editor, Steve Crawshaw, East European Editor, and the foreign desk of the *Independent*; Bohdan Ciapryna and Stephen Oleskiw of the Ukrainian Information Service; and Peter Shutak and Taras Kuzio of the Ukrainian Press Agency.

I'm most grateful to Sir Rodric Braithwaite, Paddy Hands, Tony Millan, Peter Millar, and Antony Wood who commented on drafts, and I particularly appreciate the skill, support, and commitment of my editor, Nick Sayers, and all the team at HarperCollins – editorial, design, production, rights, marketing, and sales – who are proving that big doesn't have to be impersonal or inefficient.

Sole responsibility for use of any information supplied and any inaccuracies therein rests with me.

John Hands
London

Note: Ukrainian place names have been used where these have now come into common use. Most Russians (and that includes Russian characters in the novel), however, still refer to the Russian names that were used officially when Ukraine was part of the Soviet Union, eg. Kharkov for Kharkiv, Lvov for Lviv.

ABBREVIATIONS

GRU — *Glavnoye Razvedyvatelnoye Upravleniye*, Chief Intelligence Directorate (of the Armed Forces General Staff)

IRA — Irish Republican Army

KGB — *Komitet Gosudarstvennoy Bezopasnosti*, Committee for State Security

NKVD — *Narodnyi Kommissariat Vnutrennikh Del*, People's Commissariat for Internal Affairs (a predecessor of the KGB)

NSB — *Natsionalna Sluzhba Bespeky*, National Security Service (of Ukraine)

OMON — *Otryady Militsii Osobogo Naznacheniya*, Special Purpose Militia Detachment (OMON was formed in 1987, largely from soldiers who had served in Afghanistan, with the ostensible purpose of controlling urban riots. In theory OMON troops, known as the 'Black Berets', were responsible to the Interior Ministry in Moscow; in practice they worked closely with the KGB)

OUN — *Organizatsia Ukrainskykh Natsionalstiv*, Organization of Ukrainian Nationalists

RUC	Royal Ulster Constabulary
Rukh	Popular Movement (initially for perestroika, then for independence), in Ukraine
UPA	*Ukrainska Povstanska Armia*, Ukrainian Insurgent Army

One can only be crucified in the name of one's own faith

ARTHUR KOESTLER, *Darkness at Noon*

MAP OF UKRAINE AND WESTERN RUSSIA
Moscow
Gulf of Finland
Baltic Sea
ESTONIA
LATVIA
LITHUANIA
Moscow
Tula
POLAND
BELARUS
RUSSIA
SLOVAKIA
VOLHYNIA
Chernobyl
Kiev
Dnieper
Lviv
Khmelnitsky
Derezhnya Missile Field
Kharkiv
KHARKIV
GALICIA
TRANSCARPATHIA
UKRAINE
Bug
Kirovograd
Dnepropetrovsk
DNIEPER
DONBAS
Donetsk
Pervomaysk
Missile Field
MOLDOVA
HUNGARY
Odessa
Sea of
Azov
ROMANIA
CRIMEA
0
150 Miles
0
100
200 kms
Black Sea

ONE

Bone-chilling cloud seeped down into the snow blanketing the flat countryside and almost extinguished the dawn. Through this mist glimmered the headlights of a small red car probing its way along a treacherous road.

The passenger shifted his position. Civilian clothes sat uncomfortably on General Marchenkov's large frame. His chauffeur, Warrant Officer Boldin, also wore a parka and casual trousers, and was driving his own Zaporozhets instead of the General's Volga. This subterfuge, and the secret meeting at a dacha forty kilometres from the Ukrainian capital of Kiev, increased Marchenkov's anxiety.

His physical courage he had proved in Afghanistan. For this the Army had awarded him the Order of Lenin. His father had been proud of him then, as proud, he said, as when Stalin pinned the identical medal to his uniform after he had helped liberate Kiev from the fascists in 1943. Marchenkov knew what Papa would think of him now. Perestroika had been bad enough for the old man; the disintegration of the Soviet Union, whose socialist values he had spent his life defending, had turned his bewilderment into bitterness; but what his son was about to do, Papa would see as the ultimate betrayal.

The car stopped at a crossroads. Earthen ramparts loomed ghostly in the mist: the eleventh-century fortifications of Belogorod, place of exile from the court of Kievan Rus, when Ukraine and Russia were one. 'It's the road to Luka,' Boldin said. Marchenkov nodded. They drove across a bridge. Below, the River Irpen was frozen into silence.

Luka village, a scattering of corrugated-iron-roofed cottages, materialized and vanished. Boldin took the next turning on the left. The windbreak of trees that had guided them from Belogorod was no more; only an occasional poplar loomed suddenly from the verge of this lonely road.

Marchenkov had disobeyed orders once before, back in 1991 when he had refused to send his troops onto the streets in support of the attempted coup. At the time he, like others, had simply done nothing. It was a much greater step to take the initiative. Now he must banish self-doubt and nearly thirty years of Soviet Army discipline if his moral courage were to match his physical courage.

'What shall I do, sir?' Boldin had stopped the car. A figure was approaching. Beyond, in the swirling shroud, stood a white Moskvich saloon with its boot lid raised. Marchenkov was late and he didn't want to be identified, but he could hardly leave the poor devil stranded in these conditions. 'Offer him a lift to the next village, but say nothing else.'

Boldin lowered his window. The man, who was wearing a black woollen hat, leaned down and spoke through the scarf wrapped round the lower part of his face. 'My battery's flat. Do you have a jump lead?'

Boldin looked to Marchenkov. The General nodded. Boldin got out and the man followed him to the rear of the car.

Both passenger doors of the Moskvich opened. Both passengers wore combat fatigues and black balaclavas that covered all except eyes and mouth. One reached into the opened boot and pulled out a rifle.

Marchenkov twisted round to try and find Boldin, who carried a regulation-issue Makarov semiautomatic pistol. The squat, tough driver-cum-bodyguard reappeared, both arms raised, followed by Woollen Hat who was pointing a hand gun at his back.

One of the men in combat fatigues aimed his rifle through the driver's opened window. 'Out!' he shouted in Ukrainian.

Marchenkov climbed out. While the rifleman kept him covered, the other masked man pushed Marchenkov's chest against the side of the Zaporozhets and forced his arms across the roof. He kicked Marchenkov's legs apart and frisked him. 'Stay like that,' said Woollen Hat, who seemed to be in charge. 'Now the other one.' The man shoved Boldin next to Marchenkov, removed Boldin's Makarov, and stuck it in his belt.

The way they held their guns told Marchenkov that these men were professionals. He decided to try a reasonable approach. 'What do you want?' he asked in Ukrainian.

'Just do as you're told, General.'

General! They knew who he was. He turned his head to face Woollen Hat. 'I demand to know whom you represent.'

Woollen Hat laughed. 'Is that right? We stopped taking orders from the likes of you long ago.' He waved his hand gun towards the Moskvich. 'Get in the boot.'

'If it's money you want . . .'

Woollen Hat sauntered up to Boldin, turned him round, and pointed his gun at Boldin's forehead. 'Get in the boot or I shoot him.'

Boldin's eyes opened wide in alarm – or was it surprise? He began to speak, but the click of the gun being cocked silenced him.

It was vital that General Marchenkov kept his appointment with Roman Bondar. 'There's some mistake . . .'

'There's no mistake.'

The Ukrainian pressed the nozzle of his gun against the middle of Boldin's forehead, just above the line of the eyebrows. He nodded towards the boot of the Moskvich.

Marchenkov didn't move.

Boldin's head rocked back to the crack of the gun. When it rebounded a jet of blood squirted out from a small round hole above open fluttering eyes.

With the back of his sleeve the terrorist leader wiped away the blood that had splashed onto his cheek.

Boldin's knees crumpled. He slid down the driver's door of the Zaporozhets. One hand jerked out to try and grab the wing mirror for support. Narrow jets of blood pumped out rhythmically from his forehead, carving jagged lines of bright scarlet in the snow.

He slithered down to a sitting position, back against the car, legs splayed out in front of him. A final half-hearted squirt fell onto his chest, and then the hole just trickled blood. His body keeled over. The blood staining the snow that pillowed his face was darker than the frozen jagged lines.

'Now will you get in the boot?' the terrorist leader said.

'I spit on your grave.'

The rifleman slowly advanced towards him, pointing his rifle at Marchenkov's chest. The barrel was almost touching him when the rifleman, with well-practised speed, pulled the barrel back and swung the rifle round to smash the stock against Marchenkov's temple.

When Marchenkov struggled back to consciousness he found himself gagged and trussed and squashed into a car boot. The lid was open. He saw the midriff of one of the terrorists, heard laughter and then a voice. 'I wouldn't be in his shoes for all the Kremlin gold.' The boot lid slammed down, plunging him into darkness.

TWO

Strident ringing cut through the darkness. Taras Stepaniak groaned.

The ringing stopped and a light blazed. Stepaniak burrowed under the duvet and found the soft warmth of her thigh. He nuzzled to within scent of his musky target before his hair was grabbed and his head pulled back. Her voice was gentle but businesslike. 'Time to get up, Taras.'

He shook his head free. She was sitting up in bed, the black silk duvet cover round her waist, naked but demure. He stretched like a cat. Not just an Englishwoman for him, but a blonde English rose, with full breasts, class, and a luxurious house in London's fashionable Holland Park. He'd settle for the lifestyle.

'Out,' she insisted. 'Henry's plane will have landed at Heathrow by now. I need to change the bedclothes before he arrives.'

An English rose, he sighed, but a practical one. 'Where's he been?'

She smoothed down his thick black hair. 'Kiev. Again.'

'Tell him to stay a few days next time, or better still, a few weeks.'

'Not a chance. Trying to do business there drives him round the bend.'

'That's the fault of the communists.'

'Henry says it's only the former communists who know how to get things done.'

'That's the fault of the Russians.'

Her breasts quivered as she laughed. 'You're all the same. Henry says Ukrainians are all talk and no action.'

'Is that right?' Stepaniak slithered back under the duvet. She pressed her knees together and pulled them up to her chin. 'Out! I said.'

His head emerged from underneath the duvet. He pulled a face and rolled onto his back. He stared up at the crystal chandelier hanging below an elaborate moulding; this was the first bedroom he'd slept in that was lit by a chandelier. At the age of thirty-five, Stepaniak felt he was entering the prime of life. If his years in the West had added a few pounds to the taut, muscular body of his youth, they had also softened his chiselled Slav features into a slightly worn vulnerability that women found appealing. They had also taught him the techniques of making a woman laugh and making her feel important.

He turned his head towards her. 'If you were Henry, would you advise the bank to invest there?'

'But I'm not Henry.'

He leaned up and licked her right nipple. 'I can taste the difference.'

She giggled.

'Will he?'

'Will he what?'

'Advise the bank to invest in Ukraine?'

She shrugged. 'Henry thinks there's a lot of potential in agribusiness, and also in unexploited mineral reserves in eastern Ukraine, but before the bank puts in big money it wants to be assured about long-term stability in the region.' She traced a finger down his nose to his lips. 'What Henry thinks is always terribly boring.'

'I've a cure for boredom.'

'Taras, I'm serious. Out.'

He rolled out of bed and crawled on the floor, searching for his clothes. Was it just escape from boredom, or did the excitement of betrayal turn her on? He found his paisley boxer shorts and climbed into them. 'Do you ever feel guilty about deceiving Henry?'

'No. What the eye doesn't see, the heart doesn't grieve for.'

'Why do you do it?'

It was she who now stretched languidly. 'Because,' she said, 'you're bloody good in bed.'

He stopped in the act of pulling on his jeans, leaned across the bed, and kissed her ear lobe. 'Don't tell me,' he whispered, 'tell your friends.'

'Bastard!'

He pulled back to dodge the pillow, tripped over the jeans around his knees, and fell onto the large flokati rug.

She grabbed a second pillow and raised it above her head ready to strike.

'When you're naked and angry you excite me,' he said and looked down at his shorts.

She sank back onto the bed, helpless with laughter. She reached down and put her hand round his stiffening penis. 'Taras Stepaniak, you're incorrigible. But save him for next time. You really must be out of here *tout de suite*.'

The street lamps were switched off at sunrise, and heavy massing cloud darkened the tree-lined Georgian terrace. Stepaniak pulled up the collar of his black leather blouson against the biting wind. It looked like rain, or even snow. Little point in going back to his flat when the office was so near. He lit a cheroot, took a deep, contented drag, and strolled towards a Holland Park Avenue already blocked with early morning traffic. It looked like poor old Henry was going to be late again.

He left the market debris of Portobello Road, turned into a flaking cream, early Victorian terrace, and stopped. A light shone from the basement halfway along the terrace. Neither he nor his two colleagues ever arrived at the Ukrainian Press Bureau before ten. Four women – early morning office cleaners by the look of them – were walking towards him. When they drew level, Stepaniak threw his cheroot into the gutter and rolled his eyes. 'Excuse me, ladies, I get very nervous walking up this street on my own. May I hide behind your skirts?'

The youngest, a sassy blonde in a miniskirt, looked at the crotch of his tightly fitting jeans. 'You can hide *inside* my skirt, ducky.'

'Sharon!' said the tall one whose hair was hidden by a turbaned scarf. The other two sniggered.

Stepaniak stayed close behind them, so that they blocked sight of him from the house. He kept them giggling with suggestive banter until he reached the house. The gate in the black, wrought iron railing was open. Light escaped from a gap at the top of the curtains covering the basement window.

Stepaniak edged down the stone steps and pressed his ear to the window. Only indistinguishable voices, two, perhaps three. He put his key in the door lock, turned it, and pulled upwards on the door knob to take the weight off the hinges before he pushed the door open. He gently released the knob and left the door ajar. His trainers made no sound on the rubber-tiled corridor.

He listened outside the closed door to the main office. The voices belonged to Evhen, Volodymyr, and the BBC World Service. He relaxed. But what the devil were they doing in at this time? He shaped his right hand like a gun inside his blouson pocket, burst open the door, and yelled, 'Freeze!'

A startled cry came from Volodymyr, whose podgy fingers dropped the radio in fright. 'Christ, Taras, you nearly scared the life out of me.'

Stepaniak affected an attitude of surprise. 'I'm sorry, Volodymyr! At this time of the morning I assumed you must be the KGB.'

The earnest Evhen was not amused. He put on his plastic-rimmed spectacles to look for the batteries that had burst from the back of the now-silent radio. 'What are you doing here at this time?'

'Did Maria Bondar phone you as well?' Volodymyr asked.

'From Kiev?' Stepaniak asked.

'You don't know?'

'Don't know what?'

'Maria phoned me at home an hour ago,' Evhen said. 'A Russian general's gone missing.'

'Good. Provided he hasn't taken any tanks with him.'

'He's been *kidnapped*,' Volodymyr said.

Stepaniak pondered this information. 'I still think a tank will fetch a better price than a general.'

'Taras, be serious for a change. The general's driver was shot through the head, and his car was daubed in blue and yellow with the initials UPA.'

Stepaniak glanced at the pictures on the office wall, idealized portraits of stern-faced men wearing khaki-green uniforms, commanders of the *Ukrainska Povstanska Armia*, lionized by Ukrainian émigrés as freedom fighters against the occupying Soviet Army and branded by Soviet history books as Nazi collaborators and traitors. 'The Ukrainian Insurgent Army?' said Stepaniak. 'These guys cannot be serious.'

THREE

From the other side of darkness came the muffled sounds of voices. General Marchenkov woke instantly. His spine tingled at the first sign of human contact for . . . for how long? He had no idea how many hours or days he'd been incarcerated in this stale, black hole, feet tied together, hands tied together behind his back, with a short rope binding feet and hands to a hot steel pipe that gurgled incessantly. He was weak from lack of food and drink, his head throbbed from the rifle blow, and his mind had been filling the black void with images more horrifying than any he'd seen on the battlefield. He breathed deeply and slowly to reduce the pounding of his heart.

The scraping of the key in the lock grated his eardrums. A blinding shaft of light shut his eyes. Marchenkov squinted to see a man standing in the brightness of the opened door. He had seen the man only once before, but every detail was etched on his memory, from the domed head, bald on top with thick brown hair at the sides and back, to the Roman nose and cleft chin jutting out from a gaunt face. But what had transfixed the entire audience at a General Staff Academy lecture shortly after the attempted coup of '91 were the man's intense, grey eyes and deep, confident voice. Senior officers, floundering in a sea of suspect loyalties and uncertain futures, seized on every word as he scorned the plotters while affirming the heroic tradition of the Army as the invincible shield of the Motherland. At the end all the officers, many of whom were his superiors in rank, jumped to their feet and applauded for more than ten minutes.

The light was switched on, a small bulb hanging lopsidedly from flex. The low room was shabby and dusty and cluttered with noisy steel pipes joined by stopcocks. The man, dressed in a dark blue, padded ski jacket and black trousers, was followed by half a dozen people. Marchenkov recognized the three who had captured him. How many more Russian officers had these terrorists kidnapped?

'Colonel Krasin, have the bastards harmed you?' Marchenkov shouted hoarsely.

Krasin said nothing. The two armed men in battle fatigues dragged a rickety wooden table from the end of the room and positioned it underneath the light bulb. Woollen Hat arranged three chairs on one long side of the table and a fourth at a short side. Krasin's grim face tensed into a smile that bared a row of perfect, white teeth. 'Why should they harm me?' The other men in civilian clothes waited until Krasin took the centre chair before they sat down.

Marchenkov's numbed mind tried to take it all in. 'You? You've defected to this Ukrainian terrorist group?'

'On the contrary,' said Krasin, 'it is you who stand accused before this tribunal of betraying Russia.'

One of the guards put down his Kalashnikov assault rifle and unsheathed the bayonet strapped to his belt. He leaned over Marchenkov and cut through the rope that tied him to the pipe and the rope that bound his ankles. 'Stand before the tribunal!' Woollen Hat barked.

Marchenkov struggled to his feet. The guard pushed him underneath the light. His shadow fell over the men on the other side of the table. To Krasin's right sat a man with a broad Slav face and a black Cossack moustache; to his left, a balding, slack jowled man with two large moles on his cheek; and, at the side, a weasel face wearing steel-framed spectacles. Only Krasin and Slav Face returned his gaze. 'Who are these people?' he asked Krasin.

'Members of a military tribunal. Their names are not important.'

'Military tribunal my arse. Where are we? Where are my superior officers? Where is the charge sheet? Where is my defence counsel?'

Krasin's voice was relaxed. 'These are extraordinary times, they require extraordinary measures. Proceed with the charges.'

Weasel Face read from a file in front of him. 'Marchenkov, Aleksei Fyodorovich, Major General commanding the 25th Motor Rifle Division, you are hereby charged with the following. First, that you disobeyed an order, classified top secret, to transfer eighteen Tochka and twelve R-17 missiles to Major Stanis of the Custodial Troops for transportation to General Kolinko of the 4th Guards Tank Division at Kursk.'

Marchenkov's stock of nuclear warheads had been shipped to Aramas-16 for dismantling in accordance with the Commonwealth of Independent States' agreement on disposal of the former Soviet Army's tactical nuclear weapons, but the battlefield missiles, which could also deliver conventional or chemical warheads, were to remain as part of the Ukrainian Army's armaments. He had suspected that the order to secretly transfer the missiles across the border to a Russian division had been issued by local commanders without reference to Moscow, but Krasin was from the General Staff. He called their bluff. 'No such order was given by the high command.'

'Don't talk to us about the high command,' Slav Face said. 'NATO has succeeded in disarming and breaking up the Army without firing a shot, and all the high command do is lick American arses and sell off our weapons for dollars in overseas bank accounts.'

'I warn you, Colonel,' Marchenkov said, 'the penalty for sedition is death.'

Krasin glanced at the two men with Kalashnikovs slung over their shoulders. 'Why did you disobey the order, General?'

'You know perfectly well,' Marchenkov said. 'It contravened the arms agreement between Russia and Ukraine that was ratified by both parliaments.'

'Fuck parliaments,' Slav Face growled. 'Self-serving politicians passing laws that everybody ignores while the nation sinks deeper into anarchy.'

How many times had Marchenkov heard sentiments like this from his own officers? But this was no barrack room debate: his life was at stake. He stood as erect as he was able. 'Colonel Krasin, kindly inform your colleague that, whether he likes it or not, we are now living in a democracy.'

The bald top of Krasin's head gleamed in the light of the single bulb as Krasin stared up at Marchenkov. 'A democracy! So we can be like the West. What has this Western democracy brought to our country? I'll tell you what it's brought, General. It's brought profits for the criminals and speculators, unemployment and hunger for the people, and humiliation for the armed forces.'

'You sound like the putschists of '91,' Marchenkov challenged. 'Why didn't you join them?'

Krasin spoke as though he were dealing with a particularly stupid child. 'General Marchenkov, you disappoint me. Did you think I would support a collective of drunks, incompetents, and communist has-beens? Not only were they incapable of restoring order and self-respect for the Motherland, their blundering effort set back the patriotic cause. But this is a digression. Let me put it simply. If you think we will accept parliamentary agreements that provide Ukraine with battlefield missiles which they can use against us, you must be, at best, extremely naïve.'

How far did this conspiracy extend? With so many rumours and counter rumours circulating in the armed forces, Marchenkov hadn't known whom to trust. He regretted now that he'd confided only in his wife and his driver about his decision to tell Roman Bondar that Russian commanders were conspiring to thwart the Russo-Ukrainian arms agreement. His driver was dead, he doubted that these fanatics would let him live, and Lera would be too frightened to tell anybody.

Weasel Face cleared his throat. 'Second, that you did compound this insubordination by the treasonable act of arranging to reveal details of the secret military order to an enemy of the state, the convicted criminal, Roman Bondar.'

A wave of nausea drained the strength from Marchenkov's body. His knees buckled and he leaned on the table to steady himself. He no longer cared for this farce of a tribunal or for his own safety, the only thing that mattered was to know who had betrayed him: Lera, who had pleaded with him for the sake of the children not to go and see Bondar, or Grigori Boldin, the driver whose life he had saved at the siege of Khost. He stared at the smirking Slav Face and gambled. 'Why did you have your informer killed?'

'He'd served his purpose. Besides, he knew too much.'

Thank God it wasn't Lera, but betrayal by Boldin was almost as bad. How much had he been paid, or had the bitterness of the officer corps spread through the non-commissioned ranks even to the driver whom he had treated as one of the family? Suddenly the room swayed. Woollen Hat grabbed him.

'Untie his wrists and bring him a chair,' Krasin said.

Marchenkov sank onto the chair. He rubbed his wrists to try and restore circulation. When he had followed his father into the Army, everything had been simple and straightforward. You obeyed without question your superior officers, who took their orders from the high command, and the high command acted on behalf of the people. The people, in turn, looked up to the armed forces as guardians of the territorial sovereignty of the state. And now . . . ?

'Give him a drink,' Krasin said.

Woollen Hat brought a flask and poured out amber liquid into an enamel mug. Marchenkov held the mug in both hands and savoured the sweetened tea.

Krasin intertwined his fingers, rested his hands on the table, and looked at Marchenkov with the solicitude of a family doctor. 'General Marchenkov, you come from an honourable military family. You served in Afghanistan with distinction. The charge of treason is a grave one, a capital offence. I am under pressure to exact the ultimate penalty. But I understand that you did not actually meet Roman Bondar and pass on secret military orders. In view of your previous good record, I shall give you an opportunity to redeem yourself and the good name of your family.' He smiled invitingly. 'Join us, and your future is assured.'

Marchenkov said nothing.

'We want the name of every officer at regimental commander level and above stationed in Ukraine whose loyalty is to the Ukrainian state,' Krasin said.

So this was the purpose of the charade. 'I assume you have the names of those who signed the oath of allegiance to Ukraine?'

Krasin spoke to him man to man. 'We both know that means nothing. Most signed simply to preserve their jobs, their housing, their children's schooling, and their pensions. I'm sure you thought of Lera and your boys when you signed. I want to know only about those officers who are prepared to fight for Ukrainian independence.'

The bastard. Not all those who had signed the oath of allegiance to Ukraine had done so for mercenary reasons. Many, like himself, believed the Army should never have been used to preserve the Soviet empire against the wishes of its peoples, and that every independent country had the right to control its own armed forces. But why had Krasin gone to these lengths to try and rob the Ukrainian Army of its defensive missiles and ascertain the loyalty of its commanders? 'On whose authority are you acting, Colonel?'

'A loyal officer does not question. He obeys.'

Marchenkov put the mug of tea on the table. 'You accuse me of disloyalty and then you ask me to break my oath to the Ukrainian state and betray my colleagues? It is you who disappoint me.'

Krasin's face hardened. 'And Brutus was an honourable man. I may not have had your privileged background, Marchenkov, but at least I know where my loyalties lie.'

'On the third of April 1965,' Weasel Face said, 'you took an oath of allegiance to the Motherland and solemnly pledged to defend her with your life.'

'There are many who would have you shot simply for swearing loyalty to this so-called independent state,' said Slav Face.

'So-called?' said Marchenkov. 'You're living in a fantasy world, my friend. Ukrainian independence is a fact.'

'The only historical fact,' said Slav Face, 'is that these lands have always been one. Moving the capital from Kiev to Moscow did not alter this fact. The only fantasy is an independent Ukrainian state, dreamt up by fascists in Galicia province.'

Marchenkov looked at Krasin. 'I see no point in continuing this conversation. Your chauvinist colleague is living in the past.'

'Perhaps,' said Krasin, 'he has a better sense of history than you give him credit for. What is the historical justification for an independent Ukrainian state? Three years in the last thousand years. Three years after the collapse of Tsarist authority when opportunists declared an independent democracy, then a monarchy, and then a military junta that fled the country.'

'Because the Red Army invaded Ukraine.'

'The Army restored order,' said Krasin.

'The Army reclaimed what belonged to Russia,' said Slav Face. 'And if you think that the historic consciousness of Mother Russia will permit opportunist Ukrainian politicians now to appropriate one handful of sacred Russian soil, then you are very much mistaken.'

'You're all mad,' said Marchenkov. 'There's no turning back.'

Krasin's voice carried an unnerving edge of authority. 'We shall see how much longer this second period of Ukrainian independence outlives the first. In the meantime, the names please.'

'Go to hell.'

Krasin shrugged. He bent down to reach inside a briefcase, removed a semiautomatic pistol, and placed it on the table. 'Do you know what this is?'

Marchenkov glanced at the big, stainless steel, black handled gun. 'Compensation for an inadequate prick.'

For a moment Krasin's mask of self-control slipped, revealing blind fury. He regained his composure and pushed the gun across the table. 'I suggest you take a closer look.'

Marchenkov hesitated. He reached out and picked up the weapon. It wasn't one he'd seen before. It was larger and heavier than a Makarov. He found the safety lever on the left-hand side and released it. 'Are you suggesting I do the honourable thing?'

'Honourable suicides are for honourable men.'

'In that case . . .' Marchenkov took a two-handed grip on the gun and raised it to point at Krasin's face.

From behind came the angry CLACK CLICK of a Kalashnikov being charged. In front, Krasin slowly raised his arms, his fingers clenched to form fists.

Marchenkov summoned his reserves of willpower. Weak though he was, he held the gun unwaveringly at an imaginary spot in the centre of Krasin's forehead. 'Put down your rifles,' he said.

'Go ahead and shoot,' said Krasin.

Marchenkov sensed all eyes were on him, but he kept the gun's sight on its target.

Krasin looked him in the eyes and uncurled the fingers of his right hand to reveal a narrow rectangular black metal case with a yellow stripe down the centre. He laughed, and the others joined in like hyenas. Krasin reached across the table with his left hand, took the unloaded gun from Marchenkov, and pushed the magazine into the base of the handle. 'To deal with the IRA, the Royal Ulster Constabulary wanted a more powerful gun than the Walther PPK, and so they acquired the Ruger 89. It can kill at longer ranges than the Walther but, of more immediate interest, it inflicts greater damage at short ranges.'

Marchenkov had to show Krasin that he wasn't cracking under the strain. 'I thought the Russian Army was selling off arms, not buying them.'

'If you'd examined the gun more closely as I suggested,' said Krasin undeterred, 'you would have seen that the serial number has been filed. But not enough to prevent an assiduous law enforcement agency from tracing this gun back to the RUC.'

'Stop playing games, Krasin.'

Krasin continued in his quiet, reasonable manner. 'This particular gun was stolen from the RUC by the IRA. Among other achievements, the IRA have developed certain punishment techniques. On the floor with him.'

Woollen Hat and one of the guards pulled Marchenkov out of his chair and spreadeagled him face down on the floor.

He heard a double click, and then felt a hard object pushed into the back of his left knee. Krasin's voice was close. 'Remember that this is not a puny little Makarov. Perhaps now you will also remember the names of those officers who are committed to fighting for Ukraine's independence.'

Marchenkov tried to swivel his head round. 'May you rot in hell.'

The ear-splitting bang burst into a paroxysm of pain just above his knee, sending jagged impulses of energy – like electric threads – to his stomach. His fingernails broke as he clawed a hold on the concrete floor. The excruciating pain lasted a minute or so that felt like a week before it subsided into numbness. Sweat dripped from his cold brow and blotched the concrete.

'You moved your leg, not very honourable.' A foot pressed

down on the back of his right calf and the gun nozzle was rammed tightly into the back of his knee. 'Perhaps you'll give me the names now.'

Marchenkov resolved not to give Krasin the satisfaction of an answer. His head pounded, his mouth was pressed into the dry concrete, his broken fingernails scratched deep in anticipation. He tried to slow his breathing and tell himself that no pain could be worse than that he'd just experienced. But he was wrong. When it came, the explosion tore apart every fibre, every molecule, every atom of his kneecap, shooting a million bolts of pain down to the sole of his twitching foot. Then nothing. Not even numbness below the knee, only a warm wetness spreading up from the knee.

'If you insist on being a traitor in life, Marchenkov, I shall make you a hero of Russia in death.'

Still Marchenkov said nothing.

'So be it. The Irish are Celts, such a romantic race. We Slavs are noted for our cruelty. Pull down his pants.'

Woollen Hat sniggered and pulled Marchenkov's trousers down to his knees, and then his underpants. Marchenkov felt warm steel pushed into the cleft of his buttocks. Oh my God, not this. He bit hard on his lip.

'I understand you've become a Christian.'

'He was baptized by an Orthodox priest on the eighth of September 1991.' Weasel Face's voice.

The nozzle pressed hard into his anus.

' "Greater love hath no man than this, that a man lay down his life for his friends." John, Chapter 15. Aleksei Fyodorovich, the men you are protecting are not your friends. They do not deserve your protection. They are traitors to Russia and her Army. You are a son of Russia and a man of honour. Give me their names and remain a living hero of Russia.'

'Thank you, Krasin,' Marchenkov said through clenched teeth, 'for reminding me how I should face death.'

'What's that?' Krasin snapped, pushing hard on the gun.

'May God forgive you and have mercy on your soul . . .'

The loud bang reverberated in the steel piping. His anal canal screamed in agony. The fire spread. Intense pain seared down to his knees. White flashes shot from his spine through his body and exploded into fragments before his eyes, as though his network of nerves were overcharged with sensation. The fires and flashes raged and burst. Slowly they burned out, leaving only a coldness: a numbness down from the waist, a shivering up from the waist.

'Well, Major?'

'I'll take a look.' An unfamiliar voice. It must be slack jowled Mole Face. Marchenkov tries to turn himself over, but he can't. He feels nothing at all below his waist. He tries to pull himself forward with his hands. He can't. His legs are dead weights. He hears footsteps approaching. He uses his elbows as levers to drag himself away.

Mole Face stops him by grabbing his wrist. When he bends over to feel Marchenkov's pulse, his breath smells of brandy. 'Fast and feeble.' He pulls up Marchenkov's shirt tail to take a better look at the slow steady stream of blood trickling from the anus. 'Considerable internal haemorrhaging. I'd give him two to three hours.'

'Did you hear that, Marchenkov? Up to three more hours of agony. I can put you out of your misery now if you give me the names.'

Marchenkov's shoulders heave with silent laughter. He's not in any agony. He feels nothing, only a curious light-headedness. He sees a bright light.

'Your answer?'

'May God the father of all creation receive my spirit.'

'Then God will have to wait three hours, like He did for Christ on the cross. Very fitting. Let's go.'

Marchenkov hears the scraping of chairs and the sound of footsteps, and then Slav Face's voice. 'Are we leaving him unguarded?'

A dry laugh from Krasin. 'I don't think General Marchenkov will be walking far.'

FOUR

'It's your Uncle Pavlo,' said Volodymyr, clutching the handset of the extension telephone mounted on the wall next to a portrait of the bald and white-bearded Mykhaylo Hruszevski, the president who proclaimed Ukraine's short-lived independence from Russia in 1918.

'It's too noisy here,' said Stepaniak. 'I'll take it in Evhen's office.'

Evhen peered from behind a computer screen. 'Don't be too long, the phone hasn't stopped ringing.'

That was an exaggeration, but several national papers had rung to ask about the UPA. Stepaniak left the larger basement room of the Ukrainian Press Bureau, with its fax machine, two Macintosh computers, and a dot matrix printer shrilling out yet another press release to be photocopied thirty-four times. He closed the door behind him in the smaller room, picked up the handset from the master telephone, and waited until he heard the extension being put down before he said, 'Taras here.'

'It's been a long time, Taras,' the deep voice said. 'I'd like to see you again. I'll be at Westminster Bridge at two.'

'I'll do my best, Uncle.' He put the phone down.

'Evhen,' he said, when he returned to the main office, 'my uncle's in London. He'd like to see me for lunch. I may be back late.'

'OK, but don't be too late. We've still to get the *Herald* out after we've finished the press releases.'

'Sure,' said Stepaniak. The press releases that went straight into the wastepaper baskets of Britain's newspapers, and the *Herald* whose every word was read by émigré children guilty about enjoying a Western standard of living while cousins they had never seen struggled to build an independent nation.

The day was cold and sharp. Engraved on the landscape far beyond the downward sloping grounds of Kenwood House were the City's Natwest Bank skyscraper, Saint Paul's Cathedral, the Post Office Tower, and the Houses of Parliament, almost as clearly as their images were engraved on the copper strip inside the small, wrought iron viewing pagoda. And below the labelled panorama were engraved the words

Earth has not anything to show more fair

from Wordsworth's sonnet, 'Upon Westminster Bridge'.

It was ten past two. Stepaniak bent down to tie the laces of his trainers and look up at the underside of the block to which the copper panorama was fixed. No chalk mark. Nevertheless, he wandered back towards the Nightingale Lane entrance to Hampstead Heath, dallied in front of the gate to the herb garden, and decided to examine the herbs. Only one old lady, in fur coat, flowered hat, and dark spectacles, sat on a bench facing the sun dial in the upper half of the garden. The herbs here held little interest for Stepaniak. He descended the stone steps to the deserted lower section and examined the beds between the gravel path and the high brick wall. He showed particular interest in the herbs marked by a small green sign

Bed Number 7
Jerusalem Sage
Red Sage
Creeping Thyme

The gnarled tree, between the herb bed and the wall, attracted his attention. He even felt its texture. There was nothing in the hollow at the back of the tree next to the wall. Damn.

He had nearly three-quarters of an hour to wait before the fallback meeting. He walked the long way round to the ponds, past Kenwood House and through the more rugged East Heath.

It was still only ten to three when he reached the gravel path separating the fishing pond on his left from Highgate Men's Pond on his right. At the end of the path he walked up the grass slope and perched on a bench overlooking the Men's Pond. He lit a cheroot and looked distractedly towards the half-dozen hardy fishermen seated along one side of their pond, impervious to the cold and to the roaring of the diesel powered model boat failing to be controlled by a Hampstead child and his father.

'Do you want to come?'

The man with short-cropped hair and moustache, who wore a black leather blouson like his own, but tight, black leather trousers instead of jeans, was carrying a rolled-up towel.

Stepaniak looked at the cold grey water of the pond below the diving board. 'I'm no masochist,' he grinned.

'Suits me,' said Black Leathers.

Shit, Stepaniak thought. Then he spotted a stout man approaching along the path between the two ponds. 'My friend's here.'

Black Leathers looked at the man whose oversized face appeared to have been dragged down by gravity, with his hooded eyes, sagging cheeks, downturned mouth, and triple chin. 'I thought you said you weren't a masochist.'

Stepaniak stood up from the bench and went to meet the man known to him as Pavlov and, in exceptional circumstances, as Uncle Pavlo. 'Just in time. You saved me from a fate worse than death. Why the hell weren't you at Westminster Bridge?'

'I was being observed.'

Stepaniak remembered the old lady in dark glasses. 'You're paranoid. Where's the money?'

Pavlov looked around. 'Let's walk. I'm taking it to Jerusalem sage if the way is clear. You can collect it after half past three.'

'You've got it with you? Give it to me now.'

'Moscow rules,' said Pavlov sharply.

'Jesus Christ. Moscow rules nothing these days. Why the phone call at the office?'

Pavlov stopped for breath near the top of the path that climbed to the white stuccoed Georgian frontage and orangery of Kenwood House. 'I tried to phone you at home last night, but there was no reply.'

Stepaniak thought of Pavlov's wife, a dumpy woman one generation removed from the head-scarved *babushki* who swept Moscow's streets with broomsticks. He grinned lasciviously. 'I was pumping a source.'

Pavlov scowled, and then said spitefully, 'You won't be doing that for much longer. You've been recalled.'

'Shit!' He was just beginning to reap the fruits of eleven years undercover in London: eleven years patiently gaining the trust of paranoid Ukrainian émigrés who thought every newcomer was a KGB agent; eleven years creating conspiracies that reinforced Moscow Centre's paranoia and justified increased operational funds to build up a decent income for himself. A young couple, walking hand in hand in the grassy bowl that formed a natural amphitheatre below Kenwood House, paused to look across the lake to the dome-roofed pavilion where open air concerts were given each summer. Stepaniak thought of all the English pleasures he'd been promising himself: the concerts and museums where you could pick up interesting women, historic places like Brighton and Bath where they could take you for weekends, the good life beyond the émigré community which he had barely explored. The prospect of returning to an impoverished Moscow on a captain's salary in roubles appalled him. 'Who gave the order? Volkov?'

'The telegram was signed Sedov.'

'Who's he?'

Pavlov shrugged.

'What's the reason?'

'I don't know.'

'As an intelligence officer,' said Stepaniak, 'you'd be the last to find out.' It could hardly be dissatisfaction with his work: he'd received no instructions that he'd failed to comply with, and his reports told the Centre what it wanted to hear. In fact, in the last two years, he'd had very little feedback, and that was usually a sign of Moscow's approval. Best to look on the bright side. 'Ah well, perhaps they want me to find this missing general.'

FIVE

The voice on the phone was curt. 'If you want to find General Marchenkov, wait outside the Central Railway booking office on Shevchenko Boulevard. Between seven and ten past seven, one of the public telephones will ring. The caller will identify himself as Taras Borovets.' The phone went dead.

Christine Lesyn let the eighteen-month-old copy of *Vogue* slip from her lap. This could be the break she needed. She picked up the telephone, heard the engaged signal before she dialled, and cursed Soviet technology. It took four attempts before she got through from her apartment in Kiev to the *Correspondent*'s bureau chief in Moscow.

'Sounds interesting,' a laid-back voice replied. 'Does anyone else have the story?'

'I do not think so,' Lesyn replied in competent English.

'Check it out and phone me straight away if it's genuine. Be good.'

Lesyn collected her notebook, mini cassette recorder and camera, and put them in her handbag next to her hairbrush and her make-up. High cheekbones gave her face a classical beauty marred only by a nose that was too long. She brushed her shoulder-length bronze hair in front of the large hall mirror. She wanted to shed six kilograms, but what could you expect in a country like this? Once she was living in the West, she would eat the health foods they had there and she'd soon look like one of those models in *Vogue*. She was reapplying her lipstick when the phone rang. She hesitated, and then picked up the handset.

'Hi, Christine, it's Jane. It looks like another slack day for news tomorrow, so we're having Michael's farewell party tonight at my apartment. We'd love for you to join us.'

'It is good of you to invite me,' Lesyn said, 'but I am afraid that I do not feel so good.'

'Another migraine?'

'Yes. I shall have some rest. But do let me know if there is any more news on the Marchenkov story. I shall leave my answerphone on.'

'Of course I'll let you know. I hope you feel better.'

Dressed in her long Finnish-made grey suede coat and sheepskin-lined brown suede boots, Lesyn walked quickly up the hill outside her apartment block to the car park of the Moscow Hotel, Kiev's largest and once its most imposing, with a spectacular view over the Soviet city's grandiose centrepiece, the October Revolution Square. The yellow concrete tiles missing from the outside, and the stench of urine pervading the inside, caused the hotel's fall from grace long before Ukrainian nationalists desecrated the square. Lesyn gave the attendant one hundred coupons and unlocked the door of the new Zaporozhets that she would eagerly have traded for any Western car. The petrol gauge showed one quarter full. She hoped Marchenkov wasn't far away.

By five to seven she was hugging herself and stamping her feet on the frozen slush next to the open telephone kiosks outside the Central Railway booking office. She hated the cold. It was almost ten past seven when one of the phones rang. Taras Borovets was brief and precise.

She climbed into her car and drove up the broad boulevard lined with trees as bare as the shops now closed for the day. She continued past the central obelisk in Victory Square where the road became Victory Prospekt, the main highway to Lviv, but at the next major road junction she turned off and headed south-west towards the Brezhnev high rise apartment blocks of Borshchagovka district on the outskirts of the city.

Twenty minutes after leaving the phone kiosk she parked her car on a dimly lit, ice covered estate road on which children were playing ice hockey with homemade sticks. She warned them to keep clear of her car before she searched for the block that

Borovets had named. It was on the edge of the estate and she found the keys to the basement exactly as he had described: underneath a large stone at the foot of the tree outside the rear entrance.

The first key turned easily enough. The green wooden door creaked open and she groped in the dark for the light switch. She stepped carefully down the concrete steps from the store room, reluctant to dirty her leather gloves on the grimy metal handrail. The second key grated in the lock of the rusty metal door. She pushed the door open and peered into the basement. She coughed. No answer. She switched on the light. Rows of pipes, crisscrossing in the usual botched Soviet fashion, snaked around the walls and most of the ceiling of a room that seemed to be empty, save for a table and chairs below the bulb hanging from a length of flex. Then she saw the trail of blood.

She found him face down, hands reaching out for a warm pipe in a corner of the basement. His trousers were down around his knees. Dried blood caked his naked buttocks. Blood also stained both trouser legs. She took off her gloves and gingerly felt his chafed right wrist for a pulse. The hand was cold, the pulse non-existent. She turned his head round to make sure it really was General Marchenkov. When she saw the white face that had appeared in all the newspapers the day after his driver was found shot, she gasped. This *was* the story she needed.

A wave of panic overtook her satisfaction. She hurried to the door and locked it. Heart beating quickly, she sat down at the table and told herself that all she had to do was take care and cover herself; she mustn't be frightened out of a story like this which would help her secure a staff post with the *Correspondent*. She noticed an envelope on the table. She replaced her gloves and opened it. It contained a single, typed sheet

> Foreign soldiers out of Ukraine and out of Ireland!
> Death to representatives of imperial powers!
>
> UKRAINIAN INSURGENT ARMY

She copied the message into her notebook, wrote down all the details, and took half a dozen photographs of the body. She turned off the lights, locked both doors, stood in the freezing snow, and shivered violently.

Stupid, unsophisticated public telephones that couldn't connect to any number outside Kiev. The post office on the estate was shut. She strode back to the apartment block, went in by the front entrance, and rang the first doorbell she saw. 'Excuse me, there's been an accident. Do you have a telephone?'

The old woman shook her head and tried to close the door, but Lesyn's foot was in the way. 'Who has a telephone?'

'The Karpenkos, apartment 32,' the old woman said.

Lesyn ran up chipped concrete stairs and banged on the door of number 32. It opened an inch or so. 'Who's there?' asked a man's suspicious voice.

Lesyn put on a distraught smile. 'I'm so sorry to trouble you. There's been an accident. I must telephone my boss's brother in Moscow.'

No response.

'I'll pay for the call,' Lesyn said, showing a dollar bill.

The door opened and closed quickly behind her. An unshaven man in a tracksuit took the dollar bill. 'The phone's over there.' Both he and his wife watched her carefully.

Lesyn gave them a dazzling smile and put her handbag down on the sofa that doubled as a bed. 'It's a very personal call.'

The couple looked at each other and walked reluctantly through to the next room, but left the door ajar. Lesyn closed it before picking up the handset. She swore under her breath when she heard the engaged tone. Ten infuriating minutes later she managed to contact the *Correspondent*'s bureau chief in Moscow.

'Are you sure nobody else has the story?' Jonathan Smythe's voice had lost its laid-back drawl. 'Right. Give it to me again from the top.'

When she finished, he said, 'Had he been kneecapped?'

'I do not know what you mean by this "kneecapped".'

'Where exactly were the wounds in his legs?'

'I am not sure.'

'Look, this is what you do. You go back there and write down every single detail: precisely how many gunshot wounds he has, precisely where they are, which was the one that caused death, what expression is on his face, every possible detail, right? And we must get some photographs.'

She was indignant. 'I have told you. I have made six photographs.'

'I mean professional pics, wired to London before midnight Moscow time, that's eleven your time, right? Do you know anyone who can do it?'

'Will this story be on the front page?'

'I'll be surprised if it's not the splash. But I need all the details, and good pics will help.'

'You will tell Martin Harvey that this is my story? It will be in my name alone, you promise this?'

'Promise, but can you get pics wired to London?'

'I know an English boy who does freelance work for Reuters. He sends his photographs by wire.'

'Great. Ring him. Tell him there's three hundred dollars for exclusive pics wired to the *Correspondent*'s London office before eleven your time.'

'Three hundred dollars?'

'Go to four hundred if necessary. I'll cover.'

'What about the militia?'

'Get the details and the pics first. Then call the cops. Stick with them. Write down everything they say, then phone me with the lot.'

'I am telephoning from the apartment of a stranger on the estate. It is very difficult.'

'OK. Look, I'll get London to call your apartment at quarter to eleven Kiev time. We'll be tight up against a deadline, so you must be ready to dictate your report. Use the slug FUKE2.ADD. I'll already have given them the bones.'

'How many words do you want?'

'On a piece like this, as many as you need. Good hunting.'

Andrew Mitchell's phone kept ringing. Then she remembered the party. 'Hi, Christine,' he answered from Jane's noisy apartment. 'They said you had another migraine.'

'Yes. But I found a story. I need photographs of a man in a dark basement to go by wire to the *Correspondent* in London before eleven o'clock. Two hundred and fifty dollars for an exclusive. Can you do it?'

'Tell me where and I'm on my way.'

She hesitated by the public telephone kiosk on the estate. She had remained calm while Mitchell had enthused about the story and the photographs, but he was an English boy, he didn't know the militia like she did. Alone, she was frightened again. For political reasons they would have to arrest somebody soon. She dialled the Bondars' apartment.

Maria's voice radiated warmth. 'Christine, it's good to hear from you. It's been so long.'

'I need to speak to your father.'

'Daddy's in bed. It's his lung again; the doctor insisted he stay in bed for forty-eight hours. Can I help?'

'No. It's urgent. I must speak with him now.'

Roman Bondar, too, sounded surprised and delighted to hear from her. 'You must come round for supper soon.'

'I've found General Marchenkov. He's been murdered. I need to call the militia, but I'm afraid. Will you help?'

Lesyn heard a sharp intake of breath from Roman Bondar, followed by a bout of wheezing. Then Bondar's voice said, 'Of course. Don't you worry, Christine. I'll phone Lieutenant Colonel Petrosyan of the National Security Service. He'll take care of you.'

SIX

Colonel Nikolai Krasin's telephone connection from his office in Moscow to an office in Kiev suffered no delay. 'Tell the British Ambassador off the record that you cannot guarantee the safety of his Foreign Secretary next week. Explain that, for obvious reasons, neither you nor the Government can admit this officially, and so you will greatly appreciate it if the Foreign Secretary develops an illness which forces him to postpone the visit. The Ambassador will understand.'

SEVEN

Finding General Marchenkov was one job he wouldn't be needed for. The six-column photograph under the *Correspondent*'s masthead showed the mutilated body. Below, the headline announced

Russian General 'executed' in Ukraine

Brutal terrorist murder reveals link with IRA

Stepaniak read the gory details. He shuddered when he reached

> Dr Dmytro Ivakhiv of the Kiev Militia said that for the bullet to have shattered the spinal cord, the gun must have been held upside down so that it fired up through the anal canal. Death was caused by slow internal haemorrhaging, and took place several hours after this third gunshot wound. The probable murder weapon has been found, and a spokesman for the National Security Service, which has taken over the case, said they were confident of being able to trace its origin.

He barely glanced at the single paragraph blobbed at the end of the article

● The Foreign Secretary has postponed a planned visit to Kiev to discuss Ukraine's application for associate membership of the European Community, *writes our Diplomatic Editor*. A spokesman for the Foreign Office said that the Foreign Secretary has a heavy cold.

Stepaniak put down the paper and looked out of the aeroplane window. Khaki coloured forests, lightly dusted white, patched the solid white carpet below the plane as it descended to Moscow's Sheremetyevo-2 Airport. Only the runways were clear, black slashes on a snowfield from which red-and-white banded radar masts and single-storey buildings grew. The plane landed with a bump, taxied in over sheet ice, and waited half an hour before a ground crew was found to bring out a set of mobile steps. Back to the USSR. Nothing, it seemed, had changed except the name.

Even the name hadn't changed on the gold-on-green insignia of the immigration officer's khaki uniform. From behind the glazed upper half of his booth, the young man peered at Stepaniak and at the mirror system which gave him a view of Stepaniak's rear. He spent a long time examining Stepaniak's papers, which had been carefully prepared years before. Stepaniak resisted the temptation of asking who in his right mind would want to be an illegal immigrant into Russia. The officer made a telephone call before returning his papers and allowing him through to collect his luggage.

A customs officer stopped him. 'Open your suitcase.'

'I've nothing to declare,' Stepaniak said.

'Open your suitcase.' Manners hadn't changed either.

Stepaniak hauled the bulging suitcase onto the table and unlocked it.

The customs officer rummaged through. 'What are these?'

'Come on,' said Stepaniak, 'you know you can't get any in Russia, and even if you can they're as safe as a sieve and as sensitive as rubber boots.'

'Do you have an import licence for them?'
Stepaniak grinned. 'I'm a healthy growing boy.'
'Half a suitcase full of Western condoms for personal use?'
'It's my personal mission to combat AIDS in Russia. Have a box.'
The customs officer put three boxes in his pocket and cleared Stepaniak's luggage.
At last Stepaniak passed through into the airport entrance hall. Grey light filtered through the glass walls at the far end. Travellers in Western clothes gazed at signs in Cyrillic script, others waited aimlessly for delayed flights, Muscovites in imitation Western clothes busied through the chaos as though they had a purpose, and half a dozen men, roughly dressed, most unshaven, closed in around him. He hadn't expected a reception committee.
'Taxi?' two of them said at the same time. Stepaniak remembered stories he'd read in the newspapers and chose the smallest driver.
'Currency,' stated the short man who wore a leather jacket.
Stepaniak nodded.
He followed the man and his suitcase through the slush to the short term car park. The car, to Stepaniak's surprise, was Japanese and, though grimy, seemed relatively new. 'Where have you been?' the driver asked, offering him a cigarette from a Marlboro packet as they drove out of the airport.
Stepaniak declined, gave him a cheroot, and lit one for himself. 'Europe,' he said in Russian.
'Long trip?'
'Eleven years.'
'You should have stayed. Even Poland's a better place to live now. What were you doing?'
'Providing technical assistance to our socialist friends.'
'And now they've thrown you out? Christ! When we were powerful they came begging for help. We gave it to them. Free of charge. We put them back on their feet after the War. We kept on supplying them with oil for next to nothing. Now we're in a mess, what do they do? Piss on us. I know what I'd do with the

ungrateful bastards. I bet you felt like spitting in their faces when you left. Got a job to come back to?'

'Fortunately, yes,' said Stepaniak. 'There's always work for my trade.'

'Well, count yourself lucky. Eleven years, you say? You'll never recognize the place. No jobs, no food, no respect, no law, no order, no nothing, while those so-called democrats sit on their arses and argue all day. They never actually *do* anything. Look at that,' he said, pointing his cheroot past Stepaniak to his right. Two massive, grey granite plinths, one bearing two heroic granite soldiers, the other a grateful granite peasant and a grateful granite worker, supported the imposing black and gilded wrought iron gates to what once had been the Warsaw Pact headquarters. 'It seems like only yesterday that half the world feared us. Now, even Ukrainians take over half our army and start shooting our generals. And what do our so-called leaders do? Crawl on their knees to the West with a begging bowl. It's fucking humiliating. Is this what we won the War for?'

The car pulled up, as instructed, outside the Children's World store in Lubyanka Square. The driver nodded over his left shoulder. 'Are you sure you don't want me to take you across the square?'

Stepaniak looked past the driver, beyond the central cylindrical plinth on which a flimsy white, blue, and red tricolour had replaced the statue of 'Iron Felix' Dzerzhinsky, to the Lubyanka, the ochre Italianate *palazzo* made notorious by the KGB, which dominated the square. 'Certainly not. What do you think I am?'

'That's all right then,' said the driver. 'The fare's twenty dollars. For one of those bastards it'd be forty.'

Stepaniak grinned as he crossed the street that ran downhill from Lubyanka Square, separating the side of the Children's World store from the side of a modern eight-storey, light grey granite building. So much for glasnost: when Stepaniak had left Moscow for his undercover mission, Chebrikov was transferring the KGB headquarters from the Lubyanka to the new building that Andropov had commissioned. Stepaniak walked round to the front entrance of the modern building on Great Lubyanka Street, known as Number One, now the headquarters of the Russian Ministry of Security.

The armed guard telephoned from his booth just inside the heavy wooden door. He put down his telephone and said, 'You're to go to Number Twelve. Lieutenant Colonel Filatov is expecting you.'

Stepaniak crossed Great Lubyanka Street by the traffic lights at the end of Number One. On the other side of the street a No Entry sign marked Furkasovsky Lane, behind the Lubyanka, where black KGB Volgas were guarded by militia and plainclothes officers. The next block on Great Lubyanka was an older building, whose double sandstone columns, separated by six tiers of windows, supported a solid, top storey. It had been used by Dzerzhinsky as the first Moscow headquarters of the Cheka before he requisitioned the Lubyanka. When Stepaniak had visited Number Twelve on the eve of his departure, builders had just begun converting it into a new KGB social club. The armed guard telephoned, turned to Stepaniak and said, 'Lieutenant Colonel Filatov is in Room 231. Up the staircase, straight through the memory room, and it's to your right.'

Stepaniak left his suitcase with his parka in the cloakroom at the side of the cathedral-like foyer, with its white-speckled black marble pillars rising from a white marble floor. He climbed up the marble staircase, curious to see what remained of Chebrikov's grand plans for a KGB memory room. He pushed open the door and entered a shrine. A twice-life-size aluminium head of Lenin stared at him from a pedestal in front of a back lit, stained glass window at the far end of the room. The rabble may have removed Felix Dzerzhinsky's statue from Lubyanka Square, but here the memory of Saint Felix was still revered with his bronze death mask, his desk, and other sacred relics. Stepaniak meandered through the wood-panelled room and examined the other mementos. On a table lay the Union flag found in the pocket of Sydney Reilly when he was arrested on one of his single-handed expeditions to overthrow the Bolshevik government. In an adjoining room, captured old machine guns and rifles testified to the victory of the NKVD over UPA fascist bandits in Ukraine during and after the Great Patriotic War. A pen that fired bullets, spectacles whose arms contained poison, and a transmitter capable of compressing a message and sending it to an overhead spy satellite were exhibited as spoils of the Cold War. Side altars venerated Philby, Burgess, Maclean, Blunt, and other undercover agents. A false-bottomed suitcase and bomb-making equipment demonstrated the need for an intelligence service to combat drug smuggling and organized crime. The message was clear: spies always had been, were, and always would be, indispensable for the State's security; only the enemy changed.

Ukrainian émigré organizations had outlived their usefulness. Stepaniak wondered what new adversary the Centre wanted him to spy on. Mafia gangs were dangerous. Stealing technology appealed to him much more: it meant a big expenses account in the West.

Lieutenant Colonel Filatov looked less like a spy master and more like a second-hand car salesman on the Old Kent Road. Tall, slightly stooping, with receding hair and plastic-rimmed spectacles, his grey striped jacket didn't quite match his grey striped trousers, and his blue polyester tie didn't quite match his blue nylon shirt. Only two telephones stood on his desk; clearly he wasn't very important. 'Sit down, Captain Stepaniak,' he said, indicating a hard wooden chair in front of his desk. 'This office looks after arrangements for former officers of both the Security Ministry and the Intelligence Service.'

'Not quite the posting I had in mind,' Stepaniak got in quickly. 'It would be a pity if all my expertise and experience were wasted on a desk job.'

Filatov sighed. 'You're not being offered a posting. You're to receive a pension of four thousand three hundred roubles a month, and I've allocated you half of a two-room apartment on Oleko Dundicha Street.'

Stepaniak mentally replayed Filatov's statement to make sure he'd heard correctly, then he jumped to his feet. 'This is ridiculous! I want to see Major General Volkov.'

'Volkov's been freed from responsibility for the Illegals Directorate in order to concentrate on long-term development.'

'What is that supposed to mean?' Stepaniak demanded.

Filatov shrugged. 'He's been pensioned off, like you.'

Still on his feet, Stepaniak put both hands on the desk and leaned over Filatov. 'I can understand them laying off domestic headbangers, but every country needs a foreign intelligence service. I demand my right to go to the Forest* and see whoever's in charge.'

'Captain Stepaniak, please sit down. The decision has already been made. The country simply hasn't got the foreign currency to support the level of foreign intelligence operations we've been running.'

Stepaniak slumped back in the chair. 'The prime of my life and I get half of a two-room apartment on Oleko Dundicha Street plus a pension of four thousand three hundred roubles a month.'

'Think yourself lucky you're not in the Army. You'd have been offered a share of a tent in Irkutsk where it's twenty-five below. At least you'll have a Moscow apartment with central heating.'

'Thanks. Thanks a lot.'

'Look, I know it hits people hard.' Filatov opened a drawer in his desk, took out a sheet of paper, and slid it across to him.

'What's this?'

'A list of names and telephone numbers.'

'Colonel Filatov, you may think I do not possess the skills required of a new-style Russian intelligence officer, but credit me at least with the ability to read.'

Filatov lowered his voice. 'They are people who recruit former KGB officers.'

Stepaniak looked at the list. 'What for?'

'Private security organizations.'

'And what do these private security organizations do?'

Filatov's brows creased. 'They provide security for those who pay: joint ventures, cooperatives, private companies, those kinds of people.'

'Mafia?'

Filatov said nothing.

'You approve of this?'

* Officers' slang for the headquarters of the External Intelligence Service, formerly the First Chief (Foreign Intelligence) Directorate of the KGB, which is located in a birch forest at Yasenevo, about sixteen kilometres south-west of the centre of Moscow.

'Of course not. These private agencies are scum.'
'Then why are you giving me this list?'
Filatov lowered his voice even further. 'Because, Captain Stepaniak, next week I may be sitting where you're sitting.'

Stepaniak stood on Great Lubyanka Street with the keys to half an apartment in one pocket, and his wallet, holding now-precious US dollars, in another pocket. This couldn't be happening to him. From a champagne supper and a class lay in Holland Park to . . . to this. Women, and even men of his own age, trudged past him in the slush, grey faces long since drained of hope that the overthrow of communism would liberate them from the daily struggle to survive. He wanted to grab hold of one, shake him by the shoulders, and say, I'm not like you; you've known nothing else, but I have. Instead, he dragged his suitcase to the edge of the pavement and waved his arm. No taxis stopped for him. The drivers of four private cars that did stop refused to take him anywhere for roubles. He resigned himself to joining the herd who had no choice but to jostle their way down the steps to the Lubyanka metro station. He bent to pick up his suitcase. A black Zhiguli pulled into the pavement.
'Oleko Dundicha Street, please, near Filevsky Park metro.'
'Right.'
'Roubles?' Stepaniak asked defensively.
'OK.'
Stepaniak gratefully put his suitcase in the boot and climbed into the front passenger seat. Only then did he become aware that somebody was seated in the rear passenger seat. 'You know the way?' he asked the driver.
'Sure,' said the driver, who had the neck and shoulders of an American footballer. He drove down the broad, busy road that Stepaniak knew as Marx Prospekt and turned right by the light grey, multicolumned former Lenin Library onto Kalinin Prospekt. Stepaniak noticed a sign that labelled it New Arbat Street. But instead of continuing down this canyon between modern office blocks with their ground-floor shops and on across the river, the driver took the slip road onto the Garden Ring Road.
'You're sure you know where you're going?' Stepaniak asked.

A voice from behind said, 'We're taking you home.'

Stepaniak sank back into his seat and watched helplessly as the car left the eight-lane Garden Ring Road at a square dominated by a gigantic, spired apartment block and headed off to he knew not where. Vagankovskoye Cemetery passed by on the left, and a dozen railway lines jammed with stationary coaches passed underneath. They weren't going to the Forest.

Stepaniak tried to compose himself. Anything was better than living off a pension in Moscow. But the hairs on the back of his neck sent another message to his brain. Half a two-room apartment on Oleko Dundicha Street suddenly seemed an attractive prospect.

Stepaniak sat up when the driver turned off Begovaya Street by the first slip road and circled back underneath Begovaya to head down the Khoroshovskoye Highway, between the white-and-blue, high rise apartment blocks on the right and their yellow-and-white counterparts on the left.

The car stopped at a set of traffic lights. Stepaniak tensed. When the lights changed to green the driver turned right, down a narrow road bordered on the right by a modern, sand coloured, two-storey brick building, and stopped outside solid steel gates wide enough to let a tank through. Stepaniak leaned back in relief.

A young trooper wearing a holster strapped to the outside of his greatcoat left the gatehouse, which was identified only by the number 76. He carefully examined the driver's pass and looked through the window. Then he signalled, and a section of the steel gate swung back to let the car in. As soon as it stopped, Stepaniak climbed out and gazed up at the nine-storey glass building.

'I said we were taking you home.' The other passenger, a stocky man with short-cropped hair, was standing next to him.

After passing through two more identity checks, Stepaniak and his companion took a lift to the eighth floor. They walked down a narrow red carpet that ran along the centre of the parquet-floored corridor. At the far side of the building, the other man stopped outside a brown, leather padded door and knocked. A voice said, 'Enter.'

The man opened the door and said, 'Colonel Leskov, this is Captain Stepaniak.'

A bald-topped dome-headed man, who had a Roman nose and a cleft chin jutting from a gaunt face, rose from behind a desk. 'Welcome back to the Aquarium, Captain Stepaniak,' said Colonel Krasin.

EIGHT

Krasin's piercing grey eyes seemed to look into Stepaniak and read his innermost thoughts. Stepaniak averted his own gaze and examined the red striped tie, pale blue shirt, and neat grey suit that Krasin wore. Krasin's thin lips pulled back into a smile that emphasized the gauntness of his cheeks. He closed his hand round Stepaniak's just enough for Stepaniak to feel his strength.

'It's good to be back, sir,' Stepaniak said, vainly trying to recall the officer who would probably have held the rank of major when Stepaniak had been posted here.

'Please be seated,' Krasin said genially. He nodded and the other man left, closing the padded door quietly behind him.

Stepaniak sat down on a plain but well-upholstered chair in front of Krasin's desk. An antique inkwell and a tennis ball were the only objects on the polished desk top. Five telephones stood on a table next to the desk. The wall behind Krasin was solid glass, like all the outer walls of the building called the Aquarium by those who worked here. Stepaniak had always thought it an ironic name for the headquarters of the least scrutinized intelligence service in the country, known formally as *Glavnoye Razvedyvatelnoye Upravleniye*, the Chief Intelligence Directorate of the Armed Forces General Staff.

None of the usual portraits of political or military leaders hung on the other walls, just six pictures arranged symmetrically: four Russian landscapes and two photographs – one of a passing-out parade and one of eight young men holding aloft a rowing boat. A barbell rested on one of the three other chairs in the room. The only item of value, apart from the inkwell, was an elaborately carved chess set whose pieces were poised mid-game on a small table by the glass wall. Two bookcases completed the rest of a spartan room. Military manuals and texts filled one, while the other contained works of Russian literature, supplemented by Goethe, Schiller, and Rilke in German, plus Shakespeare, and some authors Stepaniak didn't recognize, in English.

'Did you enjoy your time here?' asked the man who had been introduced as Colonel Leskov.

After his training Stepaniak had been assigned to share a room twelve metres square with seven other GRU officers who made life hell for the new man. 'Yes, sir.'

'But you only stayed at GRU headquarters for six months.'

Careful, Taras, this Colonel Leskov is no fool. 'My colonel told me the KGB had selected me for a penetration mission, sir.'

'What was your response?'

Stepaniak wasn't sure what answer would please him, and so he replied, 'My colonel said that he'd objected, but he had to do what the KGB told him, and so had I.'

Krasin gave a derisive laugh. 'Under Brezhnev, the GRU leadership was corrupt, under Andropov it was corrupt and spineless, and under Gorbachev, it was corrupt, spineless, and incompetent. But' – he placed his hands flat on the desk and leaned forward – 'things are changing.' He sat back and removed two folders from a drawer and placed them neatly on the desk. He opened one. 'This top secret communication to the Centre from the head of Line N at the London Residency contains the code "91". Were you the agent?'

'May I look, sir?'

Krasin pushed the folder across the desk.

Stepaniak didn't believe it. It was a photocopy of the current volume from his product file. Written authorization from the head of Directorate S was needed just to read an illegal's file; to photocopy it was unthinkable. 'Yes,' he said slowly. 'I was the source for this report.'

'And you, presumably, obtained the material from one of your sources?'

Stepaniak nodded.

'Interesting,' said Krasin, 'but low grade. It might even have been taken directly from the *Financial Times*. Did you take it from the *Financial Times*?'

Tiny beads of sweat formed on Stepaniak's brow. He almost expected Krasin to open the second folder and take out a clipping from the *Financial Times* published the same day he'd filed his report. 'I can't remember, sir,' he said. 'Collecting economic intelligence wasn't my only task.'

'I know. And I want you to know that operational standards like this will not be tolerated if you work for me.'

'Yes, sir.'

'Good.' Krasin closed the folder, stood up, took the tennis ball, and beckoned Stepaniak to join him at the glass wall. He repeatedly squeezed the tennis ball in his right hand while he talked. 'The Army is reduced to holding its parades on Khodynka Field, in private like some third-rate mercenary outfit, instead of marching through Red Square.'

Beyond the rear of the GRU complex, a vast sea of concrete extended between military railway lines as far as the rear of the former Warsaw Pact headquarters, the stadium of the Central Army Sports Club, and a helicopter terminal. 'It's a disgrace,' Stepaniak agreed.

'We need to restore pride,' said Krasin, continuing his hand-strengthening exercises with the tennis ball in his left hand. 'And for that, we need self-respect, discipline, and dedication.'

Discipline and dedication were for mugs. 'You can rely on me, sir,' said Stepaniak with all the sincerity he could summon.

'Good.' Krasin's genial smile returned. He sat down and opened the second folder. 'I see you have Polish blood in you.'

Stepaniak, too, resumed his seat. 'Not as much as Felix Dzerzhinsky.'

The smile vanished: only one man cracked the jokes round here. 'Did you enjoy your eleven years in England?'

The colonel was scrutinizing Stepaniak's reactions; this man could spot a lie at fifty metres. 'Yes, sir,' Stepaniak answered honestly.

Krasin nodded. 'Your father was Ukrainian?'

'East Ukrainian,' Stepaniak said quickly, 'and my mother was Russian.'

Krasin stared into his eyes. 'I wonder where your true loyalties lie, Captain Stepaniak.' He pursed his lips. 'Tell me, what do you believe in?'

Stepaniak had not thought about that question for years. Perhaps he had believed in communism once. Perhaps at kindergarten in Kharkov when the first song he was taught glorified Lenin: 'always the best friend of children'. It was Uncle Lenin who wanted him to clean his teeth every day, and smiling Uncle Lenin who was happy when he did whatever his teacher told him to do. Perhaps he still believed when he went to school at seven years of age and his reader began with the immortal words: 'The first country of socialism in the world became the first country of children's happiness in the world.' As an Octobrist he listened in awe to the true story of fourteen-year-old Pavel Morozov, martyred by the private farmers for reporting to the authorities that his father was hiding grain from the State during the collectivization campaign of 1932. The young Stepaniak volunteered to be a *zvenovoi*, reporting to the teacher on the conduct of the other children in his group. But the promised children's happiness never materialized. After school other boys hit him because in class he'd told the teacher that they had not finished their homework or had made a joke about Lenin. (He learned to get his revenge by informing on them privately.) And while his teachers referred to his father as a model Soviet citizen and protector of State and Party, Stepaniak saw the reality: a bully who used his position as a KGB major to line his own pockets, drink himself stupid, and beat up his mother at home. Stepaniak joined the Young Pioneers and, dressed in blue trousers and white shirt, with a red scarf round his neck, he marched and stood guard outside the war memorial in Kharkov's Victory Park, just like the KGB guards did outside Lenin's tomb, not because he believed any longer but because he heeded the words of the only teacher he ever respected. Leonid Kozlovsky was an historian, a Jew, and a womanizer. 'Taras,' he said when the young Stepaniak was summoned to stay behind because his essay was politically incorrect, 'it's all shit. You're smart enough to see that, but remember, while you can think what you want, you can't say what you want. Not if you want the good things in life.' And that had been Stepaniak's philosophy ever since. The crucial question here was: what was the right thing to say? Last month orthodox communism, last week reformism, yesterday radical democracy. Today the best bet looked like patriotism. 'I leave beliefs to the intelligentsia, sir. I simply want to do my patriotic duty.'

Krasin smiled his approval. He swivelled his chair so that he faced out over Khodynka Field. 'I may be able to help you realize your ambition, Captain.'

Stepaniak had passed the test; only one question remained. 'Will it involve wet jobs, Colonel? You see, I wasn't trained for that.'

Krasin swivelled back. 'I'm aware where your particular talents lie. Your mission will be similar to the one you've been undertaking in England, but with two differences. First, you will perform to a higher standard, and second, you will penetrate Ukrainian organizations in Kiev, not in London. Do you foresee any problems?'

'No, Colonel. Just tell me what you want.'

Krasin put his hands behind his head and leaned back in his chair. 'We need to give you a work name. Let me see. Stepaniak, Taras Sergeyevich. Stepaniak, T.S., out of England and into the wasteland. You shall be Eliot.' He laughed.

Stepaniak joined in the laughter, though he didn't understand the joke.

'Your local controller will use the name Lomonosov.'

'What are the contact procedures?'

'He'll make contact once you're established, and then give you a procedure for the future. You have two main targets. First, the UPA. I want you to find out as much as you can about this Ukrainian terrorist organization. I suggest you employ your particular expertise on Christine Lesyn.'

'The London *Correspondent* journalist who found General Marchenkov's body?'

'The same. Lesyn appears to have connections with the UPA. Your second target is Roman Bondar.'

Stepaniak grinned. As part of his job at the Ukrainian Press Bureau in London he'd written a profile of Roman Bondar, former political prisoner turned Ukrainian politician, who was one of the leaders of the Ukrainian national movement, Rukh. And he'd researched the article by talking extensively on the phone with Maria. 'No problem. I know his daughter. At least I've spoken to her a lot on the phone. She works in the external affairs department of Rukh.'

'Indeed,' Krasin said. 'They're an organizational shambles, with a high staff turnover. In fact, they're badly in need of an English-speaking press officer just now. Your work for the Ukrainian Press Bureau in London will have earned their trust. You're perfect for the job.'

This was all too neat. It was time to show Colonel Leskov that he wasn't dealing with another moron. 'One question, Colonel. Did you arrange my recall from London and my redundancy from the intelligence service?'

Krasin smiled. 'Do you want to work for me?'

Stepaniak nodded. 'Yes, sir.'

Krasin picked up one of the telephones. 'Get me the Rukh office in Kiev on the public line.' After a few moments a telephone rang. He gave the handset to Stepaniak and picked up another phone to listen.

When someone finally answered, Stepaniak said in Ukrainian, 'I'd like to speak to Maria Bondar, please.'

Eventually a bright voice said, 'Maria here, can I help?'

'It's Taras Stepaniak.'

'Taras, good to hear from you! How are things in London? I heard that you'd left the Ukrainian Press Bureau.'

'That's why I'm phoning. I decided I can't stay in Britain while you're all struggling to build a nation. I want to help. I don't mind what I do as long as you think it's useful.'

'Taras, that's wonderful. When are you coming?'

Krasin held up three fingers.

'In three days.'

'Marvellous. How are you coming? Plane or train? Give me the details and I'll come and meet you.'

Krasin shook his head.

'You have too much to do without wasting your time at airports. I'll phone you when I'm in Kiev.'

'I look forward to that.'

'Me too. It means a lot to me.'

Stepaniak and Krasin put down their telephones at the same time. Krasin smiled. 'Impressive.'

Stepaniak sat back and took out a packet of cheroots.

'Not in this office and, if you take my advice, not at all.'

'Yes, Colonel.'

Krasin stood up and led Stepaniak to the door.

'There is one operational question, if I may, Colonel.'

'Yes?'

'In Britain, the worst that could have happened was to be caught and imprisoned. Then the KGB would have picked up someone in Russia and arranged an exchange.'

Krasin nodded.

'But in Ukraine?'

'What about Ukraine?'

'What protection will you supply, Colonel? I mean, look what happened to General Marchenkov.'

Krasin put his arm around Stepaniak's shoulder and turned to look Stepaniak straight in the eye. 'Put your trust in me and have no fears about meeting Marchenkov's fate.' He bared his teeth in a smile. 'We know how to look after our own people.'

NINE

All roads may lead to Rome, but all railway lines lead to Moscow. The grandiose foyer of Moscow's Kiev Station was packed with former citizens of the empire. Flat-faced Eskimos and Mongols in long-haired goatskin or reindeer coats jostled with hawk-nosed Georgians and Armenians, Central Asians in colourfully beaded felt overcoats, and the Slavs of Russia, Belarus, and Ukraine. Parents shepherded children, plus an assortment of cheap, battered suitcases and bursting cardboard boxes held together by string, through the gaps between other families who overflowed from red benches to cover most of the marble floor; youths, many in military uniform, lounged against the marble walls and Tuscan pillars.

Stepaniak sought refuge in the restaurant, where an attendant guarded the door against a restless crowd. Stepaniak spoke English and was let through. Above head height the restaurant was the neoclassical palace built for the last Tsar: plain white marble pillars with gilded capitals supported an immense, pale green, vaulted ceiling. Below head height seven decades of Soviet reality reigned: empty dishes and full ashtrays littered the few tables occupied by those fortunate enough to have been admitted by the doorman, while the vacant laminate-topped tables were laid with ill-assorted cutlery. Stepaniak chose one with fewest items missing. It took his most charming smile to lure a waitress from the group who nearly outnumbered the diners.

At the fourth shake of the waitress's head, Stepaniak gave up ordering from the long menu and asked what appetizers were available.

'Capital City Salad.'

He nodded. 'And which soups?'
'Capital City Salad.'
'For the main course?'
'Stroganoff.'
'Anything else?'
She was bored. 'Stroganoff.'
'OK. Stroganoff. Followed by ice cream.'
'No ice cream.'
Stepaniak knew that things were bad, but even so, a Moscow restaurant without ice cream was like a McDonald's without hamburgers. He was finding it difficult to keep smiling. 'What do you have for dessert?'
'Tea.'
He sighed. 'One tea. And a beer.'
'No beer.'
He put a dollar bill on the table. She shrugged and picked it up.
Half an hour later, as Stepaniak was about to leave and find his train, the waitress returned with a tray containing a can of beer, a glass of tea, a small glass dish holding a sculpted pyramid of what appeared to be potato, and the main course.
'May I have a glass for the beer?'
She gave him a strange look, searched through the cupboard at her desk, and returned with a glass dessert bowl.
The 'stroganoff' consisted of lukewarm gristle floating in a fatty sauce over cold greasy rice. He pushed it away and, for the first time, sympathized with those who had been sent to the gulag.
He lugged his suitcase through the throng in the foyer, pushed his way down a wide corridor, and stepped out into the cold black night. Snowflakes cascaded down cones of weak white light from high platform lamps as he hauled his case up the steps onto Platform 13. His sleeping car was at the far end of the long, blue train, and he only just managed to clamber aboard before a porter slammed the door shut and the train lurched out of the station at precisely 20:20. Having the trains leave on time seemed the one remaining organizational feat of the former Soviet empire.
The train was lumbering past tall industrial chimneys blanching the night with their mushroom clouds of pollutant before he

located the door to his two-berth compartment. Disappointingly, no nubile young woman awaited the delights of his suitcase, only an overweight, lugubrious man with slicked-back thinning hair who wore a creased, dark grey, polyester suit. He looked enviously at Stepaniak's Western parka and jeans. Vatslav Krikalen introduced himself as an official of Moscow's Vneshekonombank, making the latest in an interminable series of visits to Kiev to try and resolve the dispute over the former Soviet bank's assets claimed by the National Bank of Ukraine.

'I'm a journalist,' said Stepaniak as he lifted his suitcase up onto the rack.

Krikalen carefully unlocked his status symbol, a black plastic-coated metal executive briefcase, and removed a paper bag. He delved into the bag, and his sausage fingers emerged holding two sandwiches, one of which he offered to Stepaniak. Stepaniak couldn't taste whatever paste was spread meagrely between the thick white slices, but he didn't care. He was grateful for anything that would fill his stomach and take away the foul taste of the restaurant's pigswill.

Krikalen's gloom lifted when Stepaniak opened a bottle of duty-free Scotch. Krikalen produced a plastic cup from inside his briefcase and watched as Stepaniak filled it. He put the cup to his lips and drank greedily. When all the whisky was gone, melancholia returned. After complaining about the unreasonableness of Ukrainians, he belched, stood up, and removed his suit, tie and shirt to reveal flannel pyjamas. He placed his suit on a metal hanger and clambered into his bunk.

With bread and half a bottle of Scotch inside him Stepaniak was feeling much more like his old self. He was even tempted when the compartment door opened and the conductress gave him an appraising smile. She was young and pretty, if plump. Krikalen's beady eyes were on the two glasses of tea in traditional metal *podstakanniki* that she carried. With a resigned glance in Krikalen's direction, Stepaniak returned her smile and gave her a five-dollar tip. This expansive gesture was worth it if only for the expression of disbelief on Krikalen's face. When the bank official recovered, he gulped his tea and burrowed underneath his blue blanket with the elegance of a stranded whale finding water.

Stepaniak stripped down to his vest and boxer shorts, climbed into the bunk opposite, and turned out the light. It was rather extravagant to give her a tip equal to her monthly wage. It was also equal to the monthly pension he'd just escaped from. That had been a close shave. If his father were alive, he would doubtless complain that Stepaniak always landed with his bum in butter, but the crude bully never appreciated how Stepaniak used his brains to get what he wanted. The young Stepaniak had seen from his mother's side of the family the privileged lifestyle of the military *nomenklatura*. He persuaded his grandfather, General Pashkov, to pull a few strings and secure his acceptance at a military academy. Once there he cheated to obtain top grades in English and in a Political Theory that was bullshit in order to gain a place at the GRU training school and so avoid combat in Afghanistan. Nor was it by chance, as his bonehead of a father thought, that he had been recruited by the First Chief Directorate of the KGB for what every agent wants most of all: work in the West. He had taken great care to impress a KGB colonel's daughter with more than his command of English and Ukrainian. But this new job *was* a stroke of luck, even if Leskov had arranged it all. The KGB was in a mess, but the more secretive GRU, which had a foreign intelligence budget larger than the KGB's, was well placed to pull the levers of power in the new Russia.

Leskov had an intimidating presence, but Stepaniak believed he had him well under control. Leskov was a Russian patriot, probably fanatically so, but he was also a career officer, no different from the others in that respect. All Stepaniak had to do was tell him what he wanted to hear. It was going to be a cushy number. His first two targets were women. What more could he ask? He settled down and, despite the snoring from the bunk opposite, drifted off into a contented sleep with thoughts of the good times to come.

TEN

When she bounced up from behind the small desk, the top of Maria Bondar's head barely reached his chin. Her blonde hair was brushed back and held in a ponytail by a blue-and-yellow striped ribbon. If all the elements of her face had been in proportion she would have been beautiful, but saucer-like brown eyes, a nose bent at the bridge, and a mouth that instinctively opened into a wide smile dominated a small high-cheekboned face as delicate as porcelain. Firm, high breasts, like those of a well developed schoolgirl outgrowing her uniform, pressed against a much washed blue denim shirt too small even for her slender body. The shirt was tucked into a pair of shapeless Polish-made jeans. Stepaniak knew that the woman inside this teenager's body was approaching thirty.

'Taras, welcome to Kiev! It's great to meet the man behind the voice.'

The grip of her small hand was surprisingly firm. He held onto it and looked into her eyes. 'I tried to guess what beauty lay behind your voice, but my imagination pales before the reality.' He brought her hand upwards and brushed it with his lips.

She blushed, and in her confusion said, 'Where are you staying? How is London? Is it snowing there? I've a million and one questions to ask you, but first I want you to meet Les Koval, head of the secretariat. You said you wanted to help. I think I've got just the job for you.'

She led him down a corridor lined with torn linoleum, and up bare wooden stairs. Without knocking she opened a door into a cacophony of three arguments and the radio broadcast of a debate in Parliament. No one looked towards them from the three groups, mainly young people in shoddy informal clothes, who were disputing with the fervour of the single-minded. Maria led him through the blue-grey haze of tobacco smoke to a desk in front of a faded and curled election poster on an institution-green wall. Behind the laminated desk, on which sat a Macintosh Classic and the transistor radio, a man with thinning sandy hair and a large walrus moustache was trying to conduct a telephone conversation.

When Maria introduced Stepaniak, Koval shook his hand while continuing his telephone call with the handset cradled between shoulder and ear. At last he finished. He looked Stepaniak up and down. 'How long were you with the Ukrainian Press Bureau in London?'

'Full time for seven years, but I'd been helping part time before that.'

'Maria thinks we need an English-speaking press officer. We can't afford to pay much.'

Stepaniak gave Koval one of his sincere looks. 'If it was money I was interested in, I'd have stayed in London and got a job with a national newspaper.'

'How long do you plan to stay in Kiev?'

'As long as you need me.'

Koval turned to Maria. 'Tell Oksana to fix him up with a six-month visa. If he stays longer we can make it permanent.' He returned his attention to the telephone and began dialling.

'I see,' said Stepaniak, as Maria led him away.

'Oh, don't be put off by Les's manner. He's cynical about everybody, not just those from the diaspora.'

'You've had problems with them?'

'I wouldn't say problems. Many came over, especially from Canada, eager to build a nation. Some of the Rukh workers who'd been struggling for the nationalist cause since the days of Shcherbitsky found their energy' – she screwed up her face – 'wearing, I suppose you'd say. And some of those from the diaspora found our ways . . . well, many of them became disillusioned and left. But,' she said brightly, 'you're different, I can tell.'

'How can you tell?'

'For a start, you're older.'

Stepaniak laughed at her gaucherie. 'Thank you very much.'

'I didn't mean . . . Oh, well, anyway.'

He smiled and said nothing.

'Come and meet the others in the press office,' she said quickly to hide her embarrassment.

The two women, both in their twenties, eyed Stepaniak before exchanging furtive glances of approval. One was plain and wholesome and, with her dungarees and her hair in plaits, might have come straight from milking cows on a village farm, while her raven-haired colleague wore a vermilion lycra dress that emphasized her roly-poly figure.

When Maria had gone, the plain one shyly approached Stepaniak and asked his advice on a press release she was drafting. Stepaniak's eyes lingered on her breasts. She blushed. The draft was rubbish.

'It makes it appear that Rukh has split into half a dozen warring factions, like Solidarity in Poland.' Stepaniak smiled confidingly. 'It may have, but we can't let the public think that. Let me work on it. I may need some files.'

'I'll get them for you,' the roly-poly girl said eagerly.

Stepaniak began redrafting the press release about Rukh's response to the Government's proposed ultra-conservative economic programme. A group of nationalist deputies in Parliament were planning to vote with the ex-communists who formed the Government, to the fury of the radical democrats, the Greens, and most other groups that had formed Rukh as a popular mass movement for independence. Roman Bondar was summoning a meeting of the squabbling Rukh leaders to thrash out a united front. It confirmed Leskov's assessment of the role Roman Bondar played in Ukraine's fragile new democracy.

After his two colleagues finished work, Stepaniak went to Maria's room.

'Hi! How was your day?' she asked.

'After you left me, the sun vanished behind black clouds.'

Her cheeks flushed. 'There's been no sun all day.'

He looked into her eyes and said, 'I'd like to repay your trust in me and celebrate my first day at work by taking you out to dinner.'

'That . . . that sounds nice. When were you thinking of?'

'Now.'

'Now? But . . . Daddy will be expecting me for supper tonight.'

'You cook for your father?'

'No. Mother does that.'

'That's settled then. My first day at work is today.'

She came to a decision. 'I'll phone Mother. I'll be ready in half an hour.'

When he called back, she was still typing on an old portable typewriter. 'Sorry,' she said, 'nearly finished.'

He helped her into a parka and wondered whether the baggy jeans hid skinny or fat legs. On balance he hoped they were skinny.

'Where are we going?' she asked.

'I was hoping you'd tell me. It's years since I was in Kiev.'

She thought and then said, 'There's a restaurant on Victory Prospekt. We can walk.'

Snow was falling again when they crossed Victory Square to the Lybid Hotel and tramped through the slush past the multi-storey Ukraine State Department Store whose window displays resembled an Oxfam shop in a recession. A uniformed man opened the restaurant door to say that it was closed.

'Being a doorman at a restaurant isn't a job,' Maria said in frustration, 'it's a state of mind. Why do they always close restaurants at meal times?'

'So the staff can eat, of course,' said Stepaniak.

Her frustration dissolved into laughter.

'Where to now?' he asked.

'We could go back to Victory Square and try one of the restaurants at the Lybid Hotel.'

'No,' he said decisively. 'I'm staying at the Lybid until I find a place of my own, and I've sampled their so-called food. I want this to be a celebration, not a penance. What about some of these cooperative restaurants I've heard about?'

'Well,' she said, 'I've been told there's one next to the Architects' Union on Pushkin Street. But it's expensive.'

'This is a celebration. Let's go.'

She went to the pavement. The first car she waved pulled up. 'Come on,' she said.

'Are you sure there's a restaurant here?' he asked when they stood in front of the white neoclassical façade.

'There's only one way to find out,' she said, and opened the unmarked door to the left of the main door to the Architects' Union. On a landing below a dozen marble steps a man dressed in a pullover and cord trousers stood next to a table. Maria led the way down.

'A table for two,' Stepaniak said.

'We're full,' the man said.

'What's the problem?' Stepaniak asked. 'Will a thousand coupons solve it?'

'There's no problem, we're full.'

'Then maybe five dollars.'

'I told you. We're full.'

Three burly youths, two with freshly scarred and bruised faces, came down the stairs. The owner nodded to them and they walked past and down another flight of stairs.

'I see,' said Maria sweetly. 'These are your favoured clients?'

'Certainly not,' began the man. Then he saw Maria smiling innocently at the three as they took up their positions in front of a door at the bottom of the stairs. He beamed. 'We are full, but for a lady as charming as you I will make an exception.'

Maria's face lit up. 'Thank you.'

They left their outer coats in the cloakroom, and the owner led them down past the three bouncers into a small basement dining room with three long and three small tables that would seat a total of about forty. It reminded Stepaniak of a church basement converted to serve tea and biscuits for the faithful after Sunday's main service, except that bland Eurovision-style pop songs warbled from a cassette player on a shelf. If this was the height of Kiev sophistication, the sooner he completed his mission the better. Only one table was occupied. 'Make up another table,' the owner said to the waitress, and led Stepaniak and Maria to a corner table laid for two.

Maria's eyes opened even wider at the plates of stuffed fish, smoked salmon, smoked sturgeon, red caviar, pickled herring, cold meats, crabmeat salad, strips of cold chicken, and fish paste surrounding a plate of brown and white bread and a dish of butter.

'I thought there was a food shortage,' Stepaniak said.

Maria lowered her voice. 'I've never seen anything like it. I think the stuffed fish is pike. I last saw that at my cousin's wedding nearly ten years ago.'

'I'll order some wine,' Stepaniak said.

'There's drink here,' she said, pouring him out a glass of pale red liquid from a flagon. '*Mors*. Full of vitamins, very good for you, Taras.'

'But to celebrate we shall drink something that's also very good for you.' He beckoned to the waitress. 'The wine list, please.'

The waitress gave him a bottle of chilled white wine instead.

'*Rkatsytelie*,' said Maria, studying the label. 'It's from the Crimea. It's very good.'

'Do you want to order the main course now?'

'Goodness, I don't think I'm going to manage all this.'

He smiled and poured her another glass of wine. He followed her eyes as they swivelled round in fascination. A party of eight came to the table next to theirs. The men were dressed in expensive leather jackets or smart Western-tailored suits, while the women showed deep cleavages and long legs in sheer tights. Maria leaned across and whispered, 'I've never seen mafia bosses before.'

The taped music was replaced by a violinist who ranged from sentimental Hungarian rhapsodies to a gypsy version of 'Yesterday'. Stepaniak poured more wine into her glass and employed a technique that rarely failed. He asked her about herself, then said very little and gazed directly into her eyes. As her voice washed over him he imagined that he was untying the ribbon and letting her hair fall loose about her face, that he was unbuttoning and then parting her shirt, that his hands were caressing her willing body. His eyes smiled confidently as she searched for words to fill his silences, as a blush tinged the top of her cheeks, as her hands repeatedly brushed back wisps of hair that escaped the ponytail, as her fingers nervously refastened the third button of her shirt. She was going to be easy.

'But tell me what you believe in, Taras,' he heard her say.

'I believe in the power of positive thinking.'

'Right! Half the members of Rukh don't really believe we can build an independent Ukraine without the management experience of the former communist apparatchiks. But if you believe in something strongly enough you can make it happen.'

He looked into her eyes, smiled, and imagined the moment of slowly easing himself into her. 'Don't doubt it.'

'Are you . . . are you laughing at me?'

'No.' He put his large hand reassuringly over hers. 'I'm admiring you.'

The blush deepened. 'I think we'd better go now.'

'So do I,' he said softly.

Maria took two slices of brown bread and the plate of fish paste, and made a large sandwich which she wrapped in a paper serviette.

He looked quizzically at her.

'For your breakfast tomorrow morning. I'm worried you don't have proper food at that hotel.'

'I appreciate your concern for me,' he said while his eyes looked into hers. 'You will come back to the hotel for a nightcap.'

'Goodness, no,' she said, handing him the wrapped sandwich. 'Daddy will be worried. He was expecting me before ten. It's well past eleven already.'

He sighed to himself. 'I'll take you back.'

'Certainly not. It's in the opposite direction. There's a bus I can catch that goes near home.'

'I insist.'

'You're very determined, Taras, just like my father. But Daddy will appreciate it.'

The bus stopped at the Friendship of Peoples Boulevard in the less fashionable part of Pechersk district which housed the Parliament building and most government offices. Stepaniak accompanied her up the quiet street off the boulevard and along the path between white lawns to the dimly lit porch of a three-storey block of apartments. 'I've really enjoyed this evening, Maria,' he said. 'You've made my return to Ukraine very special.'

'I've enjoyed it too,' she said.

He leaned down to kiss her. She drew away like a frightened rabbit and covered her embarrassment by scrabbling in her handbag. She pulled out a bunch of keys and inserted one in the lock. 'Thank you for a lovely evening,' she stammered.

He smiled, waved, and turned away. So, she was playing hard to get. She may have won the first round, but it would only make his victory all the more satisfying.

As she watched him go she clenched her tiny fists in frustration. She was twenty-eight years old and acted like an infatuated schoolgirl. What on earth had he thought of her as she'd gabbled on to try and impress him, giving opinions on politics that she'd borrowed from her father, offering views on Crimean wines she'd never drunk in order to show her sophistication, wittering on nervously about anything rather than expressing what she really felt. Was it the same old fear that made her act like this? Taras had said virtually nothing. He'd obviously been bored out of his mind. This was the last time he'd ask her out.

ELEVEN

It was time to see if Christine Lesyn proved equally resistant to his charms.

If Ukrainian girls still clung to their virginity, North American and British girls were more sophisticated. After his lack of success the previous evening, the prospect of a willing young body appealed to him. Most foreign correspondents in Kiev were stringers, mainly youngsters from the US, Canada, or Britain, who received a small retainer from their newspaper and were paid on the number of words published. Young, adventurous, and poorly paid. That would do very nicely, thank you. He smiled to himself as he walked up the stairs to Les Koval's office.

Before ten thirty was the best time to find Koval alone. After that, other Rukh officials began to arrive at the building and soon intruded with the latest gossip or conspiracy theory.

'Les,' Stepaniak said, 'sorry to disturb you, but if I'm to do this job properly, I need to cultivate the foreign correspondents.'

Koval looked up from the piles of papers on his desk. 'So cultivate them.'

'I was hoping you might fill me in on their backgrounds. The girls in the press office don't know anything about the foreign press.'

Koval shrugged. Most of the names on Stepaniak's list meant nothing to him either, until Stepaniak came to the *Correspondent.*

Koval gave a mirthless laugh. 'Our dear Christine, part time journalist and full time opportunist.'

'Part time?'

'How many Ukrainians have you met who work full time?'

'She's Ukrainian?'

Koval stretched out his arms and yawned. 'The Lesyns and the Bondars know each other from way back, in Lviv. Chrystia and Maria were contemporaries at Ivan Franko University. When Maria came to Kiev with her father after the 1990 elections, she arranged for Chrystia Lesyna to come and work in the press office here. It was a good stepping stone. After six months Chrystia became Christine and left to freelance for any Western newspaper that would have her.' He gave an earthy chuckle. 'The *Correspondent* did.'

Stepaniak offered Koval a cheroot. 'The girls in the office don't seem to hold any regular press briefings.' The two girls didn't seem to do anything much, apart from talk about boys and use the phone to find out where and when bread, milk, and sugar were likely to be available. 'How often does Christine Lesyn come here?'

'Our Christine has far grander things to do than visit our humble little offices, especially now she's become the ace reporter who tracks down missing Russian generals. If you want to meet her, I'd try Parliament. That's where she spends most of her time. Have you got a parliamentary press pass?'

'No. The girls didn't mention anything.'

Koval savoured the cheroot. 'There's a defence debate this afternoon. Yaro Melnik, the head of our defence commission, is going. Nationalist deputies are planning to hold an informal press conference during the debate. Lesyn is sure to be there. I'll ask Yaro to take you and call in at the press centre on Sadova to get you a parliamentary pass.'

'So you're our latest press officer, the one from England who took Maria out to an expensive restaurant?'

Stepaniak was unprepared both for the hostility and the appearance of Yaroslav Melnik who, reportedly, had served as a major in the Soviet Army before he joined the Rukh staff. Brown eyes burned from a pallid, intense face beneath lank, black hair and a thick, walrus moustache that covered his upper lip. A distinctly unmilitary cardigan partly covered a T-shirt. Stepaniak was tempted to ask if a walrus moustache was *de rigueur* for male

Rukh staff. Instead he smiled and said, 'Delighted to meet you, Yaro.'

Melnik ignored Stepaniak's proffered hand. 'Les says that you worked for the Ukrainian Press Bureau in London. I've a cousin in London. Maybe I'll give him a ring.'

Stepaniak wondered who this man's cousin might be. He was pretty sure his cover would stand up, but rival factions among the émigrés often accused each other of being infiltrated by the KGB. Complications like this he could do without. 'Fine,' he said, 'and in the meantime Les said you'd be kind enough to get a press pass for me and show me the ropes at Parliament.'

'It's not my job,' said Melnik, 'but Sadova Street is across the road from the Parliament building. If you want to go, I'm leaving now.'

'Whatever suits your convenience,' said Stepaniak.

It had stopped snowing, but snow lay thick over frozen slush on the wide pavement outside the Rukh building. Stepaniak rubbed his gloved hands together and wondered which of two battered old cars and a van parked on the pavement belonged to Melnik.

'I left the company BMW at home today,' said Melnik as if reading his thoughts. He walked past the parked cars towards the trolley bus stop on Taras Shevchenko Boulevard. Ten freezing minutes later they pushed themselves into a packed number 9 which trundled off and downhill.

Gone from the faces on the bus was the submissiveness Stepaniak remembered from a dozen years before, the brief muttered exchanges, the stealthy glances to spot which fellow passenger was an informer. Now there was a weariness that occasionally erupted into heated complaints about the lack of meat, fish, and vegetables. One wizened war veteran berated a young man wearing a blue-and-yellow enamel badge on his jacket, blaming all the country's ills on independence. 'Silly old fool should go and live in Russia,' Melnik said to Stepaniak.

At the end of Taras Shevchenko Boulevard, the trolley bus turned left into Kreshchatik. This had been the pride of Soviet Ukraine: the Champs-Élysées of the east, with six lanes of traffic bordered by chestnut-tree-lined pavements as wide again; on either side, eight-storey Stalinist baroque blocks of apartments and offices, with ground floor shops filled with the best the Soviet Union produced; and at its centre, the vast October Revolution Square, with wide granite terraces stepping up the hillside to the massive red granite Lenin above four bronze fighters for the Revolution, and higher still to the Moscow Hotel that dominated the skyline.

Stepaniak saw only a couple of customers through the large window of the Central Market dairy annex where peasants sold their milk and cheese at market prices. On the opposite side of Kreshchatik a long queue waited outside the State dairy with its affordable prices and empty shelves. The trolley bus stopped in the renamed Independence Square. A green wooden fence, daubed with stickers and graffiti, surrounded the place where Lenin and his fighters had once stood. The new 'monument' summed up for Stepaniak what this bunch of amateurs had to offer to replace a system that, for all its faults, had put food in people's bellies.

They alighted at the far end of Kreshchatik, by the glass and yellow-tiled Dnipro Hotel on the square Stepaniak had known as Leninsky Komsomol. Ahead, the snow-covered slope of Pioneer Park rose from the square. Crowning the slope was a huge stainless steel arc, like a silver rainbow, that commemorated the 1654 reunification of Russia with a Ukraine liberated from the Poles. 'That's the next to come down,' said Melnik as they waited in the square for another trolley bus to take them up the street renamed Hruszevski. Reunification survived rather longer than the three-month presidency of Hruszevski after the 1918 declaration of independence, Stepaniak was tempted to tell this arrogant bastard.

The officials at the Parliamentary Press Office showed less suspicion than Melnik about Stepaniak's press credentials. Stepaniak followed an impatient Melnik across Hruszevski Street, where temporary barriers prevented pedestrian access to the Parliament building. Melnik pushed his way through the crowd of petitioners, waiting in the bitter cold with their placards demanding increased wages for increased prices, no more rent rises, and compensation for Chernobyl victims. Melnik and he showed their passes and a militiaman waved them through a gap in the barriers.

Trying to keep abreast of Melnik, Stepaniak slipped on sheet ice covering the empty square in front of the six-columned neo-classical portico of the former Ukrainian Supreme Soviet. Melnik didn't stop. Stepaniak caught up with him at the door to the right of the portico. They left their coats in the cloakroom and climbed two flights of red carpeted marble stairs to a deserted press lobby. 'They'll all be inside,' Melnik said.

From the back of the press gallery Stepaniak looked down into the octagonal chamber, which was illuminated by an immense chandelier suspended beneath the domed glass roof and by a battery of bright television lights. The hammer-and-sickle bas-reliefs on the eggshell-blue walls appeared more durable than the blue-and-yellow Ukrainian nationalist flag propped up in the white niche that had contained a statue of Lenin. Below the flag the chairman sat at his elevated desk, vainly attempting to keep order. Many deputies had left their desks, which were arranged in curved rows focused on the chairman, and were crowding the speaker's rostrum beneath the chairman. At the rostrum the Defence Minister, when he could be heard above the angry heckling of the deputies, assured ethnic Russian soldiers that they had nothing to fear in Ukraine and that the National Security Service would hunt down without mercy the killers of General Marchenkov. If Hruszevski's parliament had been as shambolic as this, Stepaniak reflected, it was little wonder he hadn't lasted long. 'Which one is Christine Lesyn?' Stepaniak whispered.

'The one whose bronze hair comes out of a bottle,' replied Melnik.

Most of the reporters were young and informally dressed in sweaters or cardigans and jeans. The woman with the well groomed, shoulder-length bronze hair wore a grey suit. Stepaniak moved round the back of the press gallery to get a better view. Her nose was too long, but he certainly wouldn't kick her out of bed.

At the end of the Defence Minister's speech the chairman stage-managed the debate to the fury of a group of deputies who stormed out. Most of the reporters left, and Stepaniak followed them down one flight of steps to the large central lobby outside the deputies' entrance to the chamber. Here, a dozen deputies took turns to accuse the Defence Minister of subservience to Russia. Christine Lesyn appeared bored.

As the informal press conference came to a ragged end, Stepaniak approached her. 'Excuse me,' he said in English, 'I couldn't help noticing how fluent your Ukrainian is.'

'But . . .' She stopped and smiled. 'You really think so?'

'You must be a special correspondent from England.'

She graced him with a dazzling smile. 'Why do you think so?'

He nodded towards the group of young reporters who were comparing notes and translations. 'These others aren't in your league.'

'Really? Actually, you are right in one way. I am trained as journalist, while most of these boys and girls are just here for experience after university. But I am Ukrainian. Christine Lesyn.'

'*The* Christine Lesyn?'

'You have heard of me?' Her surprise was as authentic as the colour of her hair.

'I tried to guess what beauty lay behind the elegance of your reports, but my imagination pales before the reality.' He took her proffered hand and brushed it with his lips. 'Permit me to introduce myself. I'm Taras Stepaniak from London. I've just become a press officer for Rukh.'

'Pleased to meet you, Taras. It is interesting that you should think I am English.' She was content for him to keep hold of her hand while his eyes roamed unashamedly over her body.

'In London you would pass unnoticed except, of course, for your beauty.'

'Really?' Her eyes returned the scrutiny. 'Martin Harvey – do you know Martin Harvey, he is deputy foreign editor of the *Correspondent*? – well, Martin also said that my English is perfect.'

Stepaniak did know Martin Harvey. The self-admiring little shit had rejected Ukrainian Press Bureau articles on Ukraine by announcing that he only accepted copy from impartial professional journalists. 'Of course our paths crossed, but in London I had to deal with the foreign editors of most of the major papers.'

'This is very interesting, Taras, because I may come to work as journalist in London. Martin has more or less promised he will find me a position with the *Correspondent*.'

Flat on your back if his performance follows his reputation, Stepaniak thought. 'With your work on the Marchenkov killing, I'm sure many of the editors I know will be eager to employ you.'

'Really?'

She had swallowed the bait – hook, line and sinker. 'I think we should get to know one another better,' he said. 'What about dinner?'

'I like that. When?'

'Tonight.'

'Now I have this boring story to file. You call for me at eight. Here is my card. My apartment is on Karl Marx Street, above the Lancôme shop.'

The owner of the Lestnitza Restaurant in the basement of the Architects' Union building greeted Stepaniak warmly. His expression froze when he saw not the lady with the delightful smile but yet another woman baring cleavage and legs. With a resigned shrug he led them to the same corner table, which was covered with the same *zakuski*. Stepaniak poured out glasses of the *Rkatsytelie*, asked Lesyn about herself, and then gazed directly into her eyes. At the end of the meal, when he suggested they go back to the Lybid for a nightcap, Christine Lesyn said that her apartment was much nearer.

She opened the apartment door, took off her suede coat and shoes, and said, 'It is very convenient to live above one's perfume shop.'

Stepaniak smiled and placed two fingers over her lips. The two fingers traced a tantalizing path down her neck and breast to the top of the button-through dress she'd changed into for dinner. She stood in the hall while he slowly, ever so slowly, undid each button, his eyes not leaving hers. His hands were like velvet on her flesh when he eased the dress from her shoulders and helped it slide to the floor. Her nipples hardened when his left hand caressed her right breast, while the fingers of his right hand felt their way down the back of her hair onto her neck, down her tingling spine and over the nylon of her black slip until they spread out so that hand and fingers could fondle her left buttock. With a sharp intake of breath she parted her legs as his fingers inched into the crease between her buttocks and gently probed towards the lips of her vulva. She was flushed and weak at the knees as her own fingers groped with the buckle of his belt. The more frantic her fingers became, the more leisurely did his hands slide the straps of her slip from her shoulders and massage the thin material down her body and over her hips. His hands cupped her buttocks and lifted her up his body. She wrapped her legs round his waist and her arms round his neck, and he carried her through into the bedroom.

She was kissing and biting his hair as he let her slide down his body onto the bed. She reached up to claw down his trousers and pull his shorts away from his growing penis while he shrugged off his shirt. For a moment he loomed naked over her. Then he bent towards her. As she moaned and squirmed on the bed, he slowly peeled away her bra, tights, and briefs with his hands while his mouth followed and explored the exposed flesh and the crevices between. Urgently she spread her legs and thrust her pelvis towards him but he, wordlessly this first time, would not hurry.

He brought her to a climax three times that night, but when she woke in the morning he was gone.

TWELVE

Christine Lesyn took even less time than he'd expected before she contacted him. 'I have two tickets for Parliament's Independence Day celebration next week at the Kiev Hotel,' she said over the telephone. 'Would you like to come?'

'If you are there, nothing would give me greater pleasure,' Stepaniak said.

'It begins at eight, so you collect me at seven thirty.'

She was wearing a black, imitation silk dressing gown when she opened the door. 'I will not be long time,' she said to impress him with her English.

While she continued putting on her make-up, he wandered round the apartment. 'How many rooms do you have?' he called out.

'Four, apart from bathroom and toilet.'

'All to yourself?'

'Yes.'

This was amazing. The doors, the dining table and chairs, and the cabinets in the dining room were solid wood. Fine Turkmen, Armenian, and Kazakh carpets covered much of the parquet floor and draped several walls. Posters of the British Houses of Parliament, Buckingham Palace, and Marilyn Monroe filled other spaces. The cast iron, scroll footed bath and the pedestal hand-basin were enamelled and stained yellow, the chrome taps were large and dulled with limescale, but the white tiles were uncracked and the water flowed freely. The sink, oven, and oak kitchen cabinet gave the tiled kitchen a solid, pre-War appearance, spoiled only by a modern German fridge and posters of the Beatles, but here too everything worked. From the window of the spacious living room, which was on the top floor of the six-storey cream-and-turquoise baroque building, he could see down Karl Marx Street, across Kreshchatik, to the eight-storey Stalinist Central Post Office that abutted Independence Square. This was Kiev's equivalent of a Mayfair apartment. 'How did you manage to get this place?' he asked when he returned to the bedroom.

She looked at his reflection in her large dressing-table mirror. 'The owner was administrator of former Communist Party Central Committee. Officially I pay him two thousand coupons a month. Unofficially the *Correspondent* pays my monthly retainer into his London sterling account.'

She turned round. 'Since it is Independence Day celebration, do you think I should wear traditional blouse? My grandmother gave me hers.'

He saw from the bedside clock that it was already eight o'clock. 'If you want.'

From a drawer at the bottom of the walnut wardrobe she removed a white cotton blouse embroidered with delicate patterns in red, green, yellow, and blue. She untied her dressing gown and let it part. Underneath she was wearing a black underwired half-cup bra and black bikini briefs. She held the blouse to her neck. 'Does it suit me?'

'Sure.'

'I think I have to change my bra. The black will show through this material.'

He nodded.

She removed her dressing gown and stripped off her bra in what she clearly thought was a seductive manner. He looked at the clock.

She selected a white lace bra and finally pulled the blouse over her head. She examined herself in the mirror. 'Actually, the red embroidery clashes with my lipstick,' she concluded. 'I shall have to change blouse or lipstick.'

He decided which would be the quicker. 'The lipstick.'

He was wrong. At half past eight he said, 'I was hoping we wouldn't miss the speech by Roman Bondar.'

She paused in the act of brushing her hair. 'Independence and democratic government will enable Ukraine, with its population, agricultural and mineral resources, size, and strategic position, to become one of leading nations of Europe. This potential will be realized by hard work in field and factory, and tolerance in street and legislative chamber. It will be crowned with membership of European Community.' She turned round. 'Now you have heard it. The thirty-minute version does not add anything.'

'But why did they choose Bondar to give the keynote speech? Why not the President or the Prime Minister?'

'They are not stupid, you know. On Independence Day it is important to show a united country. Bondar is the only West Ukrainian the Government trusts, and he is the only national figure the West Ukrainians trust. This is why Government arranged for him to be elected Chairman of Parliamentary Foreign Affairs Committee. They can bring him out to impress foreign delegations, and most of the embassies will be represented there tonight.'

'Interesting,' said Stepaniak. 'But do you think we might actually see this event at first hand?'

It was nearly half past nine when their taxi pulled up outside the Kiev Hotel, a glass and concrete high rise block across the street from the Parliament building. Stepaniak took both coats to the cloakroom, but he still had to wait five minutes while Lesyn reapplied her lipstick and rebrushed her hair in front of the wall mirror at the foot of the staircase leading up to the first-floor hall.

The sounds of an accordion, drums, xylophone, and violin came from the hall. Evidently the speeches were finished. Stepaniak opened the door and saw Maria Bondar, in traditional blouse, long billowy red skirt and red boots, dancing with Yaroslav Melnik. Her feet barely touched the ground, her hair swirled around her head, her eyes sparkled, her mouth opened wide in laughter. Jealousy stabbed him to the core.

'What are you staring at?' Christine Lesyn asked.

'The musical instruments,' he said.

'Traditional,' she said sarcastically. 'They are desperate to invent historic culture.'

She inspected the *zakuski* on the tables that lined one wall of the wood-panelled room. 'Not up to the standard of the Lestnitza Restaurant,' she said to be overheard. Her voice took on a shriller tone when she spoke in Ukrainian; it wasn't difficult to imagine her trading insults in the market place. Eventually she selected some bony smoked salmon, blinys with soured cream, and pickled mushroom. 'You'd think they would supply better wine than this.'

Stepaniak filled his plate and poured himself a large cold vodka.

Lesyn promenaded across the room, which was decorated with blue-and-yellow flags and tridents, and blue and yellow balloons and streamers. She chose a table that gave a good view of the groups of guests standing and chatting with their hosts in the centre of the hall. 'I do not see many people from the West, but the one over there in grey suit is Canadian Ambassador. And of course you know the Prime Minister, who is talking with head of National Security Service.'

Stepaniak's eyes were elsewhere. Maria Bondar, her cheeks flushed, was sitting at a corner table and drinking a glass of orange that Melnik had brought her. 'Excuse me,' Stepaniak said, 'there's somebody I must have a word with.'

'Taras, are you joining us?' Maria exclaimed in delight. Melnik stared.

'I'd love to, and I was also hoping to see your father,' Stepaniak said.

Maria pulled a face. 'Daddy's gone off with the British and the German Ambassadors. Typical.'

'We considered it unacceptable that the European Community delegation postponed its visit just because the British Foreign Secretary had a cold,' Melnik said as though he held Stepaniak personally responsible.

'Oh, Yaro,' Maria said, tousling his hair, 'don't be so pompous. Let's make this the happiest day since the human chain.' That had been the most magical day of her life since her father's release from the labour camps. It was impressed on her memory even more than the referendum the following year, which had inevitably confirmed Ukraine's independence. There had been nothing inevitable about the eve of the seventy-first anniversary of Hruszevski's declaration of an independent Ukrainian People's Republic. When she stood next to her father on a temporary platform in front of the gigantic granite statue of Ivan Franko, her heart was pounding with fear. Ahead, the banned blue-and-yellow nationalist flags outnumbered the umbrellas above the sea of faces that stretched uphill to the trees at the top of the park. Members of the Lviv militia – fresh-faced troopers barely out of school and officers she had been to school with – looked up at the platform, uncertain where their allegiance lay. Behind, between the Doric columns of the university's first-floor portico, leather jacketed thugs of the KGB were talking into two-way radios. Barking came from beyond the trees, where a score of trucks lined up in front of the Dniester Hotel on Mateiko Street. Beside the trucks stood the dreaded OMON troops, who had exchanged their black berets and khaki combat jackets for steel helmets and bullet-proof vests, and their wooden truncheons for either long, hard rubber batons and plastic riot shields or else assault rifles. She gripped her father's hand, and his bass voice began to sing *Schche ne vmerla Ukraina*, the first line of the Ukrainian national anthem, 'Ukraine shall not perish'. The words were taken up by those on the platform, and then, like a swelling wave, the anthem spread through the park, out to the line of people holding hands in a human chain that stretched down to Pobedy Square, up Semsotletiya Lvova Street, and along half a million people who lined the 500-kilometre highway through Ternopil, Rivne, and Zhitomir to Kiev. At that moment she knew the tide of independence could not be stopped. 'How I wish you could have been there, Taras,' she said.

'I'm afraid it wasn't safe for me to return then,' Stepaniak said.

'So you tell everybody,' Melnik said.

Maria frowned at Melnik.

'I was at this end of the chain,' Melnik said, 'in Saint Sophia's Square. And so was that bastard.' He nodded towards an elegantly dressed, silver haired government minister who was chatting jovially to Les Koval. 'He told us to disperse. I asked him to join us and he screamed out that he would have us all shot. Now he knows more verses of *Schche ne vmerla Ukraina* than I do.'

'Yaro!' Maria protested. 'If you're going to be so crabby, I shall dance with Taras.' She stood up. 'Come on.'

Stepaniak was taken aback. 'Who, me? I can't dance.'

She laughed and took his hand. 'It's easy, I'll show you.'

His protests were to no avail. 'Just relax and be yourself,' she said.

Suddenly, that was the last thing he wanted to be. As Maria led him onto the dance floor to a foot-stamping *hopak* being played with gusto by the four-piece band, he just wanted to be somebody who could share her uninhibited joy. She didn't laugh at his uncoordinated attempts, but encouraged him with smiles that lit up her whole face. He tried hard to please her and, after half an hour, she was saying, 'That's wonderful, Taras, I knew you could do it.'

'I'd better get back to Christine,' he said reluctantly. He couldn't remember the last time he'd enjoyed so much innocent fun.

'I didn't realize dancing was among your many talents,' Christine pouted.

'Maria Bondar was very insistent,' he said, trying not to smile.

'She can be very wilful when she sets her mind to something, just like her father.'

'Do you want to dance?'

'I have a migraine. I want to go home.'

'I've a cure for migraine,' he said, reverting to his normal persona.

Lesyn, accompanied by Stepaniak, made a regal exit, taking a detour to wave her farewells to several people, including Maria Bondar and a glowering Yaroslav Melnik.

Her mood had improved by the time they reached her apartment, and an hour later her migraine had disappeared.

She snuggled up to him. 'You don't have to live in that horrid hotel, you know, Taras. This apartment's big enough for two. Why don't you move in here?'

THIRTEEN

From his room in the Lybid Hotel Stepaniak peered through binoculars across Victory Square where five roads meet. The early morning sun cast chestnut branch shadows on the yellow three-storey Rukh building that pointed towards the hotel from the intersection of two of the roads. The front door was closed. No cars were parked on the snow-covered pavement between the chestnut trees. Nothing moved behind the tall uncurtained windows. The blue-and-yellow flag fluttering from the rooftop pole was the only sign of life.

Fifteen minutes later the door to Les Koval's office opened just wide enough for one person to see inside. Stepaniak's eyes darted round the room to confirm that nobody was there. He let himself in and closed the door silently behind him. The smell of stale tobacco smoke hung in the air.

Stepaniak removed his bunch of skeleton keys from the pocket of his leather blouson. The filing cabinet yielded without protest. Methodically he searched through each file in each drawer, tracing the creation, and often unexplained death, of committees, commissions, and councils that grew amoeba-like in such profusion that coordinating committees were needed to coordinate the work of coordinating councils. Through this confusion Roman Bondar emerged as the one man who made things happen. But of the UPA there was no trace.

Stepaniak leafed through the papers between the Macintosh Classic and the overflowing ashtray on Koval's desk. He began to read a draft policy document from Yaroslav Melnik demanding that former communists be banned from the posts of Minister of Security, Minister of Defence, and Minister of Foreign Affairs.

The telephone rang. Stepaniak held his breath. His ears strained to detect any other sounds. Nothing. The telephone stopped ringing. He wondered why Melnik had written the paper: there was no chance of the policy being adopted. The other documents were petitions, nothing of interest.

He moved round the desk and opened the three unlocked drawers. Expenses claims, invoices, receipts, press cuttings, pencils, pens, paperclips, rubber bands. The rattling of his keys in the stubborn lock of the fourth drawer was joined by the click of the door handle. The door began to creak open.

Stepaniak froze. The draught from the opening door sent shivers through the fine particles of dust that danced lazily in the transparent beam of sunlight slanting from the dirty window across the grey metal filing cabinet to the scuffed green linoleum floor.

'Les, I was just about to phone you,' Stepaniak said. 'When I saw nobody here, I was worried that you might be ill.'

'We had a late night this morning,' Koval yawned. 'I doubt if most of the others will be in before midday.'

Stepaniak moved aside and, as Koval passed, he unbunched his right hand inside his pocket and released his keys.

Koval sank into his chair. 'What do you want?'

'It's the Marchenkov murder. The only thing the foreign correspondents are interested in is the UPA.'

The sleep left Koval's eyes. 'I'd like to get my hands on those murdering bastards. All they do is give the nationalist cause a bad name.'

'Right,' Stepaniak agreed, 'but what do I say to the correspondents?'

Koval fingered his walrus moustache and uttered a statement he'd made many times before. 'Rukh policy is quite clear. Rukh insists that all non-strategic forces and matériel of the former Soviet Army stationed on Ukrainian soil now belong to the Ukrainian Army, and if Russian officers do not accept this they must seek a transfer to a regiment in Russia. But Rukh is committed to peaceful means to achieve its objectives and condemns all violence. Rukh neither knows nor approves of this so-called UPA. Will that satisfy them?'

'I'll do my best. But who are these people?'

Koval took one of Stepaniak's cheroots and leaned forward to come within range of Stepaniak's lighter. 'I've no idea. The best person to ask is the NSB officer in charge of the investigation, Lieutenant Colonel Petrosyan. He's one of our people. Did you meet him last night at the Independence Day celebration?'

'No. I left early.'

Koval exhaled with a grin. 'So I noticed. Did you sleep with her?'

'I didn't sleep a wink.'

Koval's laugh turned into a cough as he choked on his smoke. He shook his head. 'Nice apartment, I'm told.'

'Very nice, and very central.'

'You sound as if you're thinking of moving in.'

Stepaniak shrugged. 'She's offered, but . . .'

'But it might cramp your style. My God, we have a *kavaler* in town.'

'You sound as if you know the form, Les.'

'I'm a happily married man with two children.'

'And before that?'

Koval grinned. 'Here's Petrosyan's telephone number.'

Stepaniak stood outside the forbidding grey granite National Security Service building on Vladimirskaya Street. The last time he had been here the brass plaque proclaimed 'KGB Headquarters, Ukrainian Soviet Socialist Republic' and he had been accompanied by his controller from the Illegals Directorate of the First Chief Directorate of the KGB in Moscow. He came to be briefed for his undercover mission to London on the links – many of which, he subsequently discovered, were imagined – between illegal nationalist groups in Ukraine and émigré organizations. His controller, an intelligent and sophisticated man who had an excellent collection of American jazz records, scathingly referred to the domestic branch of the KGB as thugs. Stepaniak found the Ukrainian Republic HQ officers less thuggish than his father, who had recently retired as a KGB major in Kharkov, but they did display a far greater vehemence towards their nationalist countrymen than did his Moscow controller, as though they, as Ukrainians, were determined to prove their loyalty to their bosses in Moscow. Stepaniak, now a GRU secret agent working for Rukh, was amused by the prospect of meeting a Rukh secret agent working for the KGB successor organization in Ukraine.

Lieutenant Colonel Petrosyan's eyes glinted conspiratorially when he shook Stepaniak's hand. He was a squat, affable man with wavy black hair, and only the mud on his black loafers spoiled an immaculate attire of royal blue cashmere suit, pale blue shirt, and striped tie. His office was similar to the ones Stepaniak remembered from his previous visit: characterless institution-green walls but hung now with Ukrainian landscapes instead of Party and KGB portraits. Petrosyan walked to the window and looked out over the rear courtyard to the grey granite KGB hotel and social club where Stepaniak and his controller had stayed. 'A pleasant day, Taras Sergeyevich. I've been too long indoors. We can talk about the Marchenkov investigation while we take a stroll.'

The mud on Petrosyan's loafers was fresh, and Stepaniak thought it too bloody cold to be pleasant, but if Rukh's man in the security service preferred to communicate with Rukh people outdoors, so be it.

They left by the front entrance, next to the interrogation centre, on Vladimirskaya Street, and Petrosyan turned right, along the pavement bordered by stark bare trees.

When they were out of range of the building, Stepaniak said, 'I see they've changed the pictures inside.'

Petrosyan gave a throaty chuckle. 'And the brass plaque on the wall outside.'

'What about the top brass inside?'

They had reached the point where Vladimirskaya Street opens out into Bogdan Khmelnitsky Square, an expanse of tarmac sweeping round an oval park in which a granite horseman reins his steed atop a granite hill, a memorial to the Cossack hetman who freed Ukraine from the Poles and reunited it with Russia. 'When will they change him?' Petrosyan chuckled and crossed the street.

Stepaniak followed him through the gate of the Saint Sophia Bell Tower, a colossal four-tiered wedding cake crowned by a golden dome. Petrosyan stopped in the square in front of Saint

Sophia's Cathedral, an extravagance of a score of green helmet-shaped cupolas surrounding a central gilded dome. 'This was the Kiev end of the human chain for independence,' Petrosyan said. 'Are you a believer?' He chuckled and walked inside the cathedral.

Petrosyan's habit of asking an ambiguous question, and then chuckling and moving off before a reply, disconcerted Stepaniak.

'It's only baroque on the exterior,' Petrosyan said as they walked past the mosaics of the chancel apse. 'Since you were interested in the paintings in my office, I thought you would be interested in this.' He led Stepaniak to a shadowy side aisle and stood before a wall. A dark oil painting ended prematurely part-way up the wall; above an uneven white border stood faded pink figures against a faded blue background. 'If you're skilled enough to peel away the seventeenth-century oil painting, you reveal a whitewashed background. Carefully remove the whitewash and you expose the original eleventh-century fresco of Yaroslav, the greatest ruler of Rus.'

Stepaniak stood behind him, uneasy with the way Petrosyan had taken control of their meeting. 'Colonel, I'm not sure what all this has to do with Rukh's interest in the Marchenkov case.'

'We men of letters must look beneath the surface, do you not agree, Mr Eliot?'

Petrosyan turned from the fresco to face Stepaniak. He chuckled. 'Lomonosov's the name. Our mutual friend Leskov sends his best wishes, and also this envelope.'

FOURTEEN

Fascism. It was the old standby, but it never failed. Stepaniak had often put a fascist slant on Ukrainian Press Bureau publications to discredit the Ukrainian émigré movement in Britain, and so he wasn't surprised that Leskov now wanted him to do the same for Rukh. According to Petrosyan, a reporter from CNN was in Kiev to film a background feature on the Marchenkov murder: the reporter was Jewish. The only challenge was to do it subtly, so that the fascism didn't appear to be the ravings of a crank.

Stepaniak's two colleagues in the press office usually joined a six o'clock bread queue and never reached the office before ten thirty. He was sitting alone in the drab room pondering on the best way to give Rukh a bad image when Maria appeared. The recollection of her encouraging him round the dance floor brought a smile to his face. 'Hi.'

'Good morning, Taras. You said you were only staying at that hotel until you found a place, so I've found a place,' she blurted out as though she'd memorized the lines.

'Well . . .' She wasn't wearing those shapeless jeans, but her denim skirt covered the top of her boots, and he still didn't know if her legs were skinny or fat.

'Ivan's been asked to go to Lviv for at least twelve months to set up a marketing cooperative for sugar beet farmers. Sonya's going with him, and they're leaving Anatoli – their son – with her father, so that's ideal.'

He was baffled. 'Ivan? Ideal?'

'Ivan is the husband of Sonya, my cousin – it was at their wedding that I last had stuffed pike, you remember – and their apartment's only twenty minutes' walk from here and the rent's only five hundred a month including heating.'

Her enthusiasm was infectious. Maybe Les was right, and moving in with Christine would cramp his style. 'You're an angel, Maria. When are we off?'

'Friday, after work. I'll take you there.'

When Maria had gone, Stepaniak's mind drifted back to the Independence Day dance – and Melnik's hostility towards him. A smile slowly creased his face. He picked up the telephone, dialled the Zhovtneva Hotel, and asked to speak to David Myers of CNN television.

The smile was even broader when he dialled Christine Lesyn afterwards. At ten o'clock she would still be in bed. He used his low, sexy voice. 'It's Prince Charming with his early morning call . . . No, I can't come straight over and do that,' he laughed. 'One of the people at the office has offered me an apartment . . . No, it's not like that . . . Yes, I know I said that I'd move in with you but . . . Listen to me, Christine . . . It's five minutes' walk from here . . . No, wait, listen to me, please, there's something else, CNN . . . That's right. I promised I'd introduce you to some British editors, well, I have a better idea. I thought that with your looks, you'd be perfect for television, and so I was planning to introduce you to a team from CNN, but if you feel that I . . . Today . . . Of course I still do. Meet me in the hard-currency bar of the Lybid at five thirty . . . Me too.' He put the phone down and thumped the air in triumph. A close call at one point, but killing three birds with one stone was always satisfying.

'Thank Christ you've arrived,' said David Myers. 'We have a problem.'

Behind Myers in the ground-floor Rukh conference room, the CNN sound recordist, lighting engineer, and cameraman lounged next to aluminium cases containing their equipment. The two girls from the press office were dutifully arranging rows of chairs below the platform which supported a table in front of a huge blue-and-yellow flag.

'I'm here to solve all your problems,' Stepaniak said expansively.

'No one here speaks English,' said Myers with the unravelling patience of a man used to American efficiency, 'those two girls are setting up a press conference for fifty instead of a one-to-one interview, and that earnest guy over there is hanging around like a spare prick at a wedding.'

'That's OK,' said Stepaniak. 'We'll put a chair in front of the table for you so you have the flag in the background, and the "earnest guy" is the one you're going to interview.'

'Him? Gimme a break. Can't you get me this Roman Bondar, or somebody that someone's heard of, for Chrissakes.'

'Yaroslav Melnik is head of the Rukh defence commission. He's your man to ask about getting rid of Russian soldiers from the Ukrainian Army.'

'He'd better be good. Charlie, why haven't you set up the mikes already?'

'You never listen,' Charlie complained. 'The two table mikes were stolen in Moscow, one of the neck mikes broke and we can't get it fixed in this godforsaken place, so we're down to two neck mikes and a boom.'

'Surprise us all and use a little initiative, Charlie. I'll have one of the neck mikes, fix Mr Stepaniak up with the other, and use the boom on laughing boy over there who's going to be sitting the other side of that table.'

It took a further hour before sound and lighting levels satisfied Charlie and the lighting man, who had to stand on a chair to keep his main spot focused. 'Do you think we can actually begin now?' Myers asked from his seat across the table from a suspicious-looking Melnik.

'Why don't you do just that?' Charlie replied.

'Ready, Taras? OK.' Myers stared at Melnik. 'Why did General Marchenkov have to die?'

Stepaniak interpreted, and Melnik began his answer. After two minutes Myers stabbed a forefinger at Stepaniak. Stepaniak interrupted the monologue and interpreted. 'That is the wrong question to ask. To understand the situation Ukraine finds itself in now, you have to understand the situation that existed before 1939 . . .'

Myers rolled his eyes. 'Tell him to get to the point, for

Chrissakes. Does everyone round here speak like this? No fucking wonder nothing gets done in this place.'

Half an hour later Charlie was holding the boom with the enthusiasm of someone fishing for perch in a dried-up river bed, a glaze had fallen over the lighting man's eyes, and the cameraman said, 'That's thirty-two minutes – without your reaction shots.'

'You want my reaction? I'll tell you my reaction. I got better footage from a goatsfuck interview.'

'A what?' Stepaniak asked.

'Just how does it feel?' Myers stood up. 'Mr Stepaniak, is this the best you can do?'

'Yes. Unless you want to meet the woman who found Marchenkov's tortured body.'

'You serious? What are we waiting for, for Chrissakes. Ed, don't waste any more of that film.'

Christine Lesyn was waiting in the gloomy hard-currency bar on the first floor of the Lybid Hotel. She was wearing her hair Dynasty-style, while the power shoulders gave a late-eighties feel to her businesswoman's suit. Myers looked up from her legs and said, 'Pleased to meet with you, Christine, what would you like? Charlie, here's a hundred, get the drinks, and I'll have a club soda with the usual. I'm parched.'

Charlie grumbled, took the orders, and went to the small pine bar, while Stepaniak steered them to a table near the door.

Lesyn added nothing to the account published in the *Correspondent*. Myers finished his third drink and said to Stepaniak, 'I need a new angle. I got nothing here I can use. And all that historical shit from Melnik was a complete waste of film.'

'You can't expect Yaro to be candid at this stage,' Stepaniak said casually.

'What is that supposed to mean?'

'Look,' Stepaniak said, 'there's no danger to Russians or any other ethnic minorities here, provided, of course, they accept the conditions that are necessary for building a Ukrainian nation.'

Myers put down his glass. 'Go on.'

Stepaniak loosened his tie and nodded to Charlie to refill his glass. 'Let's face it, throughout our history we've been governed by Russians, by Poles, by Lithuanians, by Germans, by just about everybody except pure-blooded Ukrainians. That's got to change.'

'How?'

'You've seen the state we're in now. We've been left devastated by the Soviet empire, just like Germany was left devastated by the First World War. A majority of Ukrainians are facing hunger and joblessness, while a minority are collaborating with foreign capitalists and moneylenders who want to exploit Ukraine's great natural wealth and use its people as cheap labour. And all our politicians do is argue about what should be done without actually *doing* anything. That's Western-style liberal democracy for you, it's just not suited to the conditions we're facing.'

'I see,' Myers said. 'You'll have another drink, Taras? Charlie. So what do you think is needed?'

Stepaniak began to slur his words. 'Like Germany in the twenties and thirties, indeed like all countries where the parliament can't agree on the measures that must be taken, we need a driving force that is above party politics, that will act decisively in the interests of the entire Ukrainian nation. Such a driving force will implement a regime of national solidarity and discipline in order to restore Ukrainian self-respect.' He noticed out of the corner of his eye that Lesyn was writing furiously in her notebook. 'Never again shall Ukraine be ruled by foreigners. And when I say Ukraine, I mean all the lands that historically belong to the Ukrainian nation.'

'Are you talking of territory beyond your agreed borders?' Myers asked.

'Agreed borders!' Stepaniak swallowed another whisky. 'Those borders were imposed by Stalin. He took away the eastern part of the Donbas and gave it to Russia.'

'I see,' said Myers. 'But what about the Russians who live in Ukraine? What rights will they have?'

'Most non-Ukrainians will be able to stay – provided they understand that this will be a state governed by ethnic Ukrainians in the interests of the Ukrainian nation and not by foreigners and moneylenders.' Stepaniak gave him a lopsided grin. 'I guess that those who know what's good for them will want to go back to their ethnic homelands, though.'

Charlie and the other CNN crew stopped drinking and watched. Myers might be a self-opinionated Jew, but they had seen him tease out too many good stories not to respect his professionalism.

Myers shrugged. 'I don't see any evidence of this driving force.'

Stepaniak looked round the bar and lowered his voice. 'How many political parties do we have? Thirty? Forty? There's a new one formed every week. Rukh, on the other hand, represents the interests of the whole nation. Under the leadership of Yaroslav Melnik, Rukh will acquire the power to enforce the interests of ethnic Ukrainians.'

'Well, Mr Stepaniak, this is interesting. I take it you'll repeat all this to camera tomorrow?'

Stepaniak put down his glass of Scotch and stared at Myers. 'What are you trying to do? Trick me into publicly disclosing Yaro's plans?' He climbed unsteadily to his feet. 'Fuck you.' He lumbered out of the bar.

He closed the door behind him and then leaned his back against the door.

'Jesus. This is the story.' Myers' voice. 'But how the fuck are we going to make it stand up. Any ideas? Charlie? Ed?'

'I wrote it down in shorthand.' Lesyn's voice. 'I can tell all this to your viewers.'

A pause. Then Myers' voice again. 'He said you were Ukraine's top investigative reporter. Now, Christine, if I was to introduce you as the reporter who found Marchenkov's body and who's been investigating the rise of fascism in Ukraine . . .'

'We could cut to voice-over part of the Melnik footage . . .' said Charlie.

A grin split Stepaniak's face in two.

FIFTEEN

It had been a good week for Stepaniak, and he fully intended to crown it with the one conquest that had so far eluded him.

After work on Friday he took his suitcase to Maria Bondar's office, where she waited in a woollen hat and a long coat. She smiled shyly and picked up two bags. Stepaniak took advantage of her temporary helplessness and kissed her. 'To what cave of delights are you transporting me?'

She blushed. 'Sonya's apartment is on Uritskogo Street.'

'I shall summon a chariot.'

'It's not far from the railway station and Station metro, and it's on a tram route and a trolley bus route,' she explained unnecessarily as the taxi dipped underneath the railway bridge and went up Uritskogo where the driver executed a U-turn across tramlines and parked outside one of the medium-rise apartment blocks that bordered the road.

The door to the apartment block had no lock, and the lamp in the dingy entrance hall had no bulb. A man stepped into the lift ahead of them. Stepaniak held the door open while Maria squeezed past him into the cramped lift. 'Which floor?' Stepaniak asked.

'Not yet,' Maria said. 'It will only go to one floor at a time.' He put his suitcase down in front of him so that he was pressed next to Maria. Did he detect a trace of perfume? When the man left at the fifth floor, she said, 'Now push the button for the top floor, button nine.'

'But twelve is the top button.'

'There are no floors above nine. The top three buttons aren't connected to anything.'

When the lift came to a halt and the door opened, he stood in the lift doorway so that Maria had to brush past him into the dark landing. The bulb was also missing from the lamp here. Maria stopped at a heavy steel grille blocking the corridor that led to two apartment front doors. She selected a long key from a key ring and turned it twice in the square, solid steel lock. A cell-like door swung open. 'Daddy won't come here since Sonya had this fitted. He hates it. He says it brings back bad memories. But there was a robbery here last year and Sonya is very nervous. You must be careful too, Taras. This is not Lviv or London. Kiev can be a very dangerous city.'

Only after locking the grille door behind them did she unlock the apartment door. She put down her bags, took off her woollen hat, and shook her hair free. 'Welcome!' she said proudly. 'Do you like the apartment? It's quite new and you have two rooms all to yourself.'

Stepaniak stepped on patches of concrete that filled depressions in the green linoleum tiles covering the hall. He looked at her. 'What have I done to deserve an angel like you?' He helped her off with her outer coat and hung it on the coat rail, which swung from horizontal to vertical.

She frowned. 'I think it is only a loose screw. I'm sure you can fix it. Well, anyway.'

As she struggled to pull off her boots, he caught a glimpse of shapely thigh. So those baggy jeans and long skirt hadn't been worn to disguise skinny or fat legs, and even her loosely fitting sweater couldn't conceal those firm breasts. He peered round the door of the first room to check where the bed was.

She led him through to the kitchen, a small white-tiled room boasting flimsy pink cabinets, a yellow enamel sink, a new gas cooker that looked as though it had been designed in the 1950s, and a fridge that looked as though it had been made in the 1950s. Pots, pans, and other cooking utensils hung from nails driven into the grout between cracked wall tiles. Maria's cousin had attempted to make it homely by sticking Mickey Mouse transfers everywhere. Maria put her shopping bags on the small, pale blue, formica-topped table. 'First things first,' she said, removing a plastic cylinder attached to a rubber tube. 'You must nail this to the wall above the tap, then fit the tube onto the cold water tap.'

'What is it?'

'It's a water purifier. You've seen the colour of the Dnieper River? Nobody believes the radiation figures the Ministry issues. I don't know if it will filter out the radiation, but I think you should try. Well, anyway.'

Next she brought out a large metal Thermos flask. 'This is for you. It will make you strong.'

'Do I look impotent?'

'No, of course not. But newcomers to Kiev forget that we're less than a hundred kilometres from Chernobyl. There's a lot of illness in the region.' With difficulty she pushed back one of the sliding doors of the pink laminated wall cabinet, removed two unmatching cups, and poured out a dark red liquid from the flask. 'It's rosehip; it's very good for you.'

'Does it enhance performance?'

'Performance?' She frowned. 'It contains lots of vitamins. You can have it on its own or with sugar or honey if you can get them. I've brought you a jar of honey from the country. I've also brought you a bag of dried rosehips. You should make it in the evening. Put six tablespoonfuls of rosehips into the flask, pour on boiling water, and leave overnight.'

He sipped at the drink and decided he preferred coffee. 'Is the other bag also full of medicines?'

Her gamine face looked up to heaven for strength. 'Of course not!' She delved in the second bag and emerged with a greaseproof paper parcel which she began to unwrap. 'For your first meal in your new home I went to the Central Market. I tried to get a chicken, but they were too small and so' – triumphantly she held aloft a scrawny fowl – 'I bought a hen. It was very expensive.' She put her hand to her mouth. 'Oh dear, I shouldn't have said that. Well, anyway.'

'Anyway what?'

She blushed. 'You mustn't laugh at me.'

She seemed so vulnerable just now that he wanted to hug her. 'I'm not laughing at you.'

'At the hen?'

'No, not at the hen either. I'm just . . . I'm just very grateful to you.'

She blushed again. 'I'll cook it for you now and you can eat it later when I've gone.'

'Why?'

'Because I need to show you how the cooker works.'

'No,' he laughed. 'I mean, why when you've gone? You're not going to leave me to eat my first meal alone in my new home, are you?'

She was flustered. 'I suppose it will be all right. Well, anyway.'

'Does that mean you'll stay for supper?'

'Yes. Now, Taras, pay attention. Sonya has a matchstick jammed here to keep the ignition button permanently open, otherwise the oven's very difficult to light. The oven door doesn't open properly unless you take this lever that Ivan made' – she took a long metal rod with a bend at one end that was hanging from a nail above the cooker – 'and poke it at the door hinge *inside* the cooker, like this. There, you see, now the oven door opens wide. You light it and I'll prepare the chicken.'

The gas hissed at his burning match before exploding alight and singeing the hairs on the back of his hand. He retreated to one of the four formica-topped stools which, with the tiny formica-topped table, comprised the dining furniture. 'Do you like cooking?'

'I never get the chance. During the week Mother cooks, and at the weekend Daddy cooks. Oh dear, you think I'll make a mess of this hen. I will if you keep looking at me like that. Why don't you go and unpack?'

He went first to the small room next to the kitchen. The plastic seat kept slipping off the lavatory bowl. He needed to pump the cistern plunger a dozen times before the lavatory flushed. In the cupboard above the lavatory, rolls of brown coarse lavatory paper stood next to jars of pickled vegetables.

The colour scheme in the bathroom made the kitchen appear tasteful. The cracked wall tiles here were pink, the enamel bath an apple green, the ceramic handbasin had once been white, the collection of steel pipes climbing up one wall were painted gold, as were the large stopcocks, but the pipes running from the stopcocks along the walls to the sink and the bath remained an unpainted lead. 'Sonya said there was a problem with the hot water in the bathroom,' Maria's voice called out, 'but it's supposed to be fixed next week.' Perhaps Christine Lesyn's place on Karl Marx Street hadn't been such a bad idea after all. Thank Christ he wasn't sharing this apartment with another family.

The most important room was, thankfully, more civilized. The dark green wallpaper almost complemented the green base of the geometrically patterned Kazakh carpet hiding the floor next to the bed. A goatskin blanket covered the bed, which sagged in the middle but was commendably large. He'd never made love on goatskin. He unpacked and put his clothes in the wardrobe; the door wouldn't close. He removed the cellophane wrapper from the packet he'd taken from his suitcase, put three condoms under the pillow, and left the bedroom door open.

Two enamel pans were bubbling away on the cooker. Maria turned off the gas, carefully removed the lid of the first pan by holding the cork stuck into the ring on the pan lid, wrapped a towel round the hot enamel handle, and drained off the water from the potatoes. 'Nearly ready. Don't keep looking at me. Do something. Set the table.'

'Yes, ma'am. Straight away, ma'am. Anything you say, ma'am.'

Two place settings of the assorted cutlery occupied the whole of the table. He wasn't expecting much from the scrawny fowl, wrinkled carrots, and spongy potatoes that she'd bought, but Maria had transformed these unpromising ingredients by the deft use of cheese, garlic, onions, and some herbs he didn't recognize into a delicious meal. A very resourceful lady. Who also had shapely thighs. 'This is exquisite,' he said.

She was embarrassed. 'You're teasing me.'

Clearly she was unused to compliments, but what could you expect from an uncouth bastard like Melnik? 'Truly I'm not.' He gazed into her large luminous eyes. 'Tell me what other secret talents you possess.'

She blushed and said nothing. She had resolved not to gabble on and bore him as she had done at the Lestnitza Restaurant.

An intriguing lady. Time to change tack. 'Tell me, Maria, why didn't your father stand for president?'

'Daddy's not interested in power. He leaves that to the politicians.'

'But he is a politician.'

'He never wanted to be.' She put down her glass of Pepsi. Stepaniak had broached the one subject on which she found it impossible to remain silent. 'When they released him from the labour camp they sent him into internal exile in Kirovograd, but within a week he was knocking on our door in Lviv. You know how big he is, Taras, but you should have seen him then, he was as thin as a rake. I didn't recognize him, but he lifted me up and said, "If they think they can keep me from my daughter after fifteen years, they'd better think again!"' Her face lit up. 'Daddy and a few others freed at the same time relaunched the old human rights group as the Ukrainian Helsinki Union, and of course he was a member of the Committee for the Defence of the Catholic Church. "They'll lock you up again," my mother said. "Just let them try!" Daddy replied. I was still at Ivan Franko University, and in contact with a lot of other groups opposed to the regime. Daddy organized a Popular Front of all opposition groups in west Ukraine. The communist authorities crushed it and so Daddy' – she giggled – 'wrote to Gorbachev protesting that they were only trying to support perestroika which had bypassed Ukraine. Well, anyway, that all led to Rukh.'

'But he did stand for Parliament,' Stepaniak prompted.

'It was only in west Ukraine that we could get candidates registered. Everyone wanted Daddy to stand. The authorities organized this terrible campaign in the press against him, accusing him of being a drunkard and a gangster, but it backfired and he won over ninety per cent of the vote in his constituency.'

'So why didn't he stand for president?'

'I told you. He's not interested in power. All he wants to do is to ensure that there's an independent, democratic Ukraine. Once he's convinced that's been achieved and can never be reversed, I'm certain he'll retire to the country. That's the place he loves best, just roaming around, free, and enjoying the flowers and the trees.'

The ones who don't seek power but who have power thrust upon them are always the most dangerous, Stepaniak reflected. They can't be flattered, bribed, or coerced. Leskov was right to be concerned about Roman Bondar.

She replaced the dinner plates with two bruised apples. 'Now it's my turn. Why did you come back after so long in England? Didn't you put down any roots there?'

'Am I married, or did I have a settled relationship in England?'

'I didn't say that,' she stammered.

All women, eventually, want to possess you, but the woman hadn't been born who was clever enough to trap Taras Stepaniak. 'No, I never found the woman I wanted to settle down with.' He let his eyes smile at her. 'As for returning to Ukraine, I suppose I have the same motives as your father.'

This time she didn't avoid his gaze. 'I thought so, Taras. You and he are very similar in many ways.'

He was about to make his move when she looked at her watch. 'But, here am I, prattling on again when I should have been home hours ago.'

He put his hand over hers and said softly, 'Maria, I'd like you to stay tonight.'

She flushed a deep red and stood up. 'You mustn't think all Ukrainian girls are the same.'

'Are you referring to Christine Lesyn?'

'I never said that. It is very wrong of you to say things like that. I must go.'

'But, Maria, I didn't mean . . .'

He followed her through to the hall where she put on her boots. 'Maria, please listen to me . . .' He tried to help her with her coat, but she took it from him.

'I can manage perfectly well myself, thank you.'

She blew her nose before she put on her woollen hat. She closed the apartment door behind her when she left.

Stepaniak shrugged to himself. Then he heard a knock on the door and grinned with the prospect of comforting her – for the rest of the night. He opened the apartment door. 'Yes?'

'Please unlock the grille door for me.'

He took the large key and unlocked the grille. 'Maria . . .'

'Good night, Taras.'

He went back inside. Through the hollow wooden door he heard the sound of the lift cranking its way up to the ninth floor. He also heard her crying.

SIXTEEN

Seen from the top floor of the Ministry of Defence Building, Moscow's Arbatskaya Metro Station is a five-pointed Soviet star. For the metro traveller, the station exit is an odd-shaped red brick building distinguished mainly by the number of middle-ranking officers in Army, Navy, or Air Force greatcoats who walk with the importance of men carrying black attaché cases. Colonel Nikolai Krasin neither wore uniform nor carried an attaché case. Nor did he head towards the modern, rectangular, white marble Ministry of Defence building that the attaché-case-carriers now referred to as the Pentagon. He despised that name as he despised his fellow travellers who no longer gave priority to war veterans and women.

Krasin joined the unseemly scramble down the pedestrian underpass of the Boulevard Ring Road, past Russians who blocked half of the underpass with their flimsy wooden trestles in order to sell books, second-hand goods, and other trash, just like blacks from the south. One old man with a row of medals pinned to his shoddy overcoat was trying to go in the opposite direction. Krasin took pleasure in stepping aside for him into one of the stalls, sending packets of Marlboro and Winston scattering onto the floor to be trampled upon by passing feet or snatched at by grabbing hands.

He climbed the steps that led to the faded yellow three-storey Praga Restaurant at the top of Arbat Street. Here, in the street that had been partially restored and pedestrianized in order to preserve Moscow's cultural heritage, a small band was playing American jazz, while a young woman wearing a tightly fitting sweater and jeans took a hat round the watching crowd of a hundred or so. Krasin turned away in disgust and entered the

Praga. A waiter approached as soon as he crossed the threshold. 'The restaurant is fully booked, sir, but I can arrange a special room for twenty dollars.'

Krasin glared at the man. 'The name is Leskov. I'm here to meet Yuri Alekseyevich Tolstoy.'

'My apologies, sir. I shall conduct you there myself, sir.' The waiter signalled a colleague to guard the entrance while he escorted Krasin to the cloakroom and then to the elevator. On the third floor he led Krasin down a carpeted corridor, stopped outside a door, knocked politely, and entered. 'Your luncheon guest, sir.'

A heavily jowled man, dressed in a light grey, double-breasted suit, nodded. 'Vodka, and a good Georgian white for me. My guest doesn't drink alcohol.'

'Pepsi? Fanta?' asked the waiter.

'Narzan,' said Krasin.

Krasin had never been in one of the private dining rooms of what used to be the favourite restaurant of Moscow's literati. Age had darkened the cream paint on the walls above the teak wainscot that reached the level of the chair tops. The curtains, yellow with gold stripes, must once have appeared opulent, complementing the crystal chandelier and the wall insets, three of which were panels of the same material as the curtains. The other three panels were oil paintings of Prague; large patches of each painting had cracked and peeled away to reveal bare canvas.

'I shall bring our best,' said a new waiter when he came with the drinks.

'Make sure that includes stuffed ham and beluga,' the heavily jowled man said.

'The ham we have, sir, but I am afraid the restaurant doesn't have caviar today.'

The man put a ten-dollar note on the table.

The waiter picked it up. 'I will find some.'

'Tolstoy', whose real name was General Churbanov, didn't wait for the *zakuski* before starting on the vodka. Krasin wondered if he had walked the four hundred metres from the Ministry of Defence. He wouldn't have been surprised if Churbanov had been driven in his Chaika limousine, which would have taken three times longer because of the traffic system. The smart double-breasted suit, bought on one of Churbanov's many visits to the USA, flattered a corpulent figure that had never seen action. While Krasin was behind enemy lines in Afghanistan, Churbanov was sitting in a comfortable office in the Chief Operations Directorate of the General Staff applying old men's Great Patriotic War strategies to a guerilla war: the casualties didn't matter, only the old men's patronage counted. Because his nerve failed when his patrons backed the '91 coup attempt, Churbanov was later able to claim that he had supported Yeltsin and was duly rewarded with rapid promotion in the post-coup shake out.

Churbanov poured himself another vodka. 'I agreed that Marchenkov could be eliminated only if you were convinced that he was going to tell the Ukrainians about your scheme to take back the Army's tactical missiles from Ukraine.' He tossed back the vodka. 'I didn't authorize you to torture him as well.'

Krasin's gaunt face was impassive. 'We asked him to tell us about the loyalties of commanders in the Ukrainian Army. He proved uncooperative.'

Churbanov lit a Marlboro. 'Did you get the information?'

Krasin said nothing while Churbanov's beady eyes watched the waiter enter with a tray and set out dishes of stuffed jellied ham, beluga caviar, smoked sturgeon, smoked salmon, shredded chicken, coleslaw, and bread and butter. After the waiter had gone, Krasin said, 'We had to use other sources.' He took an envelope from his inside breast pocket. 'The officer corps who have signed the oath of loyalty to Ukraine divide into four. First, Ukrainian nationalists, strongly in favour, mainly from west Ukraine, and mainly the lowest social class of the corps. Second, the blind, a small number of Russians like Marchenkov who believe they are acting out of integrity and will loyally serve the Ukrainian Commander-in-Chief. Third, the vast majority, are the pragmatists, and they will serve whoever provides the best pay and conditions. And fourth, the coerced, whose regiments have gone over to Ukraine and who have nowhere else to go.'

Churbanov spooned half the caviar onto one slice of bread and butter. 'The Marchenkov killing was a gruesome business, Krasin. I didn't like it.' He finished off the rest of the caviar and attacked the ham. 'To cover your tracks, I've submitted a formal protest to the Ukrainian Government.'

Krasin placed a slice of smoked sturgeon onto bread. 'We should do more.'

The waiter returned with a hot dish of mushrooms cooked with onions in soured cream and topped with cheese. Churbanov's eyes lit up and he stabbed a fork into the mushrooms. 'Such as?'

When they were alone once more, Krasin said, 'First, award Marchenkov a posthumous decoration as a hero slaughtered in battle. That will be good for morale in the Russian ranks.'

Churbanov nodded slowly. 'Good idea.' He waved his fork to indicate that Krasin should help himself to some mushrooms. 'You said first.'

'Second, arrange for the Ukrainian nationalist regimental commanders to be stationed in west Ukraine.' He handed the envelope to Churbanov. 'Here is the list of commanders who should be relocated.'

Churbanov examined the list and shook his head. 'Krasin, do you think the Ukrainian Ministry of Defence will do anything we ask?' He washed down another forkful of mushroom with a glass of wine. 'The bastards do just the opposite to spite us.'

'You're seeing the American Military Attaché this afternoon at four.'

Churbanov stopped his next forkful halfway to his mouth. His eyes narrowed. Krasin poured himself more mineral water. 'Suggest to him that the Marchenkov slaying is causing restlessness among the Russians in Ukraine, especially Russians in the armed forces, and that it will ease the tension if nationalist commanders are stationed – temporarily of course – in west Ukraine until the situation stabilizes. The message will get back to Kiev who will be eager to oblige the Americans.'

'What good will that do?' Churbanov asked. 'Marchenkov's missiles are still in Lubny.' He poured himself more wine. 'Are you aware that nearly all our missiles are made in Ukraine?'

Of course Krasin was aware, but it was typical of members of the General Staff to stumble on the facts of life only after they'd allowed the politicians to conclude military agreements.

'The Dnepropetrovsk Missile Development and Production

Centre is the largest missile-producing plant in the world,' Churbanov continued. 'We built it. It belongs to Russia as the legitimate successor of the Soviet Union. Not only have the Ukrainians appropriated it, those cunning peasants are holding us to ransom over supplies of spare parts. It's intolerable.'

'Is the plant director a Ukrainian nationalist?'

'He's had to pledge loyalty to the Ukrainian state, otherwise he'd have been out on his arse, but Vladimir Sedykh is Russian.'

'Then what's the problem?'

Churbanov lit another Marlboro. 'The Ukrainian Ministry of Trade. They're refusing export licences. It's all a fix, of course.'

'But they've got to sell the missiles and spare parts to someone. Ukrainians are incapable of marketing a brothel on a battleship.'

'That may be so, but Sedykh tells me that Iranians, Iraqis, and even Chinese have been sniffing round the plant. Imagine that, refusing to sell to us and then selling to the slit-eyes!'

The waiter entered. 'For the main course I recommend baked trout.'

'Good,' Churbanov said.

The waiter left.

'It's not good, General,' Krasin said. 'Russia can hardly claim to be a superpower if it doesn't control the production and maintenance of its own missiles.'

'What do you expect me to do?' Churbanov complained. 'Set up a new missile plant overnight?'

The waiter brought in the baked trout.

Krasin waited until the waiter had left, then he said, 'The Donbas, Kharkov and Dnieper regions are Russian.'

'We've been through all that before, Krasin. We've ruled out any attempts to redraw national boundaries; it would lead to war with Ukraine.'

'Not necessarily.' Krasin filleted his trout. 'The people in these regions were bribed by promises of riches to come if they voted for Ukrainian independence. They've now seen that the Ukrainian Government can't deliver. They're discontented, nearly half of them are Russian, and most of the others are heavily russified.'

'You're wasting my time, Krasin.' Churbanov spat out trout

bones. 'They're not going to demand to become part of Russia. All the talk now is of breaking away from Ukraine and forming their own independent republics.'

'They wouldn't if they were terrorized by Ukrainians.' Krasin cut the head off his trout. 'That would soon have them demanding to join the Russian Federation.'

Churbanov sighed. 'Even the Ukrainians are hardly likely to be so stupid.' He pushed his plate aside.

Krasin's lips drew back in a thin smile. 'I imagine the UPA may well strike in eastern Ukraine, don't you, General?'

As Churbanov watched the waiter set down the pudding, his face creased with satisfaction. 'And the international community would be forced to accept the democratic decision of the people, while loyalist regiments of the Ukrainian Army were stationed safely out of the way in western Ukraine.'

'And you would control the Dnepropetrovsk missile plant.'

Churbanov smirked. 'I like it.'

'Shall I go ahead?'

'Certainly.' Churbanov dug his spoon into the dish of ice cream and brandy sauce. 'How much does Grechko know?'

Krasin's smile disappeared at the name of the head of the GRU. 'He knows only that I have agents in Lvov, Kiev, Kharkov, and Donetsk, nothing more. He knows nothing of the UPA or our meetings.'

'Good.' Churbanov nodded appreciatively. 'How long have you been a colonel?'

'Twelve years.'

'That's a long time. Why haven't you been promoted?'

'I haven't presented Grechko with the two thousand dollars he wants for a major general's star.'

'Two thousand? That's steep. Grechko always was a greedy bastard. Mind you, I think you should look upon it as an investment. A general with your abilities could earn back that sum in a year, eighteen months at most.' He drank his coffee and helped himself to a brandy. 'I think I may be able to help. Next month I'm going to the Pentagon and then I'm giving evidence before a Congressional committee. I'd like your opinion on this document.'

Krasin read the two-page document. The draft contract, in English, gave a New York agent the sole and exclusive rights to represent Yuri Alekseyevich Churbanov 'for the commercial exploitation of the said person for lectures, articles, books, television, video, cinema, radio and all other electromagnetic media, the manufacture and sale of goods, souvenirs, and all other commercial rights now in existence or hereinafter invented.'

'Clause 3 gives him twenty per cent of the gross,' Churbanov said. 'That seems high to me, but I'm not familiar with American contracts. He's told me he has good contacts at the Washington Speakers Bureau – that's the one that organized Gorbachev's lecture tour – as well as with television and newspapers. I suppose if he can deliver, he's worth his twenty per cent.'

'What do you want me to do?'

'Have your people in New York check him out. See how good he is, what other clients he has, what terms are usual, and whether there's anyone better who would also be discreet about bank accounts and so on.'

Krasin folded the document and was about to put it in his pocket when Churbanov reached across and took it from him. Churbanov's beady eyes glinted. 'If I know you, Colonel Krasin, you've already memorized his name, address, and telephone number. You don't need the document. There's a currency payment in it for you if I receive a useful assessment of this agent before the end of the month. Now, if you'll excuse me, I must leave. As you reminded me, the American Military Attaché is coming to my office. Do help yourself to more coffee.'

Krasin watched his departing back. Churbanov would be the first to go, along with Grechko.

A young waiter entered and said, 'Excuse me, sir. I understand you like caviar. I have a jar of caviar, only twenty dollars.'

'Get out,' Krasin snapped. He removed a mini cassette recorder from his inside breast pocket and a notebook from his hip pocket. He switched off the recorder, opened the notebook, and wrote down instructions for Petrosyan and his agents in Donetsk. Now the next phase of destabilizing Ukraine could begin.

SEVENTEEN

'Go take a coffee break,' Melnik said to the two girls in the Rukh press office. 'I want a word with him.' He closed the door behind them and slid the bolt.

Stepaniak's mood at failing to bed Maria Bondar wasn't improved by a heavy cold that left one ear throbbing. Melnik sauntered across the room and perched on Stepaniak's desk, one foot resting on the floor and the other swinging loosely. When Melnik folded his arms, his biceps bulged from the sleeves of his T-shirt.

'Had a good weekend?' Stepaniak asked, offering Melnik a cheroot.

Melnik ignored him. 'What's wrong with Maria?'

'What's she been saying?' Stepaniak asked guardedly.

'Nothing. That's the problem. On Friday she was bubbling with enthusiasm because she'd found you an apartment. This morning she hasn't said a word to anybody. I tried to find out what's wrong, but she won't talk.'

Stepaniak lit a cheroot for himself. 'I can't make her out either. She must be damned near thirty, but she behaves like a virgin.'

'She's not a virgin.'

Stepaniak blew a smoke ring. 'She's either a virgin or a prick-teaser.'

'She lost her virginity when she was fourteen.'

'In that case,' Stepaniak said, 'she's a prick-teaser.'

'Two KGB officers came to the Bondars' apartment in Lviv while Roman was in Perm-36. They beat up Roman's wife and raped Maria. That's when her nose was broken.'

Stepaniak focused on the cheroot between his fingers.

Melnik leaned forward so close that Stepaniak could see every single hair of his walrus moustache. 'Don't play the *kavaler* with her, Stepaniak,' Melnik said quietly, 'or you'll have me to answer to.'

He stood up and strolled to the door. Before unbolting it he turned round. 'I haven't heard yet from my cousin in London.'

When Melnik had gone, Stepaniak wrote out a note. He left the building and crossed the square to buy a bunch of flowers from the stall outside the Lybid Hotel. He gave five dollars to one of the unlicensed taxi drivers who hung around outside the hotel entrance and told him to deliver the note and flowers to Maria's room in the Rukh building. Then he went to the Lybid's hard-currency bar for lunch to see if Scotch would kill his earache.

Maria was waiting in his office, alone, when Stepaniak returned from his liquid lunch. She was wearing the same shrunken denim shirt and shapeless jeans she wore when he first saw her, but her hair hung loose to her shoulders and her small face tensed when he walked in. She avoided his gaze and began a rehearsed statement. 'Taras, thank you for the flowers and the note. I don't apologize for not staying the night because I don't believe in doing that outside marriage, but I am sorry that I reacted like a child.'

She looked so vulnerable – but it had taken more guts than he possessed to come and say that to his face.

She glanced up at him. 'I hope you're not laughing at me.'

He took her in his arms and hugged her. Her hair smelled of shampoo. Her warm body clung to his and then began to tremble. 'Stop sniffling, Maria. I don't want to catch another cold.'

He felt her smiling. She pulled away, then she cried out. 'Taras, your ear!'

'It's nothing,' he said unconvincingly.

'Have you seen it?' Maria hunted in her handbag, retrieved a mirror, and held it near his ear. He didn't want to see it, it was enough to feel it; toleration of pain was something neither GRU nor KGB could teach, and Stepaniak had a low pain threshold.

'Have you phoned the doctor?' she asked.

'I haven't got a doctor.'

'Right.' She picked up the telephone and, at the third attempt, got through. She explained the problem, confirmed a phone number, and dialled again. 'Dr Rybalka, please . . . Nadia? It's Maria Bondar. Mother said I should phone you. A Rukh worker who's just arrived from England has a sore ear . . . Are you sure? That's marvellous, we're on our way.'

'Where?' Stepaniak asked.

'Hospital.'

'I just need some painkillers.'

'Nonsense, you need that ear examining.'

'I don't want to spend all day waiting in a hospital corridor.'

'This isn't a normal hospital. It was the special paediatric hospital for the Party élite before the Communist Party was dissolved. It's got all the latest equipment and medicines. Now it's the top paediatric centre in the country and normally you'd have to wait weeks for an appointment, but Dr Rybalka was at university with my mother and she says she'll see you straight away.'

'Can't your mother just prescribe some painkillers?'

Maria looked up to heaven. 'Taras, my mother is a cardiologist. Nadia Rybalka is the centre's ear, nose and throat consultant. You've just arrived from England, you're not registered with a doctor or a clinic, so don't feel guilty about jumping the queue and getting priority treatment. Put your coat on and let's go.'

Guilt about priority treatment was one feeling he'd never be troubled with, but Soviet hospitals were places you went to pick up infections. He regretted packing his suitcase with condoms and omitting a packet of sterilized needles.

Maria flagged down a car almost immediately, and within five minutes they were entering a modern white marble building opposite a patch of waste ground on a narrow street that led to the rear wall of the Saint Sophia Monastery. The building certainly didn't resemble a typical Soviet hospital. The grey marble floor of the foyer was spotless and uncrowded, a large LCD screen periodically updated details of clinics and consultants, and the receptionists behind the solid teak desks weren't haranguing patients. Maria went past them to the elevator. She led him out at the sixth floor, and he followed her down a corridor, at the end of which a small crowd of mothers waited with their children.

When a nurse came out of one of the doors, the mothers abandoned their children and competed with each other to thrust their appointment forms at her.

'Maria Bondar?' the nurse called out. She beckoned Maria and Stepaniak to follow her into the room.

The smiling grey-haired lady in a white hospital coat wore a small concave mirror attached to a band round her forehead. 'Marusia, how are you?'

'Mother sends you her best wishes.'

Stepaniak was relieved that the consulting room was also spotless. It contained trays of gleaming steel instruments and a black leather chair of which he'd seen the like only in a dentist's surgery in England. He gave Dr Rybalka the bunch of flowers he'd bought outside the hospital. She beamed her appreciation, put the flowers in a vase, and washed her hands.

'Now, young man, please sit down in the chair and we'll have a good look at you.'

She peered down an auriscope into his ear, tutted, and said, 'I'll have to clear out the debris first. It shouldn't hurt much.'

Stepaniak's knuckles whitened as he gripped the leather armrests. Dr Rybalka selected a thin steel probe with a hooked end. She wrapped gauze round the end, dipped it in alcohol, and started to poke down his ear. She tutted and repeated the process with a new instrument. If Maria hadn't been watching he would have screamed.

Dr Rybalka turned his head round. 'Open your mouth.' She pressed a spatula on his tongue and used the illuminated head mirror to look down his throat. 'Now your nose.' She pushed a nasal speculum up each nostril. 'Well, young man, I imagine it's painful.'

Stepaniak nodded weakly.

Concern creased Maria's brow.

'You'll have to stay in for forty-eight hours at least. I'll see if the hospital has a bed that's suitable for you.'

Stepaniak began to fear the worst. 'What do I need a special bed for, Doctor?'

'It is the Republic *Paediatric* Hospital,' Maria said.

He sat bolt upright in the chair. 'You want to put me in a ward with *children*!'

Maria started to giggle and then put her hand over her mouth.

'Taras,' said Dr Rybalka, 'you have an infection in your throat and your sinuses. You have an acute infection of both the middle ear and the outer ear.'

'Can't you transfer me to an adult hospital?'

Dr Rybalka looked at Maria.

'Taras,' Maria said, 'there are no beds available, and very few medicines, at the normal hospitals. We're very fortunate that Mother knows Dr Rybalka.'

'Please don't misunderstand,' Stepaniak said. 'I'm very grateful. But I'm not staying in a hospital for children.'

Dr Rybalka studied him and then came to a decision. 'I shall let you out only under three conditions. First, that you take all the medication I'm going to prescribe. Second, that you apply a hot poultice before you go to bed and wear it while you sleep. Third, that you stay indoors as much as possible, and when you do go out, you wear a fur hat with the ear flaps down. Now, hold steady while I put an antibiotic wick in that ear.'

That evening Stepaniak was feeling sorry for himself and drinking his way through a bottle of Scotch when he heard the doorbell. Maria was on the other side of the grille. 'How do you feel?'

'Better for seeing you.'

She put a bag on the kitchen table. 'First, the hat.' She produced a black fur hat. 'It's only rabbit skin, but it's warm. I had to guess your head size. Try it on.'

The hat fitted.

'Now pull down the ear flaps.'

'Do I have to?'

'Either that or else you go straight back to the children's hospital.'

He grimaced.

'Do you know how to put on a hot poultice?'

'No.'

'I thought not, so I brought oil, cotton wool, lint, bandages, and a scarf.'

She cut an ear-shaped hole in a wad of lint, warmed the oil in a ladle over a lighted gas ring, soaked the lint in the hot oil, and held the hot lint around his ear. 'Hold this in place,' she instructed.

'It's hot,' he protested.

'So would you be if you'd been held over a gas ring for five minutes.'

She placed a thick wad of cotton wool over his ear and then wrapped a bandage three times round his head and knotted it under his chin to hold lint and cotton wool in place. Next she took a woollen scarf and tied that around the bandage.

He went to the hall and looked in the mirror; he resembled an old *babushka*. He saw Maria's giggling reflection and turned round.

'I'm sorry, Taras,' she said in a vain attempt to control herself. 'It just occurred to me that you won't be asking me to stay tonight.'

He started to laugh himself but it was too painful.

'If you're a good boy and do everything the doctor tells you to do, and your ear gets better by Sunday, you might have a surprise.'

'You'll stay the night.'

'No! Les said that you were asking about the UPA. If you're well by Sunday, I'll take you to see a member of the UPA.'

EIGHTEEN

Five days after Krasin had lunched with General Churbanov at Moscow's Praga Restaurant, Ioakim Zhukovsky wiped a napkin across his bulbous lips, brushed the crumbs from his bushy greying beard, and surveyed the world from his favourite corner table at the Aleor Club in Donetsk, capital city of the Donbas region in eastern Ukraine. Things could be better, but then again, things could be worse. He knew people would queue for good foreign fiction after all those decades of being fed nothing but ideologically sound pulp, but the *nomenklatura* who had swapped their Party telephones for Samsung fax machines still regarded publishing as their monopoly. When he had at last managed to obtain paper through a second cousin and stored it in a friend's lock-up garage, the garage had mysteriously burned down. So, who was he to complain? Perhaps Asya was right, and he shouldn't be so single-minded. You haven't even thought about the language problem, Asya had said. It wasn't just those West Ukrainians who were demanding that everyone speak Ukrainian, even the government people from Kiev had stopped using Russian. They will ban books in Russian next, and then where will this grand Zhukovsky Publishing House be? she'd asked. Diversify. Open a restaurant that serves proper food. Look at Sophia's boy. Young Efrim had converted his moonlighting car repair work into a legal enterprise, even if he did have to pay thirty dollars a week 'insurance' to a night-time security organization whose members during the day were officers of the NSB, or whatever the KGB called itself nowadays. But Efrim's business was thriving. The important thing was that possibilities now existed. Since the Lermans had returned, disillusioned with Israel, people had stopped trying to emigrate. The reverse. Wonder upon wonder, a young enthusiastic rabbi from New York had come here to help rebuild the community! He sucked noisily on his glass of tea. The rabbi's father was in publishing. Now, if he could obtain exclusive translation rights to . . . to someone like Isaac Babel or Stephen King, then those new converts to capitalism would have to come and ask to do business with Ioakim Isaakovich Zhukovsky! A nice dream. Asya always said he was a dreamer. But what is wrong with dreaming? Does dreaming harm anybody? And what better time to dream than now? He pushed the table back from his chair and stood up.

Zhukovsky was ambling along the snow-covered pavement when his dreams were disturbed by the roaring of a motorbike on the other side of the road. Motorbikes! Motorbikes! Why so loud? This was one part of westernization he did not like. At the end of the street the motorbike turned round and came noisily but slowly back towards him. Both rider and pillion passenger wore black leathers and helmets with visors that hid their faces. When the bike reached him it stopped. The pillion passenger shouted, 'Hey, Jew!'

The short-sighted Zhukovsky peered at the pillion passenger. He saw the nozzle of a gun and heard the revving of the stationary bike. The flash from the nozzle exploded inside his skull.

NINETEEN

'We shouldn't keep meeting like this, people will get the wrong idea,' Stepaniak joked as he returned with two more Scotches to a table by the window in the empty hard-currency bar of the Lybid. In February few tourists were to be found in Kiev, most businessmen stayed at the former Communist Party hotel, the Zhovtneva, and the locals didn't have the dollars.

'On the contrary,' said Petrosyan, 'the NSB wants me to meet you to find out what Rukh is up to, Rukh wants you to meet me to find out what the NSB is up to, and Leskov wants me to meet you to pass on instructions and payments.' He chuckled. 'We don't meet often enough to keep everybody happy.'

Stepaniak lit a cheroot. 'Do you ever have a problem deciding where your loyalty lies?'

Again that throaty chuckle. 'Never. I'm always loyal to the winning side. Which reminds me, Leskov was very pleased with the CNN programme. His agents in America reported that it was a great success.' He toasted Stepaniak. 'The British went distinctly cool on Ukraine when they found out about the IRA connection with Ukrainian nationalists, and now the Jewish lobby will be campaigning against American assistance for Ukrainian fascists. Your next task is to scare the Russians and East Ukrainians.'

Stepaniak drew on his cheroot. 'How?'

'Simple. Establish links between Rukh and these UPA terrorists, and feed them to the Western media through Lesyn. The Russians will be convinced it's true if they read it in the Western press.'

Stepaniak blew out a stream of smoke. 'I'm due to meet a member of the UPA on Sunday.'

Petrosyan's eyes glinted in amusement. 'That's excellent.' He chuckled. 'You know the saying, *The Russian wept when the Jew was born, the Jew wept when the Ukrainian was born, and the Ukrainian wept when the West Ukrainian was born.* Well, I think we can add to that, *And the West Ukrainian wept when Nikolai Krasin was born.*'

'Nikolai who?' asked Stepaniak.

'Nikolai Leskov, I said.'

Stepaniak pretended not to notice Petrosyan's slip of the tongue.

TWENTY

'Surely he's not a member of the UPA,' said Stepaniak while unlocking the grille outside his apartment front door.

'Don't be silly,' said Maria.

'My name is Anatoli, but you can call me Toli,' said the young boy whose wide eyes and rosy cheeks were the only parts of him not covered by a yellow bobble hat pulled down over his ears, yellow woollen scarf and gloves, a blue ski suit, and yellow boots. 'Auntie Maria has told me all about you.'

'I wouldn't believe everything Auntie Maria says,' Stepaniak replied.

'She says my bicycle is still in my bedroom,' said Toli as he ran off into the apartment.

'I hope you don't mind,' smiled Maria, who was also muffled against the cold. 'Toli's been asking for his bike and Sonya's father has the car outside. He's taking us.'

'What about Toli?'

'He's coming too.'

Stepaniak hesitated. 'Will it be safe for a child?'

The young boy tugged on Stepaniak's jacket. 'Taras, will you carry my bicycle down to Granddad?'

'Please,' Maria corrected him.

'Please,' Toli echoed.

'Taras, what have you forgotten?' Maria asked.

'I've got the keys and the bike.'

'Your fur hat.'

'But . . .'

'No buts. Unless you wear your fur hat with the ear flaps down you won't be taken on an outing to the country.'

'Yes, Auntie Maria,' said Stepaniak.

'Is she your auntie too?' Toli asked.

'No, I'm not,' said Maria. 'Taras was being funny.'

The young boy frowned.

Stepaniak wheeled the small bicycle to the lift and the three of them squeezed in. Outside the apartment block stood a white Moskvich with its boot open. A man with a black woollen hat and a scarf wrapped round his neck got out from the driver's seat.

'Taras, this is my Uncle Vasyl, Sonya's father, who's looking after Toli until Sonya and Ivan find an apartment in Lviv.'

Vasyl Ladenyuk's handshake was firm. He put the bicycle in the boot and said, 'Please,' indicating to Stepaniak that he should take the passenger seat in the front.

'Taras is sitting with me in the back,' Toli announced.

'It seems you're a popular man,' Ladenyuk said.

'I always do what I'm told,' said Stepaniak, who climbed into the rear passenger seat.

'Auntie Maria says you're a sort of journalist,' Toli said as the car drove off.

'That's right.'

'Are you a television journalist?'

'No.'

'Oh.' The disappointment was undisguised. 'I'm going to be a television journalist when I grow up.'

'At your age,' Stepaniak said, 'I wanted to be a cosmonaut.'

'What's a cosmonaut?'

'He's glued to Super Channel, watching dubbed Western programmes all the time,' Ladenyuk complained from the front. 'I keep telling Sonya she should ration him to an hour a day, but she lets him do whatever he wants.'

They passed the Sovskie Lakes, expanses of frozen water bordered by time-worn wood and stone private houses, a small patch of unbulldozed and unconcreted old Kiev in the sovietized city.

'Do you live in London?' Toli asked.

'I used to,' Stepaniak replied.

'In a house of your own?'

'Yes.' Stepaniak wasn't sure why he'd told a lie; perhaps lies now came more easily than truth.

The pavement by the Central Bus Terminal was crowded with people trying to flag a lift; buses ran only when the bus company managed to obtain increasingly scarce diesel fuel.

'Do you drive a Jaguar in London?'

'Of course, most people in London do.'

'Taras!' Maria scolded.

'Is that right? When I grow up I will become a television journalist in London with my own house and drive a Jaguar.'

The Moskvich crossed the new South Bridge over the wide and frozen Dnieper. Unfinished apartment blocks and motionless cranes littered the flat, snow covered landscape of the east bank like memorials to unfulfilled promises.

The main road through Bortnichy Forest had been cleared of snow, but the side road they turned down was covered by a hazardous mix of ice and compacted snow. Ladenyuk didn't let that slow him. The car bumped and skidded along the track through tall pine and silver birch until the forest gave way to a clearing occupied by less than a dozen single-storey cottages in their own fenced-off plots. A good place for a terrorist safe house, Stepaniak thought.

As soon as the car stopped, Toli jumped out and ran to one of the cottages. Stepaniak waited while Maria and Ladenyuk each took a brown paper package from the boot.

'You're very good with children,' Maria said as they followed Toli, 'but you should never tell them untruths. They're so vulnerable at that age, they'll believe you.'

Stepaniak laughed. 'By the time he's old enough to get a job, I doubt that he'll have many illusions left about the West.'

'He'll never be that old,' she said quietly.

'What do you mean?'

'Sonya spent the last three months of her pregnancy with Ivan's parents at a village in the Narodichi district to benefit from the fresh country air.'

'That sounds sensible.'

'Toli was born in May 1986. Narodichi is one of the Chernobyl hot spots. Two years ago Toli was diagnosed as having cancer of the thyroid.'

Stepaniak opened the gate and looked at the young boy who was already at the door, trying to reach the latch.

The door opened into the cottage's whitewashed main room, which was organized round the central *pytch*, a traditional tiled stove with steps leading to a sleeping platform above. An old man, whose sunken leathery face was rough with white stubble, rose from a rocking chair by the *pytch*. A toothless grin split his face as Toli ran to him and wrapped his arms round the old man's waist. 'May I go and play with the goat?' Toli asked.

'Off you go,' the old man said.

'Come and see the goat, Taras,' Toli beckoned.

'No,' Maria said. 'We'll join you later. Granddad, this is Taras. Taras, this is my granddad on my mother's side.'

The old man held out his hand and peered at Stepaniak. The first two fingers of his outstretched hand were missing. Stepaniak glanced round the room, but saw no signs of any paramilitary presence.

'Sit down,' the old man ordered. He took an enamel pan and put it on top of the *pytch*, and then opened the steel door underneath and pushed in several logs from a basket. He stirred the pan while Ladenyuk and Maria placed their brown paper packets on the table. The old man poked inside the packets and grinned when he removed a bottle of vodka from Ladenyuk's packet. He shuffled off and returned with three shot glasses. Only after they had all eaten the warmed-up dumplings filled with pickled vegetables, and the three men had drunk several glasses of vodka, did he sit back in his rocking chair, light a clay pipe, and say to Maria, 'So, what does your young man want to know?'

She blushed. 'Taras is not my young man, Granddad. He's returned from the West to help us build a free nation.'

Stepaniak measured his words. 'We at Rukh want to know what plans the UPA has.'

The old man peered suspiciously at Stepaniak. 'The UPA?'

'There've been some shootings,' Ladenyuk said.

'The UPA claimed responsibility for executing a Russian

general outside Kiev,' Stepaniak said, 'and for shooting a leader of the Jewish community in Donetsk.'

'The UPA! Bah!' The old man struggled to his feet and left the room.

After a while Stepaniak looked at Maria. 'Did I say something wrong?'

'These days old Omelian can forget what happened five minutes ago,' said Ladenyuk, 'but he has a vivid memory of what happened in his youth.'

When Maria's grandfather returned he was wearing an old khaki-green uniform, with baggy trousers tucked into black riding boots, and on his head a soft-peaked cap with a Ukrainian trident badge. Three medals hung from his chest. 'Captain Omelian Pavlenko of the 8th Battalion, UPA-South, at your service.' He saluted.

'I thought the UPA were band . . . er, bands of anti-Russian freedom fighters,' said Stepaniak.

Pavlenko snorted. 'You mean you thought we were bandits? Eh?' He shook his head. 'No proper Ukrainian of my generation ever called us bandits.' He sat down on the rocking chair and picked up his pipe. It had gone out. He placed the stem in his mouth, opened the oven door, put in a taper, and held the lighted taper over the pipe bowl. 'Bandits!' Spittle dribbled from his lips as he sucked hard to rekindle the pipe. 'We were "Banderivtsi", the Bandera faction of the Organization of Ukrainian Nationalists.' The tobacco glowed red. He puffed contentedly. He was no longer looking at Stepaniak; his eyes were focused on the past, on a warm Monday evening, the thirtieth of June 1941.

Seventeen-year-old Omelian Pavlenko stood on the cobbles alongside the thousands of others who had flocked from the villages to pack Market Square in Lviv. The sun sank behind the row of tall, narrow houses, casting shadows on the side of the Town Hall that, for nearly two years, had been called the City Soviet but which no longer flew the Red Flag. Pavlenko's eyes, like those of everybody else in the crowd, were fixed on the house known as the Prosvita Building. At last the door opened and the babble of conversations fell to a hushed silence. A weary Yaroslav Stetsko, clutching a sheet of paper, stepped through the opened door. When he saw the crowd he grew in stature. He looked at the sheet of paper and his voice filled the square. 'Following the liberation of western Ukraine from the Russian Bolsheviks by the German Army, the Organization of Ukrainian Nationalists, under the leadership of Stepan Bandera and by the will of the Ukrainian people, hereby proclaims the restoration of the Ukrainian state, for which entire generations of the best sons of Ukraine have given their lives. Tomorrow we begin creating a national army to drive the Russian occupiers from the rest of our lands and restore a new, just order in Ukraine. Long live the sovereign Ukraine state! Long live the Organization of Ukrainian Nationalists! Long live Stepan Bandera!'

While the crowd roared its approval, Pavlenko thought of one of the best sons of Ukraine who had given his life. His father, a village schoolteacher, had been shot by the NKVD for refusing to teach the Bolshevik version of history. The day after the OUN declaration Pavlenko joined the rest of the men in his village who met in the church and swore an oath of allegiance to the Ukrainian state and volunteered for Bandera's national army.

'. . . an alliance with the Germans?'

Stepaniak's face swam into view. 'What's that you say?' Pavlenko grunted and puffed on his dead pipe.

'Was that after Bandera formed an alliance with the Germans?' repeated Stepaniak.

Pavlenko looked at his granddaughter. 'Where did your young man learn his history?'

'Purely to drive out the Russians, of course,' Stepaniak added quickly.

Pavlenko's rheumy eyes studied Stepaniak. 'Bandera and Stetsko were arrested less than a week after they declared the restoration of the Ukrainian state. They spent the rest of the War in Sachsenhausen concentration camp.' He relit his pipe. 'We'd no sooner welcomed the Wehrmacht as our liberators from Stalin than Hitler imposed his Reichskommissariat on Ukraine and the bastard Gestapo started rounding up our people for slave labour. Bah! The bastard Gestapo were as bad as the bastard NKVD. The

German Nazis and the Russian Bolsheviks both wanted to exploit our people and our land.' He pointed the stem of his pipe at Stepaniak. 'Bandits! That's what Bolshevik propaganda called us. "Nazi collaborators" and "fascist bandits".' He spat through the open oven door. 'We killed as many Nazis as we killed Bolsheviks.'

Stepaniak had learned a different history, of UPA fascist bandits terrorizing patriotic civilians who had helped the glorious Red Army liberate them from the Nazis. 'I went to school in the east, sir,' he said, 'where you had a formidable reputation for fighting.'

'At least you learned something right.' The remaining fingers of his right hand tapped the three crosses, one gold and two silver, that hung from ribbons on his chest. 'Crosses of Combat Merit,' Pavlenko said proudly. 'The silver star on the gold cross is for wounds received in battle. My right hand. The battle of Hurby, the twenty-fourth of April 1944.'

'Where is Hurby, Granddad?'

'Kremianets Forest, in the northern part of Ternopil oblast,' Stepaniak said.

'Taras, how do you know?' Maria asked.

Stepaniak's response had been automatic, it had almost betrayed him. His father had often boasted of how his own 16th Rifle Brigade had led the NKVD troops that encircled and crushed five thousand Ukrainian fascists at their base in the Kremianets Forest. 'A relative of mine fought there,' he said.

The old man squinted at Stepaniak. 'Which battalion?'

'I don't know, sir,' Stepaniak lied. 'He'd only just volunteered. He never came back.'

Pavlenko nodded slowly. 'We were outnumbered six to one. We lost a hundred and forty men that day. Some were killed in battle, but most were the wounded we had to leave behind. The NKVD shot them. We killed over three hundred of the bastards before we managed to break out of the trap. Two to one. Pretty good, eh? Mind you, we never shot their wounded. We were a proper army with a proper military discipline, not like those bastards.'

'Why has the UPA re-formed, sir?'

The old man puffed on his pipe and looked into the distance. 'Some of our units in the Carpathian Mountains kept up the struggle until 1954.' He shook his head. 'We thought we'd get help from the West to throw out the bastard Bolsheviks but . . . But we had no chance on our own.' His eyes refocused on Stepaniak. 'We're an independent nation at long last, thank God. We're building up our own national army. Why the devil should the UPA re-form?'

'That's what we're all asking,' Maria said. 'Taras, if you want to help us build a free nation, Daddy says the best thing you can do is find out who is using the name of the UPA to terrorize Russians in east Ukraine.'

TWENTY ONE

When the two-hour liturgy was finished, Viktor Medarovich Sablin and his family remained while the church emptied into the streets of Donetsk, a city lying in the shadows of pit towers, coal tips, and steel foundries whose tall furnace chimneys pumped toxic clouds over the Donbas region of eastern Ukraine. Xenia, his wife, tried to keep the two girls occupied by having them count the lighted candles in the stands in front of the icons that adorned the walls. At last Father Leonov, dressed now in a leather-belted black cassock, emerged from the sacristy. His portly figure, together with his ever-present smile and long, flowing white beard, had prompted the children to nickname him Saint Nicholas. 'Father, I want your advice,' said Sablin.

'Then let us be comfortable,' Father Leonov said, and led Sablin across the green marble floor to one of the benches for old people by the north wall. Incense still hung in the air, mingling with the smell of the flickering beeswax candles.

'How is the Donetsk Strike Committee faring these days?' Father Leonov asked.

Sablin sat hunched, as though studying the patterns in the floor marble, before looking up to the priest by his side. 'That's the problem, Father. In '89 I urged the men to join the Siberian miners and come out on strike. When Moscow didn't honour its promises, I asked the men to strike again for Ukrainian management of the mines. When those communist hacks in Kiev didn't honour their promises, I led the men out for Ukrainian independence. And now . . .'

'And now?'

'Now they want to strike for an independent Donbas.'

Father Leonov shrugged. 'Perhaps this will solve your problems.'

Sablin shook his head. 'Nothing's changed, Father. Do you know, two plaques are still fixed to the wall of the director's office of the mine where I work: *Coal is the bread of industry* and *The Donbas is a region without which socialism will remain only a wish.*'

The priest sighed. 'Vladimir Ilyich Lenin.'

Sablin's back straightened. 'The point is, Father, that slogans won't change anything, whether they're communist, Ukrainian nationalist, or Donbas nationalist slogans. We're sitting on the largest coalfield in the world, good quality coal, not rubbish, but the unworked seams are getting narrower and deeper. The mines are dangerous and uneconomic. We need modern machinery, Western machinery that costs millions of dollars, if our children are to have any future.'

'I'm afraid the Church can't help there, Viktor Medarovich. All I can do is to urge you to put your trust in God, and He will provide.'

'But you must do *something*, Father. The men are desperate, and desperate men look for scapegoats. I tell you, some members of the strike committee think that Jew got what he deserved.'

'That was a bad business,' the priest said.

'More and more miners are blaming West Ukrainians for leaving the Donbas to its fate. You spoke in your sermon about brotherly love. It's no good just speaking about that in church. Will you come down and talk to the miners? We must do something. We must try and stop this country turning into another Yugoslavia.'

Father Leonov pondered the request. 'Let me think about this, Viktor Medarovich. But come, your poor children are eager to go home.'

Father Leonov walked with the Sablins to their car, which was parked outside the church. When they were all inside, he leaned down to Sablin's opened window. 'I will think about what you've said and I will telephone you.'

'Father, go back inside,' Xenia said, 'you'll catch your death of cold.'

The priest laughed. Sablin turned the key in the ignition. The car rose half a metre from the ground and emitted a blinding light, as though transfigured like a saint in one of the icons, before it burst apart in a thunderous roar.

The militia found parts of the detonator, which they passed on to the NSB major who took over the case. The Ukrainian NSB had no anti-terrorist experts of its own, and so the Government, to reassure the Russian population of the Donbas, accepted the recommendation of Lieutenant Colonel Petrosyan at NSB headquarters that he should seek technical advice from Moscow. A GRU lieutenant flew down, collected the samples, and flew back to place them on the desk of his superior, Colonel Nikolai Krasin. Since the parts bore a striking similarity to detonating mechanisms the British Defence Attaché had previously described when briefing him on IRA methods, Krasin took the samples to the British Embassy for an expert opinion. The Defence Attaché put them in Wednesday's diplomatic bag. On the following Tuesday he phoned Krasin to confirm that the detonator and explosives were indeed similar to devices used by the IRA.

'The person who phoned me to claim that the UPA was responsible for the killings identified himself with the codeword "Taras Borovets",' Christine Lesyn said.

Stepaniak affected drowsiness. 'So what?' he said, still lying with his back to her.

'That,' Lesyn said as she walked her fingers down his naked spine, 'was the same codeword used by the man who told me where to find General Marchenkov's body.'

Stepaniak rolled over to face her. 'That's not evidence.'

'But I've spoken to the NSB officer in Donetsk who's in charge of the case,' she insisted, 'and he says that British intelligence have confirmed that the IRA either supplied the materials or else gave detailed instructions to the UPA on how to make that car bomb.'

Stepaniak appeared reluctant to rouse himself. He slowly pulled himself up in the bed and rested his back against the carved wooden headboard. 'Look, Christine, you come from western

Ukraine. You know how badly the Russian Orthodox treated Catholics there. It was even worse than the way the British treated Catholics in Ireland. There's bound to be sympathy from Irish nationalists for our cause.'

'*Our* cause? You're condoning the murder of priests as well as innocent children?'

'Christine, be realistic. Most of the Orthodox priests in western Ukraine were KGB informers if not KGB agents. Rukh can't publicly condone what the UPA has done, but it's understandable if we aren't too worried when an Orthodox priest gets in the way of the odd bomb.'

'So Rukh *does* approve of the UPA?'

He knew what he had to say. 'Don't be so naïve. Every nationalist movement has a military wing. In the old days the OUN had the UPA.'

'But everybody knew that.'

Stepaniak shrugged. 'Sometimes it's good politics to separate them for public consumption, like Sinn Fein and the IRA.'

He could almost hear her mind working.

She stretched. 'Taras, darling, I've some work to do.'

He yawned. 'OK. I'll get up.'

'There's no need. You stay in bed if you want to.'

He slid back under the sheets. Feeding disinformation to Lesyn was like feeding jelly babies to a stupid, greedy child. But the words were no longer coming as easily as before. He couldn't imagine Captain Omelian Pavlenko putting a bomb underneath a civilian car, still less one containing children.

TWENTY TWO

Snow was falling in large flakes, like goose down, from a grey sky. Stepaniak, huddled in thought, occasionally slipped on the icy pavement of Uritskogo Street as he made his way to work. He wasn't aware of the black Volga following him down the road.

The Volga passed him and stopped. The passenger door opened. 'Get in,' a familiar voice said.

Stepaniak climbed in. 'Where are we going?'

Petrosyan chuckled. 'To a meeting of our literary circle.' He drove off towards the Rukh building, but at Victory Square he took the main road to Lviv. Soon he turned off right and went downhill to Podol, the lower town, passing a queue of cars outside a closed petrol station. Petrosyan ignored the beckoning line of people at the Podol Bus Station and headed up the long straight Frunze Street, continuing along a road bordered by drab, high rise apartment blocks.

Stepaniak never felt comfortable in a KGB Volga if he didn't know where he was going and whom he was to meet. This journey increased his unease at no longer controlling events. Both Leskov – whom Petrosyan had inadvertently called Krasin – and Roman Bondar – through Maria – had asked him to find out who was running the revived UPA. One of them was trying to use him. But which one, why, and for what purpose?

'Don't look so gloomy,' said Petrosyan, who always wore a smile and an air of confidence. 'Do you know this district?'

'No,' said Stepaniak.

'We're approaching Shevchenko Square. In the old days the area used to be known as *Kin Grust* – "Throw off your troubles".'

He chuckled. Stepaniak could imagine Petrosyan chuckling as he applied electrodes to a prisoner's penis.

The buildings petered out after Shevchenko Square. Snow was falling more heavily now on the highway that carved a straight line through a dense green forest of pines massing above an undergrowth of snow and yellow grasses. Petrosyan slowed when they reached a solid green fence on the right. He looked at his watch and pulled in to the side of the road, just before a gate in the fence. Beyond, on the left-hand side of the road, stood a squat wooden tower.

'That's where vehicles coming from Chernobyl were tested for radioactivity,' Petrosyan said. 'If they were positive, they were sprayed with water before they were allowed to proceed to Kiev.'

'Fascinating,' said Stepaniak unenthusiastically. 'Have we stopped to take a dose of anti-radiation tablets?'

Petrosyan chuckled. 'Behind the fence is Myzhgyra, the area that used to be reserved for dachas of the Party élite. After Chernobyl they decamped south to Koncha-Zaspa. We're still responsible for security here, and so it provides perfect safe houses. If anyone gets too nosy, I confide to Chernyk, the Green Party representative on the Rukh collegium, that Health Ministry officials are suppressing radiation figures for Myzhgyra. It works like a charm.'

'What *are* the radiation figures here?' Stepaniak asked.

'Who knows?' He chuckled. 'Don't worry. I don't think we'll be here long enough to be exposed to any danger, do you?'

A black Chaika limousine, with white figures on black number-plates instead of the usual black on white, left by the gate. Curtains covering the rear windows prevented Stepaniak from seeing who was in this limousine registered to the military. Petrosyan checked his watch and then drove down the short approach road before the guard had finished closing the gate. The guard didn't bother to ask for any credentials, but simply pushed the gates fully open.

Petrosyan followed car tracks down a narrow, snow covered road through the forest, passing dachas built of wood or yellow brick, until he came to a clearing that sloped gently down to the flat grey expanse of a frozen lake. A landing stage stood on a series of spindly legs that appeared to balance precariously on the ice. It led to a timbered boat house next to a two-storey stone house. Blue smoke curled up from the chimney.

'Be careful of the lake,' said Petrosyan as he parked his car next to another black Volga. 'You don't want to skate on thin ice, do you?' He chuckled and got out of the car without waiting for a reply. Stepaniak found Petrosyan's sense of humour unnerving.

He trailed Petrosyan into the house, down a corridor, and through an opened door. A log fire blazed in a stone hearth, filling the wood-panelled living room with the scent of burning pine, and reflecting flickering flames on the shiny bald top of a domed head.

Krasin rose from a large leather chair by the fire. 'Good morning, Major Stepaniak.'

'Good morning, Colonel. It's *Captain* Stepaniak, sir.'

Krasin fixed him with penetrating grey eyes. 'I never make a mistake.' He gestured to a low table set back from the fire. It was covered by plates of *zakuski*, on which a start had already been made, plus a half-empty bottle of Stolichnaya and several bottles of mineral water and glasses.

Petrosyan poured a glass of mineral water which he gave to Krasin, and then two glasses of vodka, one of which he handed to Stepaniak. 'I told you to throw off your troubles,' he chuckled. 'Congratulations on your promotion!'

Stepaniak joined in the toast to himself and held out the glass for a refill. 'Thank you, Colonel.'

'You'd better have some food to soak up that drink,' Krasin said amiably.

Relief, vodka, and the fire relaxed Stepaniak. He leaned back in the chair facing the burning logs, with the man he knew as Leskov on one side of him and Petrosyan on the other.

'You've done well, Major,' said Krasin from his left. 'In circumstances like this I think we can dispense with worknames. My name is Krasin, Nikolai Ivanovich.'

Encouraged by this reception, Stepaniak said, 'Colonel, just who are the modern UPA?'

'They are who you say they are.'

'But who are they *really*?'

Krasin pursed his lips. 'Why do you ask?'

'I met a member of the old UPA. I'm sure there's no connection with this new terrorist organization.'

Krasin raised his eyebrows. Petrosyan leaned over from his right and refilled his glass. 'Which member of the UPA did you see?'

'An old man called Captain Omelian Pavlenko.'

Krasin looked at Petrosyan.

'What relationship does he have to Roman Bondar?' Petrosyan asked.

'He's Maria's . . . he's the father of Roman Bondar's wife,' Stepaniak said.

Krasin nodded. 'So he's keeping it in the family. That makes sense.'

'Pardon?' Stepaniak asked.

Krasin sat back, rested his left ankle on his right knee, and turned his head to examine Stepaniak's profile. 'Put yourself in his shoes, Major. He is going to do everything he can to put you off the scent. He arranges for you to see his father-in-law, a member of the UPA, who tells you that the UPA is an honourable organization that couldn't *possibly* be involved in terrorism. The old man's been briefed. He's very convincing. But they've picked the wrong man to tell this story to. They didn't know that your father fought against those fascist bandits. I assume your father did tell you what they were like?'

Stepaniak nodded. As a child he'd had nightmares after his father had recounted vivid stories of UPA bandits creeping up after nightfall and garotting people in their beds. When he woke, crying in panic, his father laughed. If ever he cried after that, his father threatened to inform the UPA about him. 'But why should Roman Bondar do all this?'

'Bondar's a cunning fox,' Krasin said. 'He wants to maintain an international image as a peacemaker while covertly using his Catholic connections to get assistance from the IRA for his terrorist organization.'

'*His* terrorist organization?'

'That's right,' Krasin said.

Stepaniak put down his piece of smoked sturgeon on brown bread. 'I don't understand why he needs to organize a terrorist campaign. He's got what he wanted, independence for Ukraine, and even a Ukrainian Army.'

'Because he's a fanatic,' said Petrosyan from his right.

'Always put yourself in the enemy's shoes,' said Krasin from his left. 'The Ukrainian Government is building up a Ukrainian Army from regiments of the former Soviet Army that were stationed on Ukrainian soil. But Bondar doesn't want Russian officers, still less Russian regimental commanders, in the Ukrainian Army. He can't rely on their loyalty, especially if there's any conflict with Russia. Nor does he want Russians managing the mines and the factories in the Donbas and the Dnieper regions. He believes in Ukraine for Ukrainians. He can't demand this publicly, of course, otherwise the West would refuse to assist Ukraine, and so secretly he revives the UPA to terrorize Russians in Ukraine until the Russian community is driven out.' Krasin bared his teeth in a smile. 'Ethnic cleansing, I believe it's called.'

'And he includes East Ukrainians who only speak Russian,' said Petrosyan.

Krasin's voice was slow and deliberate. 'I want you to use Lesyn to ensure the West knows who gives the orders to the UPA.'

Stepaniak poured himself another glass of vodka. 'I can't just tell Lesyn without any proof.'

'Have you met him yet?' Petrosyan asked.

'No.'

'When you do,' Krasin said, 'ask him about Taras Borovets.'

TWENTY THREE

They went down the same road that General Marchenkov had taken. No fog obscured the view. Beyond the windbreak of trees that lined the road from Belogorod, snow covered the fertile fields on either side of them, a sun-bright white blanket stretching to the shimmering blue horizon. A happy Maria turned round from the front passenger seat of Ladenyuk's Moskvich. 'You see why Daddy likes the country so much.'

Stepaniak looked up from the card trick he was teaching young Toli on the rear passenger seat. 'Does he come here every weekend, even in winter?'

'He bought the dacha two years ago. It's very primitive, and he and my mother come out here most Friday evenings so they can work on it throughout Saturday and Sunday. It's only weekend political meetings in Kiev, or back in Lviv, that stop them coming.'

'Perhaps he should hold political meetings in the country,' said Ladenyuk, glancing to the field on their left. A peasant was tramping through the snow, a large sack on his back. His footprints led back to a haystack whose black plastic covering had been partially removed. Ladenyuk grinned. 'Your father argues that Parliament should privatize the collective farms, but that's not what the peasants want. They prefer to keep the collective farms so they can steal from them.'

'That's communism for you,' said Stepaniak, 'the exploitation of man by man.'

'What is capitalism?' Toli asked.

'It's the reverse,' Stepaniak said.

Ladenyuk laughed.

'You're both terrible men,' said Maria, trying not to laugh. 'Taras, you mustn't believe what Vasyl tells you, he's an old cynic.'

'Is that so?' Ladenyuk took one hand from the steering wheel and pointed to the large sign by the side of the road that marked the boundary of the collective farm. *DECISIONS OF THE 27TH CPSU CONGRESS MUST BE IMPLEMENTED!* 'It's going to take more than laws passed in Kiev to change the habits of generations.'

A frozen lake bordered the left turn after Luka village. The deserted road led past the place where Marchenkov's driver had been shot; the black outline of Boyarka Forest now separated snow from sky on their left. Eventually they reached breeze-block houses built for former residents of Chernobyl, and after these an earlier generation of village houses, mainly single-storey wood or brick, each stoutly fenced off from its neighbour. Only a low palisade protected the village soviet, which resembled a parish hall except that a bronze bust of Lenin instead of a cross stood near the main door. 'I think we should leave the car here and walk,' said Maria.

'Nonsense,' Ladenyuk said, and he turned off the village street. Deep, frozen ruts gouged the dirt road ahead. The wheels of the Moskvich spun and its engine protested as Ladenyuk wrestled with steering wheel and accelerator, determined not to be defeated. The car stalled, and Stepaniak and Maria had to push to re-start it. Maria said, 'Vasyl, go on if you insist, but I'm taking Taras across the fields.'

'Can I come with you, Taras?' Toli asked.

'You stay and look after your granddad,' Maria said. 'We'll meet you at the house.'

She led Stepaniak through a gap in the fence. 'Race you to the stream.'

'Make it worth my while,' Stepaniak said.

'I bet you a million coupons I get there first.'

'I don't play the small leagues. Make that a million dollars and you're on.'

'Right!' she said, and bounded downhill through half a metre of virgin snow. He chased after her, but he found the surface treacherous and she pulled ahead with girlish squeals of delight. She had almost reached the frozen stream when her legs slipped from under her and she sprawled on her back. When he caught up with her, she lay spreadeagled in the snow.

'Are you hurt?' he asked.

'Only my dignity.' She burst out laughing. 'Help me up.'

He reached down for her hand, and resisted the temptation to lower himself on top of her. Her cheeks burned bright red, whether through exhilaration or through reading his thoughts he didn't know. He pulled her to her feet and began brushing the snow off the back of her coat, but she shook herself free and ran ahead to the stream. 'You owe me a million dollars,' she shouted back to him.

'You cheating little . . .' But when he scrambled to catch her it was he who lost his footing and pitched into the snow.

On the other side of the stream the hill rose more steeply, with yellow grasses growing from the snow until, on the higher slopes, the grasses gave way to birch and pine trees. 'This is why Daddy chose this dacha,' she said breathlessly, 'because of the hills and the trees. He loves to wander for hours on his own across the fields, through woods, and up to the hilltops where he can see across the whole countryside. Mother calls him the Lone Wolf.' She led him along a path by the stream. Ahead of them an old peasant woman, black shawl wrapped tightly round her head, staff in hand, was plodding up the hillside towards the main part of the village. Her goat followed obediently, like a dog at heel. 'That's Baba Nastia,' said Maria, waving. 'She sells eggs to Daddy.'

They came to a large plot of land, marked off by a crude fence of stakes, that nestled at the foot of the wooded hill. Maria led him to a gap in the fence, and they stepped round snowed-over vegetable patches.

Maria ran ahead. 'Daddy!'

A man climbed down from a ladder resting against the corrugated-iron roof of the largest of three single-storey brick buildings. A black woollen cap failed to control Roman Bondar's unruly mass of white wavy hair. A black coarse peasant jacket, tied at the waist with cord, was too short to conceal a woollen cardigan that hung down to grey twilled trousers tucked into black leather boots. Only the bright challenging eyes in the lined face told Stepaniak that this was no ordinary peasant.

Bondar hugged his daughter. He reached down, scooped up snow in his bare hands, washed them with it, and dried them on his jacket before stretching out a welcoming hand to Stepaniak. The man was even bigger than he appeared on television. For the second time since he'd left England, Stepaniak felt that someone was looking into him rather than at him.

The door of the main house opened. Kateryna Bondar was a handsome woman but, with her grey hair in an untidy bun, her body covered by layers of dark cardigans and a long homespun skirt, and her feet hidden in black felt boots with black rubber overshoes, it was difficult to imagine she was a cardiologist. 'You're very welcome, Taras,' she said.

Stepaniak took a small bottle of duty-free perfume from the pocket of his parka. 'A small thank you for arranging for Dr Rybalka to treat my ear.'

She blushed in embarrassment. Roman Bondar looked on in approval. 'Make the beds up, Katrusia,' he announced. 'They're staying the night.'

'But Daddy!' Maria protested. 'We've only come for lunch. You can't invite Taras to stay the night.'

Bondar's eyes twinkled. 'You mean he hasn't brought his pyjamas and his toothbrush?'

She stamped her foot. 'You know that's not what I mean. There's no hot water, there's no . . . You can't ask a guest to use that lavatory! We're leaving after lunch.'

'Taras has come for lunch. What kind of hospitality do you call it if we don't offer him a drink with lunch? And if we have a drink, how can we drive back without breaking the law? You know I never break the law.'

'Never break the law!' She looked for support to her mother, but Kateryna Bondar had long since given up trying to argue with Roman Bondar once his mind was set. She went back into the main house to make up three extra beds.

'Have you asked Vasyl?' Maria demanded.

Bondar looked into the second building, which he'd converted from a barn into a garage and workshop. Only his own Zhiguli was parked there. 'He hasn't arrived.'

Stepaniak frowned. 'What about Toli?'

‘That’s all we need!’ Maria turned to Stepaniak. ‘Come on, let’s see what’s happened to that uncle of mine.’

When they left the main gate to the Bondars’ plot of land, Maria said, ‘I’m really sorry about this. I’m ashamed that Daddy should ask you to stay overnight when the house is in this condition.’

‘Don’t worry,’ said Stepaniak. It would give him more time to establish credible links between Roman Bondar and the UPA and, besides, it was fun being in the country with Maria.

Maria was still annoyed. ‘Daddy is very determined. He’s Taurus, like me.’

‘I thought you were Catholic.’

‘I am, but . . . You’re laughing at me again.’

‘Bet you a million dollars that I find Vasyl before you do.’

It was nearly an hour later that Stepaniak and Ladenyuk finally pushed the slithering Moskvich from the rutted path and Maria steered it up the drive and into the garage. Inside the third building, the summer kitchen, Roman Bondar was stirring a large pan on top of the *pytch*, while Kateryna was peeling potatoes in a sink filled with water. ‘You finally decided to join us,’ Bondar said.

Ladenyuk rubbed his hands together and leaned against the tiled wall of the *pytch*, which was the only source of heat in the summer kitchen. ‘It’s cold,’ he complained. ‘When are you going to put some heating in this building?’

‘Not before he fixes up some running water,’ Kateryna said. ‘Marusia, will you get another bucketful.’

Maria looked up to heaven, but picked up the empty zinc bucket. ‘Let me,’ Stepaniak said.

‘Gladly,’ Maria said. ‘I’ll show you where the well is.’

‘No,’ Toli said, ‘I’ll show Taras the well.’

Kateryna smiled at Stepaniak. ‘You’ve got a friend for life there.’

The light outside was fading before Bondar announced that lunch was ready. He beckoned them to sit round the carved pine table on which he’d laid plates of pickled herring, pickled cucumbers, Bulgarian peppers, and slices of Ukrainian *kolbasa*, like salami, plus brown bread and butter. Not quite up to the standards of Krasin's *zakuski*, Stepaniak thought.

Ladenyuk, still wearing his outer coat around his shoulders like a cloak, dipped into the brown packet he'd brought with him and took out a bottle of Moskovskaya. Bondar waved it away. 'You said you were cold.' He picked up a large bell jar containing a sprig of mint in a clear liquid and poured out five glasses. 'My *samogonka* will warm you better than any Russian vodka. And now, a proper Ukrainian welcome back for Taras.' He put slices of white pig fat on pieces of brown bread, cut slivers from a clove of garlic and sprinkled them over the pig fat, and handed out the *salo*. Stepaniak reluctantly took his pig fat and glass of home-distilled vodka. 'To the prodigal's return!' Bondar toasted. 'To Taras!' said the others. Stepaniak hated pig fat. 'You like it?' Bondar demanded. Stepaniak nodded. 'Good! I wager you didn't have this in England.' Bondar cut him two more pieces and refilled his glass. 'I could see you were a proper Ukrainian.'

Five toasts later Bondar removed the pan from the *pytch* and ladled out bowls of cabbage soup in which floated chunks of ham and sausage. He poured out more *samogonka* for the men; Stepaniak wished he had the courage to join Maria and her mother who were drinking mineral water.

Bondar followed the soup with pot roast meat, and still more *samogonka*. When they had finished eating, Bondar leaned back in his chair and studied Stepaniak. 'Tell me, Taras,' he said, 'what is your honest opinion of the country you've returned to.'

The alcohol had made Bondar talkative. It was a good time to probe the fascist roots of this nationalism. 'I can't tell you what it means to me to see Ukraine independent at long last, but,' Stepaniak paused, 'is it wise to have so many different political parties arguing among themselves?'

Bondar looked into the bottom of his glass. 'For over fifty years we've been saying No. No to an unelected government imposing the Russian language on us. No to Soviet schools poisoning the minds of our young. No to Soviet nuclear reactors poisoning the air we breathe. No to the Communist Party and its privileges for the few. No to working for a corrupt system. No to the KGB spying on us and running our lives. No to the imprisonings, the beatings, and the killings. Now we must learn to say Yes. Yes to hard work. Yes to democracy. Yes to tolerance.' He looked at Stepaniak. 'You know, Taras, it's much harder to say Yes than it is to say No.'

'But must we say Yes to Russian officers in our army and Russian managers of our major industries?'

Bondar thumped the table. 'If they want to become Ukrainian citizens, of course we must say Yes! We're no longer their slaves, but by God, having been slaves, how can we wish that fate on others? We must show them, by example, that the ways of the past are wrong, and that the only way forward is to practise Christ's teaching to love thy neighbour.' He shook his large head. 'These terrorist attacks on Russians and Jews are undermining our work to build a civilized state. The sooner we find these extremists and put them behind bars, the better.' He poured out three more large drinks.

'Daddy, don't you think you've had enough?' Maria said. Bondar laughed.

'Daddy! You know what the doctors said about you drinking!'

'Doctors!' he exclaimed with a sly glance at his cardiologist wife. 'What do they know? If I can survive fifteen years in the camps, then I can survive a few drinks while I talk with my friend, Taras. Isn't that right, Taras?'

'I . . .'

'Daddy, that's not fair! Taras doesn't know about the heart and bronchial problems Perm-36 left you with. Why do you have to act so macho? Taras never pretends to be what he's not.'

Christ, Stepaniak thought, why can't she be a bitch? Why can't she give me one good reason to despise her? I'm sure her old man sees through me.

Roman Bondar looked Stepaniak in the eyes. Stepaniak smiled and did his best to hold the stare. Bondar pursed his lips. 'It takes courage to be yourself. I was never that brave. That's why, I suppose, I survived.'

In the silence that followed Stepaniak asked, 'Who is Taras Borovets?'

The four adults looked at him. Stepaniak wished the earth would swallow him up.

'Taras Borovets,' said Bondar, 'was the real name of the Ukrainian partisan leader with the *nom de guerre* "Taras Bulba", who began anti-German and anti-Soviet action in the spring of 1942. He was the first to use the name *Ukrainska Povstanska Armia* for his guerilla unit.'

'There's another Taras Borovets,' said Kateryna in her quiet voice. 'It was the *nom de plume* of a history lecturer at Lviv University who wrote samizdat pamphlets about the famine that Stalin created in Ukraine in the winter of 1932–33. That Taras Borovets was arrested when his daughter was six years old. Maria next saw her father when she was twenty-one.'

TWENTY FOUR

That night Stepaniak could not sleep.

Across in the other camp bed Ladenyuk slumbered peacefully. Stepaniak lay next to the hot radiator; he pushed back the layers of blankets that Kateryna had heaped on his bed. The log fire, which heated the boiler in the main house, gradually burned out and the radiator turned as cold as the full moon that shone through the curtainless window. Stepaniak pulled back the blankets and huddled beneath them. Roman Bondar was Taras Borovets. But this Taras Borovets could never have ordered the torture of General Marchenkov, the cold-blooded shooting of a leader of the Jewish community, and the bombing of one of the Donbas strike leaders together with his wife and children and an Orthodox priest.

The moon dulled and faded into a grey impenetrable mist that materialized as if from nowhere. The mist grew lighter. Somewhere, somehow, the sun was trying to start a new day.

Stepaniak crept out of bed and quietly and quickly dressed. He held his boots in one hand and tiptoed from the spare room into the main room. He stood over the sofa that converted into a double bed. Maria lay curled in a foetal position, the afterglow of her smile fixed in sleep. Stepaniak wondered whether his own character revealed itself when he slept, or did a lifetime of deception instinctively mask his true self? He looked at Maria and hoped that it did.

Outside, on the verandah, he put on his boots. A low, pale yellow sun was burning off the mist, which vanished as quickly as it had appeared. The peace of the valley was broken by a metronomic thud from behind the garage. Stepaniak's boots crunched in the frozen snow, but Roman Bondar didn't hear his approach. Stepaniak watched the broad back of the man as he methodically swung his axe into a pine trunk that lay on the ground. Bondar stopped to wipe his brow with the back of his sleeve and in that moment sensed Stepaniak's presence.

This was the time to tell Bondar that he was being set up. To tell the one man capable of uniting the fervent nationalists of west Ukraine with the russified pragmatists of east Ukraine, the Catholics with the Orthodox, the young idealists with the ex-communist apparatchiks. Fifteen years in the labour camps that had left his faith and his charity untarnished gave him a moral authority possessed by no other Ukrainian politician. Those fifteen years of Kateryna's widowhood and Maria's lost childhood earned him the right to be told the truth. But when Stepaniak tried to speak the words, his own cowardice held them back.

Bondar picked up the axe and tossed it towards him. 'Finish off the logs, Taras, and I'll top up the boiler from the well.'

Stepaniak fumbled and failed to catch the shaft. He lowered his eyes and picked up the axe from where it lay, partly buried in the snow.

Stepaniak found the lavatory, a plank with a round hole in the centre fixed above an enamel bucket, in a hut next to the main house. Walking back towards the summer kitchen he saw Bondar with the zinc bucket. 'Where can I wash my hands?'

Bondar went to the well and filled the bucket. He disappeared into the summer kitchen and emerged with a pan which he dipped into the bucket. 'Hold out your hands.'

He had begun to pour the ice-cold water over Stepaniak's outstretched hands when Maria's voice called out. 'Daddy! What on earth are you doing?'

Hair dishevelled by sleep, and dressed in sweater and jeans, she ran down from the verandah and snatched the pan from Bondar's hands. 'Come inside,' she ordered.

Bondar shrugged. 'Women.'

Maria heated a pan of water on the *pytch*, gave Stepaniak a bar of soap, and told him to hold his hands over the sink while she poured the warm water. 'And he talks about a civilized country,' she said, embarrassed.

Bondar fried up onions and tomatoes in the remainder of the pig fat, and then added eggs and milk, while Kateryna made pumpkin porridge. Over breakfast Stepaniak began to sneeze.

'Taras has a cold,' Toli announced.

'No wonder!' Maria said.

Bondar said nothing, but got up and brought the bell jar of *samogonka*. Enraged, Maria snatched it and took it back to the outhouse. Ladenyuk grinned. Kateryna fussed over Stepaniak. 'We can't have that ear infection returning.' She went outside and returned with a bunch of red berries from a guelder rose. She mashed the berries in hot water and poured the concoction into Stepaniak's tea. 'Drink it all up. It's the best cure for a cold.'

After breakfast Stepaniak offered to wash up, but Maria said no. 'We're going for a walk. Stay there,' she said to Stepaniak, 'while I get your fur hat from the house.'

'Taras, I'm so ashamed,' she said when they were clear of the summer kitchen.

'Please, don't be.'

'My father . . .'

'I admire your father,' he said. He was glad to be able to tell her the truth.

'You do?' She began to relax. 'He means well, I suppose, but sometimes I think he lives in a different world.'

A world where words mean what they say, Stepaniak thought.

She brightened. 'Come up the hill, I want to show you something.'

He followed her up through the snow, sometimes scrambling on hands and knees, until they came to trees that they could use as supports. At last they reached the top. 'What a magnificent view,' he said, looking across the valley to the main part of the village on top of the lower ridge opposite, and beyond to the snow-covered fields stretching as far as Boyarka Forest on the horizon.

'But look here, in front of your eyes,' Maria said.

It was so cold that pinpoints of moisture were freezing in the air. Against the background of pine trees they seemed like tiny fragments of light dancing and scintillating in the rays of the morning sun. 'Diamond dust. Isn't it beautiful? I wanted to share it with you.'

Stepaniak looked from this magical display to Maria's face, rapt with childlike pleasure. Then he forced himself to look away.

TWENTY FIVE

The apartment was as welcoming as an empty tomb when Stepaniak returned on Sunday evening. The knowledge that Krasin was using him to set up Roman Bondar, and the kindness, affection, and warmth he'd encountered at the Bondars' dacha, forced questions into his mind that he didn't want to face. He removed a bottle of vodka from the fridge and took it through to the living room.

Tarnished silver samovars, icons in gilded mountings, and family photographs in fussy frames covered the top surfaces of glass-fronted veneered cabinets containing decorative unused tableware and unread books; other photographs and reproductions of rural scenes plus a couple of curled theatre posters hung from the walls. They covered cracks and damp patches that disfigured the yellowing white distemper. The ill-matching pretentious clutter reminded him of his mother's taste in decor.

He removed the embroidered white cotton towel that Sonya kept draped over the television set and switched on. He slumped back in the plastic-bound armchair while the television warmed up. An episode of *Columbo* or, better still, a sexy French film would take his mind off things. The picture stabilized into the rolling credits at the end of an orchestral concert on Channel 1 from Moscow. He leaned forward and tried the other channels. A Ukrainian reporter on Channel 2 was thrusting a large hand mike in front of an angry old man who appeared to have a bus stop growing out of his head. Channel 3 was an equally amateurish arts programme extolling an avant-garde photographic exhibition in Saint Petersburg. The black-and-white stilted melodrama on Channel 4 had pre-glasnost Mosfilm stamped all over it. This lousy set didn't have Super Channel. Damn. He flicked back to Channel 1, ready to switch off if nothing better was on offer, and heard the signature tune of a weekly news review programme. The anchorman – emulating his American role models even to the button-down collar of his shirt – headlined the items. Was this jerk Toli's role model? At the words 'revival of fascism in Ukraine' Stepaniak put down the vodka bottle and fiddled with the tuning knob to try and get a better reception.

The television images of the wailing wife by the side of Zhukovsky's open coffin and of the exploded car in front of the Orthodox church burned into his mind in a way that the dispassionate radio reports had failed to do. The anchorman announced that they had a special report which investigated the fascist roots of these terrorist outrages. Stepaniak picked up the bottle when he saw the CNN logo at the bottom right-hand corner.

They had done a good job on Christine Lesyn. The camera angles flattered her nose, and she almost fitted the part of a glamorous American TV reporter until she spoke in English. The dubbed Russian translation recalled that, in the name of Ukrainian nationalism, Ukrainians had fought alongside the invading German fascists against the Soviet Union in the Great Patriotic War. But what, Lesyn's dubbed voice asked, was Ukrainian nationalism? Was it simply the desire for an independent state in which the official language was Ukrainian rather than Russian, or was it something more sinister? The picture of Lesyn cut to Yaroslav Melnik sitting behind a platform in front of the huge blue-and-yellow flag that the girls in Stepaniak's office had arranged. The two sound bites extracted from more than half an hour's filmed interview had that pallid, intense face behind the walrus moustache saying, 'The Soviet occupation of Ukraine was simply the latest manifestation of Russian imperialism that began when Ivan III, Prince of Muscovy, called himself Tsar and claimed sovereignty over the whole of Rus, the east European country founded in the ninth century with its capital here in Kiev . . . The only reason that the Ukrainian People's Republic of 1918 did not survive was that its president, Professor Michael Hruszevski, failed to build an army strong enough to defend the borders of the Ukrainian nation.'

'There are many nationalists today,' continued the female translator's voice over the silent film of Melnik, 'who believe that the historical territory of the Ukrainian nation extends beyond the present borders, and that only an army consisting of Ukrainian nationals will be prepared to act on behalf of Ukraine. These same nationalists believe that a democratic system which gives the vote to people of all ethnic origins inevitably leads to a multiparty Parliament that cannot agree on the measures needed to build and defend the fledgling state. They believe Parliament must surrender its function to an organization better suited to solving the urgent problems confronting Ukraine today.'

The film cut to Christine Lesyn. 'These people are not prepared to identify themselves, yet. But my investigations reveal that they are laying the foundations for what they call a "driving force" that is above party politics and that will act decisively in the interests of ethnic Ukrainians.'

It was skilful and powerful. And he had been responsible.

Stepaniak spent another restless night. When his alarm clock sounded his pillow was askew. Exposed were the three condoms that had lain unused since the day Maria brought him to the apartment.

Others at Rukh were bound to have seen the television programme. He couldn't face Maria that morning. He telephoned Koval. 'Les, I've got a cold, I'm not coming in for the next few days.'

'Taras, I need you to do an English translation.'

'Ask Maria. Her spoken English isn't fluent, but she's pretty good at translating written stuff when she can do it at her own pace. Tell her there's a dictionary in my top left-hand drawer, but, Les, please don't tell her I'm not well. I don't want her round here fussing.'

'Maria's not here. One of the girls in the press office showed her an article from an English newspaper published last week. Apparently Maria became very upset and left.'

'Which newspaper was it?' Stepaniak asked, although he knew the answer.

'The *Correspondent*. We recognized the photographs and Yaro made out the journalist's name. It's Christine Lesyn. Look, if you're not well, I'll ask Yaro to come round with the article. He's spitting blood to find out what it was that upset Maria.'

'Don't bother, Les. I'm on my way.'

Stepaniak took a trolley bus down Uritskogo, underneath the railway bridge and over the green polluted River Lybid. He alighted outside the coal-fired electricity generating station whose cooling towers spewed white pollutant into the atmosphere. He walked towards the corner of Leo Tolstoy and Saksaganskogo Streets to catch another trolley bus, but a desire to delay the inevitable overcame him. Instead, head down, he walked slowly up Saksaganskogo.

Stepaniak opened the press office door. The two girls looked up nervously and then pretended to read documents on their desk. Melnik was seated behind Stepaniak's desk. He rose to his full height and waited for Stepaniak to approach.

'Good morning,' Stepaniak said to everybody in general and nobody in particular.

Melnik placed his hands on his hips. 'Did you see the programme last night on Channel 1? Did you see what that bitch did to my interview?' He stepped forward so that his face was centimetres from Stepaniak's. 'Are you still sleeping with her?'

'What programme?' asked Stepaniak. He sidestepped Melnik and hung up his parka. 'And though it's none of your business, I live at an apartment on Uritskogo, not Karl Marx.'

'Well, this is your business!' Melnik banged his fist down on a newspaper opened on Stepaniak's desk.

The *Correspondent* carried a full-page feature, with an old photograph of a UPA unit from 1945 alongside recent photographs of the bombed-out car, and of Marchenkov, Zhukovsky, Leonov, and the Sablin family. The page was headed

Ethnic slaughter threatens Ukrainian stability

Revived nationalist paramilitary group settles old scores

'What does it say?' Melnik demanded.

Stepaniak ignored him and scrutinized the piece for his own name. He reached the end. No mention of him, thank God, but . . .

'Well?'

'It's not good, Yaro. The piece says that the revived UPA terrorist organization is the paramilitary wing of Rukh.' Stepaniak waited until Melnik's outburst of expletives exhausted itself. Then he asked, 'Where has Maria gone?'

'I don't know. I hope she's gone to murder that traitorous bitch.'

The following morning Roman Bondar telephoned to ask if Maria was at Uritskogo Street. She hadn't been home for twenty-four hours.

TWENTY SIX

The middle-aged woman who opened the ground floor apartment door in Moscow's Kuntsevo district was smartly dressed in white blouse and black suit. The blonde hair that fringed her eyebrows was layered short at the back. 'I'm afraid that I'm giving no more interviews,' she said to the girl in anorak and jeans who was dripping melted snow onto the polished parquet.

'I hope you'll talk to me, Valeria Osipovna. My name is Maria Bondar.'

'You're not related to . . .'

'I'm his daughter.'

The woman paused for a moment before saying, 'I have nothing to say.'

'Kiev is a long way.'

'I'm sorry that you've wasted your journey.'

'I brought some flowers from Ukraine to the Novodevichy Cemetery and put them on your husband's grave, so I didn't waste my journey.'

'How dare you! Do you think I want murderers' flowers on my husband's grave?'

'Do I look like a murderer, Valeria Osipovna? I'm here to find out who did murder your husband. I think you know the reason he was coming to see my father that morning.'

A man with the two stars of a lieutenant general on the epaulettes of his uniform got out of the elevator and waved. Valeria Osipovna Marchenkova acknowledged his wave and said in a low voice, 'I think you'd better come inside, but I warn you, it won't be for long.'

The living room was light and airy, except for one corner. On a table, below an icon of the black-robed Vladimir Mother of God – the Mother of Tenderness – stood a silver-framed photograph draped with black silk. A candle in a red votive jar flickered before the portrait of a proud Aleksei Fyodorovich Marchenkov. His widow hadn't offered to take Maria's coat, and Maria didn't want to sit with her wet clothes on the fine leather chairs. Marchenkova, too, remained standing, her arms folded across her breasts. 'Before you start, let me make it clear that I have nothing to add to the statement I gave to the press.'

'Who prepared that statement?' Maria asked.

Marchenkova paced up and down the room before turning to confront Maria. 'Our life was shattered. I've managed to put it back together again. We have this apartment. The boys will be accepted at the Frunze Academy. They know their father was a hero. Don't try and tear our life apart once more.'

Maria looked at the portrait and the icon above it. 'General Marchenkov was a hero and a believer. The truth will never harm a man like that.'

'I don't want Ukrainian Catholics talking to me about God or truth!' Marchenkova stormed. 'Not content with seizing our churches in west Ukraine, you now bomb our priests in east Ukraine.'

'Valeria Osipovna,' Maria said gently, 'who are you trying to convince? Whoever killed your husband also killed that priest, and the strike leader and his family, and the leader of the Jewish community. I beg of you, tell me why he was coming to see my father. If we know, we might learn why he was killed and who killed him. Then we can stop others being killed.'

Marchenkova stared at her husband's portrait. Eventually she turned round and looked at Maria's left hand. 'You've never been married, have you? You can't understand what it's like to lose the man you love. Please leave me in peace.'

'I haven't lost the man I love, but I did lose my father for fifteen years.'

'He was imprisoned for a crime. That's hardly the same.'

'His crime was to tell the truth about the famine deliberately created by Stalin in the winter of 1932 that killed seven million Ukrainians. But we can't build a future based on hatred of those who hurt us in the past. Evil was done by both sides. We must make sure that evil never repeats itself.'

'Fine,' Marchenkova said, 'but don't try and involve me or my children.'

'I was with my father that morning,' Maria persisted. 'I asked him why a general was coming on a Sunday morning. I remember his very words. I don't know, my father said, but if Aleksei Fyodorovich says it's important then it must be important. Marchenkov is a man I respect. With commanders like him in the Ukrainian Army there'll never be any armed conflict between Russia and Ukraine, thank God.' She took a step towards Marchenkov's widow. 'Don't you see, unless we find out who is doing these evil things, our countries could be plunged into bitter fighting like they were in the past. Do you think General Marchenkov would want that?'

'Don't you dare tell me what my husband would want! I can't help you, and that's that.' She turned away and looked out of the window at the garden of the apartment block reserved for senior army officers. Snow clung to the chains of the children's swings and ice covered the steel slide.

'Can't or won't? What are you afraid of, Valeria Osipovna?'

'Just leave me alone! Don't you think I've suffered enough?'

'As you wish. I shall pray for the soul of your husband, but I doubt if prayers are necessary. I'm sure he is now with God.'

TWENTY SEVEN

'I tried, I did my best.' Maria was close to tears. Stepaniak put his arms round her; he didn't care if the two girls in the press office were watching.

'I wanted to help you find out who really did kill General Marchenkov and the others so you can prove to Christine that her article was wrong.'

'I know you did your best,' Stepaniak said as she sniffed into his chest. He wanted to stay like that, holding her. She was so gutsy but also so vulnerable. She clung to him now, her breasts pressing into his chest. His loins stirred, but he was late. 'I must go now, Maria,' he said into her hair. 'I have a meeting with Petrosyan to see if he's made any progress on the case.'

She stood up straight and looked him in the eyes. 'I know you'll never give up until you find these murderers. I just wish you could give me some of your strength.'

Was it really love that made her blind? In those large luminous eyes he saw openness, devotion and, above all, trust. He felt no victory: that came when a woman surrendered her body, as many women had; but no woman had ever given him her trust. For the first time in a life spent outsmarting others, he was ashamed of his deception. 'I'll see what I can do,' he said as he turned away to reach for his parka. 'I can't promise anything.'

Petrosyan was waiting in the hard-currency bar of the Lybid. 'What do you want?'

'A Scotch,' said Stepaniak, 'a large one. Why did you want to see me?'

Petrosyan went to get the drinks. When he returned, he said,

'Leskov wants Bondar exposed before the meeting of the International Monetary Fund decides on Ukraine's proposed assistance package. That gives you precisely one week.'

Stepaniak sought inspiration in the bottom of the glass. 'There are problems.'

'You've met the man?'

Stepaniak nodded.

'So you know who Taras Borovets is. That's all Lesyn needs to find out from you. You can leave her to put two and two together.'

Stepaniak finished off his drink in one gulp and went to get a refill. He took his time at the bar, thinking how best to avoid implicating Bondar. When he sat down again, he said, 'Look, for disinformation to work, it's got to be credible, otherwise it backfires and exposes the source. You forget that Lesyn has known the Bondars a long time. It's one thing fingering that arrogant sod Melnik, but frankly I don't think it's credible to imply that Roman Bondar is a cold-blooded murderer. Lesyn's bound to see through it.'

Petrosyan made a point of studying him. 'Either the drink or the promotion has dulled your brain. Do you think we are unaware that Lesyn has known the Bondars since she and Bondar's daughter were at university together, and that the London *Correspondent* knows this too? That's precisely why Leskov decided you should use her to tell the West about Bondar's terrorist connections. The *Correspondent* will publish the story if it comes from her. It's your job to ensure that she writes the story.'

'But how?'

'Tell her that Roman Bondar has become bitter.' He chuckled. 'Wouldn't you be if you'd spent fifteen years of your life in special regime labour camps, eating shit every day if you got food at all, and spending half your time in an outdoor wooden punishment cell where the temperature drops to minus thirty?'

'Bondar is a man of integrity, Lesyn knows that.'

Petrosyan shrugged. 'Bondar drinks heavily. Tell Lesyn that his integrity is soluble in alcohol.'

'I still think we need to come up with more hard evidence than simply linking Bondar to the UPA codeword.'

Petrosyan gave him a chilling smile. 'We're not here to accumulate evidence to present to the procurator. We're here to do what Leskov tells us to do. I wouldn't treat his instructions lightly.' He stood up. 'He is taking special delivery of the London *Correspondent*. You don't want to disappoint him, do you?'

TWENTY EIGHT

In the crowded Rukh building Stepaniak was more isolated than ever. For him the week was draining away to the point when he would either have to tell Lesyn the identity of Taras Borovets or else face Krasin's 'disappointment'. For the others the week was building to a pitch of expectation when the IMF would decide either to support the assistance package for Ukraine or else let the Ukrainian economy spiral into a collapse that would destroy the country's delicate political stability.

He tried to convince himself that he would only be telling the truth about Roman Bondar's *nom de plume*: if Lesyn put two and two together and made five, that wasn't his responsibility.

The door to his office burst open. Maria stood there, her small face wreathed in delight.

He tried to appear enthusiastic. 'Has America committed itself to the IMF package?'

'Read this!' She thrust a letter into his hands. It was from Marchenkov's widow.

> My dear Maria
>
> Please forgive me for the way I treated you.
>
> You were right. I was – and still am – frightened. I am frightened that the world I've salvaged may be taken away. I am frightened that my darling Alyosha may be branded a traitor instead of being remembered as a hero. Let me explain. Shortly after his body was discovered I was visited at our home in Lubny by a colonel. But this colonel wasn't from Alyosha's regiment, nor from the Ukrainian Ministry of Defence. He told me that he was

representing the interests of ethnic Russians who are serving in Ukraine. He said that Russian intelligence sources knew of a plan by a Ukrainian nationalist paramilitary group, a reconstituted UPA, to terrorize and drive ethnic Russians from Ukraine, and especially from the Ukrainian Army. He said there had been reports that General Marchenkov was cooperating with this group in order to prove his loyalty to Ukraine and thereby secure one of the top jobs in the Ukrainian Army. If it became known that my husband was on his way to a secret meeting on a Sunday morning with Roman Bondar, the man suspected of being commander-in-chief of the UPA, then people would assume the reports were true, and Aleksei Fyodorovich Marchenkov would be branded a traitor to his country. The colonel believed that, on the contrary, my husband was meeting Roman Bondar to try and persuade him not to launch this campaign, and that was why he was murdered. But the colonel said that he could never prove this. His solution, to safeguard the good name of Marchenkov, was for me never to speak of whom my husband was going to meet nor of the purpose of his meeting. If I agreed, he would arrange for me to return to Russia where he would ensure that the boys and I were treated as the family of a hero.

On this last matter the colonel has been as good as his word, as you saw from our apartment and the future promised to the boys.

But since you left, I've been plagued by guilt. I know what my dear Alyosha would think of me because, in persuading myself that the colonel's plan was the only sensible path to take for the sake of the boys, I betrayed all the principles that Alyosha stood for – and gave his life defending. Alyosha greatly respected your father. He told me that Roman Bondar was one of the few politicians he trusted, and that was why he was going to talk to him rather than to people at the Ukrainian Ministry of Defence. For days he had been wrestling with his conscience. He confessed to me that he had received secret orders to lie to the Ukrainian Government about the number of short-range missiles under his command and to secretly transfer many of them to a Russian unit across the border. I begged him, for the sake of the boys, not to do anything, but he had made up his mind to inform your father. This was the purpose of the meeting. I'm sure this was what the colonel did not wish me to speak about.

I feel better now for having written these words, but I realize that simply writing them is not enough. I worry about these secret orders. I worry that this colonel says your father is the commander-in-chief of a nationalist paramilitary organization. I am sick with the fear that our two countries may be plunged into bitter fighting, with the loss of so many young lives.

There, I have told the truth, as Alyosha always insisted I must. Do with this letter whatever is necessary to stop this series of murders that can only lead to the re-opening of old and bitter wounds.

May God bless and protect us all
Valeria Marchenkova

'I knew God would answer my prayers!' Maria said. 'I'll give the letter to Daddy so he can raise it in Parliament and demand an official inquiry.'

Matters were running out of Stepaniak's control. He needed time to think. 'I'm not sure that's wise,' he said. 'You know what happens to parliamentary inquiries, particularly if certain people don't want the truth revealed. It's better that your father isn't put in the position of having to defend himself against scurrilous charges. Let me have the letter. I think I know how best to handle it.'

'Will you? That's marvellous, Taras.' She kissed his cheek. 'I knew I could rely on you.'

The empty can of Heineken was littering the frozen slush that covered the pavement outside the Rukh building, but otherwise it was harmless. Stepaniak kicked it savagely, sending it clattering across an empty Victory Square towards the Lybid Hotel whence it came. He didn't know which way to turn. He decided to follow the can in the direction of the Lybid's hard-currency bar, but the traffic lights changed and three lanes of cars and lorries bore down on him from Victory Prospekt. He retreated onto the pavement. He could go home. But where was home? Certainly not the apartment at Uritskogo. He turned to follow the other three lanes of traffic down Taras Shevchenko Boulevard.

Head bowed against the wind, hands in parka pockets, letter burning in jeans hip pocket, he trudged past the restless queue for the number 9 trolley bus and headed for no particular reason towards the centre of the city. After he crossed Comintern Street, the iron railings of the Botanical Gardens replaced the buildings on his right. The entrance was closed. Like a prisoner he grasped the railings. On the other side stark, frosted deciduous trees spread down the slope of a hill, at the bottom of which nestled the shelter of the winter gardens.

The letter left little doubt that Marchenkov had been killed not by Ukrainian nationalists but by elements of the Russian military. *If* that was the case, then the colonel who had visited Marchenkova was very probably Nikolai Krasin. If so, Krasin wasn't simply smearing Roman Bondar by associating him with some lunatic fringe terrorists calling themselves the UPA, Krasin had organized the whole operation himself. But what lay behind it all? Why hadn't Krasin told him? Why had Krasin initially asked him to investigate the UPA? Stepaniak felt trapped in a game in which somebody had changed the rules without telling him. Or was he letting his imagination run riot? Paranoia was a contagious disease, and even a few days in Rukh were enough to become infected with the virulently anti-Russian strain.

He cursed leaving his fur hat at the office and pulled up the hood of his parka. He found refuge from the biting wind in the foyer of the University Metro Station. Standing under the light, next to the stall that sold fresh flowers, he re-read Marchenkova's letter. At the very least he now had a good reason not to tell Lesyn the identity of Taras Borovets. But if he used the letter carefully, he could also find out what the hell was going on. He put a two-kopek coin in one of the public telephones in the metro foyer and dialled Petrosyan's number.

Cold grey light fell from the barred chapel window onto the grey marble sarcophagus of Yaroslav the Wise, who united the lands of Rus and ruled over them for more than three decades in the eleventh century. Alone in the chapel, Stepaniak examined the crosses, fish, vines, and palms carved on the tomb. He wished he could believe in their power, but they were mere symbols, like the hammer and sickle, signifying the need of men to believe in something greater than themselves.

He heard no footsteps, but from the corner of his eye he saw Petrosyan, wearing a navy blue overcoat and his usual amiable expression. Petrosyan's eyes glinted in amusement. 'Why did you suggest we met here instead of the Lybid?'

'Saint Sophia's is nearer for you,' Stepaniak said, which was both accurate and untruthful. The cathedral was a place where he found some peace, a place where he had been able to think out a strategy for tackling Petrosyan.

'What's the problem?' Petrosyan asked.

'We can't go ahead with our plan to link Bondar with the UPA.' Stepaniak watched for Petrosyan's response to this frontal probe.

Petrosyan was unmoved. 'Why not?'

'Maria Bondar knows why General Marchenkov was on his way to meet her father when his car was ambushed.'

The mask of amiability slipped. 'How does she know?'

Petrosyan had asked *how* Maria knew, not what. 'Marchenkov's widow sent her a letter,' Stepaniak said.

Petrosyan pursed his lips. 'Do you have this letter?'

'No,' Stepaniak lied.

Petrosyan nodded to himself. He strolled round the marble coffin and came to a halt noiselessly behind Stepaniak. 'What reason did Marchenkova give for her husband's meeting with Bondar?'

Stepaniak turned to find Petrosyan's beady eyes staring at him. 'Don't you know?'

'I think you had better tell me, don't you?' Petrosyan's face was impassive, but the threat in his voice was unmistakable.

'She says her husband was going to tell Bondar that he'd been ordered to secretly transfer missiles to Russia. Everything points to Marchenkov being killed by elements of the Russian military.' Stepaniak watched Petrosyan's face carefully, but the inscrutable expression didn't change. 'The Ukrainians will certainly draw that conclusion,' Stepaniak prompted.

'Who else knows about it?'

'At the moment, nobody except Maria Bondar. She was going to ask her father to raise it in Parliament, but I said that I had a better plan.'

'Which was?'

'To telephone you.'

Petrosyan's face relaxed into a smile and his eyes regained their twinkle, as though he were sharing a private joke. 'Good, you've done well. You'd better get onto Lesyn immediately and tell her who Taras Borovets is.'

'But . . .'

'But what?'

A tourist guide led a group of about twenty Germans into the chapel. Petrosyan sauntered out through the stone arch to the cathedral nave.

'But no newspaper will believe that Bondar is commander-in-chief of the UPA now his daughter has that letter,' Stepaniak said when he caught up.

Petrosyan looked straight ahead. 'That's why it's vital you get in first and link Bondar with the UPA *before* the letter becomes public. By the time Bondar produces the letter, the shit will have hit the fan.' Petrosyan had led him to the eleventh-century fresco of Yaroslav the Wise that was partly covered by a layer of whitewash and then a seventeenth-century oil painting, where he had disclosed that he was Leskov's agent. 'If the shit is spread thickly enough, it's difficult to see the wise ruler beneath, don't you think?' He chuckled and turned to Stepaniak. 'To make it more difficult, steal the letter so that Bondar has no evidence to produce.'

Stepaniak turned away. His strategy had collapsed.

'You don't look very happy,' Petrosyan said.

Stepaniak tried to suppress his anger. His words came out slowly and deliberately. 'I want to know what is going on. Who is this UPA gang that ambushed Marchenkov?'

'You don't need to know.'

Stepaniak rounded on him. 'Stop treating me like an idiot! It's my hide on the line. I'm the one who's working in Rukh. Melnik half suspects me of being responsible for the CNN programme. If he finds out that I'm an agent of the Russian military, he isn't going to worry about the Geneva Convention. I can't afford to work in the dark, so start giving me the answers.'

Petrosyan shrugged. 'If you insist. The UPA is a group of former OMON troopers who were sacked by the Ukrainian Interior Ministry after independence.'

'They take their orders from Colonel Krasin?'

Petrosyan looked round the vast central nave whose every wall and pillar was emblazoned with sparkling golden-based mosaics or blue-hued frescoes, and where Japanese tourists were ignoring the signs that forbade the taking of photographs. 'I think we should say Leskov.'

Stepaniak had guessed the answer, but this didn't prevent a sickness in the pit of his stomach when he heard Petrosyan spell it out. He couldn't look Petrosyan in the eyes. He made a pretence of studying the Virgin Orans, the huge blue-on-gold mosaic in the apse that depicted the Virgin interceding on behalf of mankind. 'Did Leskov tell them to torture Marchenkov?'

'Certainly not.' Stepaniak heard the chuckle in Petrosyan's voice. 'He did that himself. He sets great store by patriotism. But of course you know that.'

Stepaniak raised his eyes from the interceding Virgin to the dome above, from which Christ Pantocrator – the Ruler of the World – looked down on him. Christ may rule and protect the world of Maria and of Marchenkova, but how could He rule and protect the world of Taras Stepaniak, a world that included Colonel Nikolai Krasin?

TWENTY NINE

The banging on the apartment door frightened Christine Lesyn. She fastened the chain before unbolting and unlocking the door.

'It's only you,' she said with relief. 'Isn't the doorbell working?' She unchained the door and let him in.

It's only me. Only Judas. Stepaniak's eyes stared from a face flushed with alcohol. She was wearing a green, long sleeved, tight dress with a low neckline that revealed the top half of firm, rounded breasts. The hem of the dress reached halfway down thighs that were ready to open. It was the dress of a whore. He had to tell this whore that Roman Bondar's cover name was Taras Borovets. This whore would then sell Bondar's good name and the IMF rescue package for a job in the West – and his escape from Krasin's vengeance.

'Taras, darling, what's wrong?'

He bolted the door behind him and pulled her to him.

She gave a nervous giggle. 'Taras, you've been drinking.'

His hand reached behind her and dragged down the zipper of her dress. He pulled the dress down from her shoulders to pinion her. He took off his outer coat and kicked off his shoes.

'Taras . . .' There was a hardness in his eyes that she had never seen before. She freed her arms and held up the front of the dress to try and cover her black bra.

He grabbed at the dress and dragged it past her hips until it fell to the floor.

'Be careful, Taras! This dress was made in Germany.'

He stood on the dress and forced her waist slip down her struggling body.

'Taras, stop it!' she shrieked. The flesh not covered by black bra and tights was white and goosepimpled.

He picked her up and lumbered down the corridor. 'What the hell are you doing!' she screamed. He swivelled and used her flailing legs as a battering ram to open the bedroom door. He staggered into the bedroom, bumping into the dressing table and sending bottles of French perfume and English skin creams crashing onto the parquet. He dropped her onto the pink candlewick bedspread and took off his clothes.

'You bloody animal . . .' she began before anger in her eyes turned to alarm. She grabbed the bedspread to cover her body, but when he was naked he wrenched the bedclothes aside, pulled off her bra, ripped off her tights and briefs, pushed her legs apart, and inflicted himself on her. He continued thrusting into her until, at last, his loathing was spent.

He left her abruptly, rolled onto his back, and stared up at the ceiling.

Her panting slowly subsided. When she spoke, it was in English. 'You are drunken pig! I thought you were different. I thought your time in England made you . . . made you different.'

'Like Martin Harvey?' he asked contemptuously.

'He is gentleman. You . . . you are Ukrainian through and through. Uncouth drunken pig, just like the rest.'

He thought of Roman Bondar, Kateryna Bondar, Dr Rybalka, and all the kindness he'd met. 'You're not Ukrainian?'

'The first thing I do when I am in England is apply to be British citizen.'

He laughed at the ceiling.

She sat up and pulled the pink bedspread over the lower half of her body. 'What is so funny? If you see yourself you know why I want to leave this country.'

'You'll be at home in England.'

'This is what Martin Harvey says.'

'In King's Cross.'

She frowned. 'What is King's Cross?'

'It's where the whores are. Not the classy ones. They're in Shepherd Market. I'm talking about your type. The cheap scrubbers.'

'You are saying these horrible things to excuse your behaviour. I do not listen. Because I sleep with you does not make me a whore you can treat like this.'

He turned his head and scrutinized her. Strands of bronzed hair hung wantonly over a face smudged with make-up. She might have been a whore of any one of a hundred nationalities plying her trade in an apartment in any one of a thousand cities. But that was unfair. Most whores that Stepaniak knew had some national pride. 'There's nothing you won't do to get a job in the West. You sell yourself, your friends, your principles, your country.'

'This is not true!'

'Oh no? What about the Bondars?'

'What about the Bondars?' she said defensively.

That hurt. He twisted the knife. 'They were friends of your family in Lviv. They gave you a job with Rukh here in Kiev. How do you repay them? By writing slander about Rukh if you think it'll give you a byline in a Western newspaper.'

'You say what you like about me, but the pieces I have written for the *Correspondent* have been good, bloody good. Martin Harvey says so.'

He turned to stare at the ceiling again. 'Your precious Martin Harvey. What does he know? What do you know? You're so busy screwing others that you don't know when you're being screwed yourself.'

'Because you do not like the stories I have written about Ukrainian nationalism . . .'

'Those stories in the *Correspondent* were just that. Stories. Fiction.'

'This is a lie and you know it!' She stared at him and her voice grated with scorn. 'You are jealous of Martin. This is it. You are afraid I will go to London without you. You are like all Ukrainian men. You think you own me. Nobody owns me!'

He rolled onto his side, facing her, and propped himself on his elbow. 'You don't know what I'm talking about, do you? You and I are whores alike, the only difference is that I know it.' He got off the bed and, naked, walked into the living room. He needed more Dutch courage in order to betray Roman Bondar.

'What do you mean, fiction?' she called after him.

He returned with a bottle of Scotch and a glass. Alcohol and anger had loosened his tongue: he'd almost said too much. 'Forget it.'

'You accuse me of writing fiction and then say forget it! I am professional journalist.'

'I said forget it!'

'Fiction! You are drunk! I suppose you think General Marchenkov was not tortured? That he was not shot in kneecaps and then shot up arse? That he did not bleed to death in agony for hours with shattered spine? I saw his body, for God's sake!'

Her reflection in the dressing table mirror exploded into a thousand fragments with the impact of the whisky glass. 'Shut up! Shut up about General Marchenkov!'

The violence of his outburst stunned her to silence.

He sank onto the bed and gulped whisky from the bottle.

She smelled his fear. And she smelled a story. She put her hands on his shoulders and felt the tightness. She pressed her thumbs into his spine and massaged upwards to ease the tension. 'You are safe from nationalists here,' she whispered into his ear. 'You can tell me all about it.'

He wrenched himself free. 'You never stop, do you?'

'I do not understand you. I do not understand why you are covering up for fascist pigs like Melnik.'

'Shut up, you stupid bitch! You know nothing.'

'Really?' her voice rasped. 'You think I do not know what is going on at Rukh? There is only one reason for you to cover up, isn't there?'

He took another swig of whisky.

'Marchenkov was ambushed on the road to Bondar's dacha. You are covering up for Roman Bondar, aren't you?'

He studied the black and white Scotch terriers on the label of the duty-free bottle – was it left here by Martin Harvey? All he had to do was to tell her that Taras Borovets was the *nom de plume* of Roman Bondar and he would escape Marchenkov's fate.

She seized on his silence. 'So that is it! That little virgin Maria has been getting to you. Cover up for Daddy and she might even drop her knickers for you.'

He dropped the bottle, grabbed her by the hair and pulled her face within striking distance. 'You leave Maria out of this! You're not fit to . . .'

Her naked terror stopped him in his tracks. He unclenched his fist and his arm fell limply.

When she saw that he wasn't going to hit her, she said spitefully, 'But it is true, isn't it? Roman Bondar is involved with UPA.'

The bottle, on its side, was almost empty. He watched the pool of whisky spread over the parquet towards his discarded jeans. His voice was barely audible. 'Marchenkov was killed by a group of "patriots" in the Russian military. They set up and control the modern UPA. They want the West to believe that Roman Bondar is the UPA commander-in-chief.'

'This is typical Ukrainian paranoia!'

'They set me up to tell you their lies. They set you up to publish their lies in the West.'

'Get out!'

He reached out and picked up his jeans. One leg was already wet with whisky. He fumbled in the back pocket for the letter from Marchenkov's widow and handed it to her. 'For God's sake, keep my name out of it.'

THIRTY

West of Moscow the Moscow River meanders through gently rolling wooded hills. At Perhushkovo the land flattens and the river bend spreads out to form a lake bordered by sandy beaches. A three-metre-high green fence with an electrified wire running along the top reserves a large area bordering the lake for dachas of the military élite. On this midweek winter's day only one dacha showed signs of life. Eight black cars – Chaika limousines or Volgas apart from a solitary Zhiguli – were parked in front of the two-storey brick building rendered with yellow stucco. The flat area of the roof, used for sunbathing in summer, was covered by snow, but the heat of the chimney exposed the surrounding green metal roofing. The bright sun in the cloudless sky wasn't warm enough to melt the snow on the rear verandah that overlooked the frozen lake, nor melt the icicles that hung like shark's teeth from the lintel above the large double-glazed window next to the rear door.

The shadow of shark's teeth fell on the plain, light oak dining table that had been made at Moscow's Lux factory, like the utilitarian leather-padded chairs round the table and the oak drinks cabinet with rounded edges that stood at the opposite end of the dining room from the oak fireplace. The furniture had been designed to complement the plain oak panelling and floor of a dacha built in the Constructivist style of the thirties. Its austerity and its Russianness appealed to Krasin; the smell of American tobacco smoke that poisoned the air did not.

'I demand an explanation.' General Churbanov flung a copy of the London *Correspondent* onto the heavily polished table. The front-page headline announced

Russian plot to destabilize Ukraine

UPA terrorists alleged to be agents of Russian military

'The President is furious,' Churbanov said, fingering the collar of his Brooks Brothers shirt. 'He's promised that heads will roll.'

Krasin looked neither at the three-day-old newspaper nor at Churbanov, seated like a judge at the head of the table. Three men sat on either side of the table; only one, from the Black Sea Fleet, wore uniform. Like a jury, all were watching Krasin at the prisoner's end of the table. His grey unblinking eyes studied their reactions.

The slim, elegant Eduard Mishin wore a smart Western-tailored suit but, unlike Churbanov, he could be mistaken for a successful businessman in Berlin, London, or New York. The Russian President's foreign policy adviser was a person whose support Krasin had cultivated. 'The Americans have asked him to set up a commission of inquiry,' Mishin said.

'Fuck the Americans.' Bogdan Gorbunov was dressed in a black double-breasted gold-buttoned uniform with the two gold stars of a vice admiral on his epaulettes.

'On the contrary,' said Krasin, 'the President should accept the Americans' advice.' His teeth bared in a smile. 'Eduard should advise him that the person best qualified to head the inquiry is Valentin, who will conclude that the UPA is a renegade gang of former OMON troopers trying to provoke the Russian population into action against Ukrainians. I shall offer to cooperate with the Ukrainian NSB in tracking them down.'

Valentin Titov, a member of the Russian Parliamentary Defence Commission, peered through rimless spectacles. 'Good thinking, Krasin.'

'That may get you off the hook,' said a petulant voice, 'but it won't stop the anti-Russian feeling in Ukraine. There've been demands to remove Russians from top jobs in the defence industry.' Vladimir Sedykh, director of the Dnepropetrovsk Missile Development and Production Centre, had grown his hair long on one side and combed it across the top of his head in a vain attempt to disguise his baldness. Krasin considered him weak.

Major General Arkady Kolinko, on the other hand, had earned Krasin's respect in Afghanistan. Now commanding the 4th Guards Tank Division, Kolinko was more comfortable in the field with his troops than seated in this overheated but curiously impersonal government dacha. He had loosened his tie and undone the top button of his shirt. From beneath black bushy eyebrows his eyes stared accusingly at Krasin. 'It doesn't stop those shits in the media asking me why I was planning to take delivery of Marchenkov's battlefield missiles.'

Churbanov leaned forward and stubbed out his cigarette in a square glass ashtray. 'I want to know how it happened,' he insisted.

'Because I was too compassionate,' Krasin said. 'I accepted the word of Marchenkov's widow that she would tell no one where Marchenkov was going and why. It won't happen again, I promise you.'

The myopic Titov's many years as the communist boss of Omsk had taught him to distrust promises made by Moscow. 'What's to stop this woman identifying you as the mystery colonel and then having the media trace you back to this group?'

Krasin was impassive. 'Valeria Marchenkova poisoned her sons and then committed suicide.'

Titov frowned. 'When?'

'Tomorrow.'

'Such action falls within our competence.' Colonel Maksim Batalov had untrustworthy eyes and a mean mouth. He'd undertaken the transition from KGB to Russian Security Ministry effortlessly: his office, files, and work in counterintelligence were unchanged. Mishin had considered it essential that the patriotic faction of the Ministry was brought on board.

'She's military,' Krasin said.

'You should have thought of that before you let her blab to the Western press,' Batalov said.

'Squabbling will get us nowhere,' Mishin said. 'A commission of inquiry by Valentin and the removal of Marchenkova are sound, short term measures. But we're still facing a major crisis in the long term.'

'Too true,' Churbanov said. 'The Ukrainians have got us by the balls. We've been forced to negotiate away most of our missiles, and now we find that we can't maintain the ones we've got left without parts from Ukraine.'

Mishin ignored him. 'This exposé produced considerable sympathy for Ukraine among the international community. The IMF agreed an even better aid package than the Ukrainians dared hope for. They no longer need to sell us their agricultural produce, and if they turn off supplies, as they've threatened in order to feed their own people, I don't see how we can prevent food riots in Russia.'

'Simple,' said Titov. 'Impose martial law until we sort out the economy and the Ukrainians. The people have seen that democracy has made life much worse than before. They'll back us this time.'

Churbanov fidgeted with his cufflinks. 'The Americans would never support that.'

'Fuck the Americans.' Vice Admiral Gorbunov stood up and walked out of the room.

'The people are coming out onto the streets for Vetrovsky,' said Batalov. 'They're saying that only he can restore Russian pride and put food back in the shops at a price they can afford. Last Sunday's rally in Manezh Square attracted over a hundred and fifty thousand.'

'Vetrovsky's a fascist,' said Churbanov, 'a madman.'

'The people call him a patriot,' said Batalov.

'When Vetrovsky spoke at the General Staff Academy,' said General Kolinko, 'he got a standing ovation.'

'We agreed that it would be too risky changing the president at this stage,' Mishin warned. 'If Vetrovsky took over, the Americans would freeze all economic aid.'

'Fuck the Americans.' Vice Admiral Gorbunov put an ice-cold bottle of vodka on the table and went to the drinks cabinet for glasses. 'It's about time we proved what we're made of. What do you say, Arkady?'

'Either this president of ours stops Ukraine pushing us around,' said General Kolinko, 'or we find somebody else who will.'

Churbanov banged the table. 'You got us into this mess, Krasin!

Your plan to destabilize Ukraine has backfired, thanks to . . . to this.' He waved his hand impotently at the *Correspondent.*

Gorbunov stopped pouring out the vodka. All eyes turned from Churbanov to Krasin.

'Gentlemen,' Krasin said, 'if it is our considered view that the Ukrainians are controlling the board, may I suggest we have little option but to take their queen and achieve mate in one move?'

'What, precisely, are you proposing?' Churbanov demanded.

When he had everyone's attention, Krasin said quietly and confidently, 'We annex eastern Ukraine.'

Vice Admiral Gorbunov and General Kolinko chorused approval, but the other expressions ranged from incredulity to outrage. 'You must be mad,' said Churbanov, 'the Americans . . .'

'Fuck the . . .'

Krasin put up a hand to silence them both. 'Very reluctantly, and only with the support of NATO.'

'I think we'd better hear this,' Mishin said. He drew deeply on his cigarette.

Krasin leaned back in his chair. 'Tell me, gentlemen, which is the one circumstance in which NATO would not only support, but even demand, our military intervention in Ukraine?'

A smile spread across Mishin's face as he exhaled. 'To fulfil our international obligations.'

The stupid Churbanov didn't understand, and so Krasin spelled it out. When he had finished, the only dissenting voice came from Gorbunov. 'I don't see why we have to stop at Khmelnitsky. Why don't we press on and take back the whole of Ukraine?'

'In an ideal world we'd do that, Admiral,' said Krasin. 'Regrettably, the world is not ideal. We can secure east and central Ukraine with minimum resistance. If we went beyond the Bug River we'd face concerted opposition from the Ukrainian Army's divisions stationed in west Ukraine and a population that would be, in effect, a guerilla army.'

'I agree,' said Mishin. 'Once we've established control over east Ukraine with NATO's backing, we're bound to find Ukrainian politicians who will accept autonomous republic status. Let the West Ukrainians keep Galicia, Volhynia, and Transcarpathia.'

Titov grunted. 'Let them fly their blue-and-yellow flag and call themselves whatever they want. We'll control enough of the agricultural land, and virtually all the mineral and industrial resources. They'll soon run out of cash to pay their army.'

'Then, gentlemen,' Krasin asked, 'we are all agreed?'

Gorbunov raised his glass. 'Here's to success!'

'In that case,' Krasin stated, declining the vodka, 'I need the cooperation of Colonel Muratov.'

Churbanov picked up one of six telephones on a side table, gave his codeword, and said, 'Get me Colonel Muratov, Ivan Vasilievich.'

Moments later a voice answered. 'Vanya,' Churbanov said, 'it's Yuri Churbanov. Colonel Krasin, Nikolai Ivanovich, of the GRU needs your help in an operation which has the support of the highest authority. Do I make myself clear?'

He paused while Muratov answered. Then, 'It's precisely to achieve that objective.' A pause. 'Good, I knew we could rely on you.'

He looked pleased with himself for the first time that afternoon.

General Kolinko refilled his glass. 'An old friend of mine, Grigori Semyonov, has taken over command of the 106th Guards Airborne Division. He has over six thousand men at Tula within an hour and a half's flying time of the targets. I can bring in another ten thousand by road and rail from the east.'

'I can organize air support from the south,' said Gorbunov.

'Gentlemen,' said Krasin, 'the operation must be mounted with surprise, speed, coordination, and surgical precision. May I suggest that the military among us stay behind to work out the logistics, and then General Churbanov can notify Ukraine, Belarus, and NATO about planned "regular troop exercises". Meanwhile, Eduard must prepare the ground for the President so that he takes the right decision at the right time.'

'That means isolating him from the boys in the pink pants,' said Mishin.

Titov snorted. 'When Krasin gives us the date, have the Ford

Foundation set up a conference in Chicago on economic liberalization for Russia. They'll all be off there like a shot.'

The others laughed. 'Good idea,' Krasin said quietly. 'I might be able to arrange something like that.'

The others looked at him. 'Colonel Krasin,' said Churbanov, 'the Motherland will be in your debt – if the plan succeeds . . .' He let the rest of the sentence hang in the air.

THIRTY ONE

A cold north wind drove the snow from the direction of the Kremlin across the frozen Moscow River. It battered the Union flag flying from the pole inside the wrought iron railings that guard the British Embassy on Morisa Toreza Embankment, directly opposite the Kremlin. Krasin's black Zhiguli stopped outside the left-hand gate where a dozen visa seekers were vainly trying to talk their way past the greatcoated militiaman. The militiaman examined Krasin's invitation card while a Russian, swathed in woollen hat, scarf, and fingerless gloves, reluctantly left the small caravan parked inside the grounds in order to open the gate. 'The drive's full,' he said bluntly. 'You'll have to park round the side, beyond the visa section.'

Krasin parked his car and strode past the line of transport containers that brought the luxuries enabling these foreigners to continue their self-indulgent lifestyle. By the time he reached the front of the two-storey white-edged ochre mansion, snow clung to his uniform. He stood in the porch, shook off the snow, and scraped his shoes. Across the river the golden onion dome atop the tall, white Ivan the Great Bell Tower broke through the swirling snowstorm as though to remind Krasin of Russia's greatness.

A tall stooping man with a thatch of white hair squinted down through pebble lensed spectacles as Krasin walked up the central, dark oak staircase. When Krasin had almost reached the top step, Sir Digby Everett beamed in recognition. 'My dear fellow,' his bass voice said, 'I'd almost given you up for lost. I'm so pleased you could make it. I did so want you to meet our new Defence Attaché since you seemed to get on splendidly with his predecessor.'

'I'm honoured that you invited me, Ambassador,' Krasin said. 'I apologize for being late.'

'I don't think we're expecting anyone else,' Everett said. 'Let me take you through.'

The Ambassador led Krasin into the crowded white ballroom. Krasin estimated that over a third of those present wore military uniform. He took a glass of mineral water from the tray of drinks offered by the waitress while the Ambassador peered round the room. A handsome, grey haired woman, immaculately attired in black cocktail dress and pearls, greeted Krasin and, without altering her smile, murmured, 'By the window,' as she passed the Ambassador.

'There he is, by the window,' Everett said. 'Already buttonholed by the Americans if I'm not mistaken.'

One lean, crew cut American in army uniform was talking earnestly to a stocky man in the blue-grey uniform of the Royal Air Force. 'Jamie,' said the Ambassador, 'I want you to meet Colonel Nikolai Krasin from the General Staff here. Colonel Krasin, Air Commodore James Campbell, our new Defence Attaché. I believe you already know Colonel Ronald Wells.'

'Ambassador,' the American nodded respectfully. 'Kolya,' he said to Krasin, 'you old son of a gun. I thought you were never coming.'

'I'll leave you military chaps to it,' said the Ambassador.

Krasin bowed his head and then turned to the British Defence Attaché. 'Welcome to our country, Air Commodore.'

'Jamie, please,' said Campbell. He eyed the small badge on the collar of Krasin's uniform. 'Paratrooper, like Ron here?'

'Alas,' Krasin said, 'now I'm just a penpusher.'

'Don't you believe it,' said Wells. 'I reckon Kolya and I are two of the fittest guys in Moscow, and we're the only two who don't drink alcohol. Right, Kolya? Tell you what, Jamie, why not grab a partner and come for a game of tennis against Kolya and me.'

'Rugby's more my game, you understand,' said Campbell. 'It's rather like gridiron but without all that protective padding you Americans feel you need.'

Wells laughed. 'I can see Kolya's going to have to get up early in the morning to put one over you. Hey, Kolya, don't look so serious, this is supposed to be a party.'

'Forgive me,' said Krasin. 'I've got things on my mind.'

'More coup rumours?' Wells asked.

Krasin shook his head. 'But it might turn out to be as serious.'

Wells stared at him. 'Jesus, I believe you mean it. What gives, Kolya, or can't you tell us?'

Krasin looked round. The score of colourful chattering coteries changed amoeba-like as members detached, circulated, and attached in the slow dance of diplomatic small talk. 'Can we be alone?'

'I don't think the Ambassador will mind if we retire to his drawing room,' Campbell said.

Campbell stood in front of the large, carved oak fireplace while Krasin and Wells sat down in blue-green damask armchairs on either side. Krasin fingered his glass. Finally he looked up. 'This is not official, and I haven't received confirmation yet.'

Wells, on the edge of his seat, nodded understandingly.

'But,' said Krasin, 'we've had a report that battalions of the Strategic Rocket Forces are planning to swear allegiance to the Ukrainian state.'

'Holy shit!' said Wells. 'Whatever quarrels they had with you about dividing up men and equipment of the former Soviet Army, those bastards agreed that all strategic nuclear missiles would remain under unified command.' He jumped to his feet and jabbed his forefinger at Krasin as though Krasin were responsible. 'The White House made it clear that we want to deal with only one nuclear power after the breakup of the Soviet Union, and that's Russia.'

'Ukrainians firing off intercontinental ballistic missiles sounds to me rather more than serious,' Campbell said.

'Fortunately,' said Wells, 'that's one thing they can't do with them, right, Kolya?'

Krasin said nothing.

'Hey, c'mon. We had General Churbanov testify before the House Armed Service Committee. I got a copy of his evidence back in the office. Your nuclear missiles have more electronic locks than crabs on a New Orleans whore. A whole bunch of codes have got to be fed in from the right people here in Moscow, in the right sequence, and within a fixed time limit, otherwise those missiles can't be fired.'

'Churbanov is a tank man,' Krasin said.

'You wouldn't be trying to tell us that your General Churbanov doesn't understand your nuclear command and control systems, would you?' Campbell asked.

'I'm saying that Churbanov read from a well prepared brief.'

'And who wrote that brief?' Campbell asked.

Krasin examined his empty glass. 'When nationalism first started pulling the Soviet Union apart, the high command became worried that Ukrainians, Kazakhs, and others might seize its nuclear weapons, and so it wanted to let them know that the missiles couldn't be used without the unblocking and launch codes that Moscow holds. The high command has been putting across that message ever since.'

'Are you saying that Churbanov lied to the House?' Wells asked.

'What Churbanov said, crudely speaking, is more or less the case as it applies to the newer missiles you call the SS-24s and the SS-25s. But there are also 130 silo based SS-19s still in Ukraine.'

'With no PALs for Chrissakes?'

'They do have permissive action links, but I'm afraid that they're much less sophisticated than you might deduce from Churbanov's testimony.' Krasin took a deep breath and pretended to steel himself. 'I'd be dishonest if I didn't tell you, Ron, that any one of two hundred technicians from the Dnepropetrovsk Missile Development and Production Centre could retarget those missiles and wire a bypass for the blocking mechanisms.'

'And jump start the missiles?' Campbell asked.

Krasin nodded.

'Jesus H Christ!' Wells exclaimed.

'Look,' said Krasin, 'I don't want to alarm you. The reports haven't been confirmed. Until now we'd always regarded the SRF troops as the most reliable in the Army.'

'Well, Kolya, I appreciate your honesty,' Wells said.

Krasin stood up. 'If you'll excuse me, I'm flying to Kiev tonight to try and find out what exactly is going on down there. I'll let you know if it looks serious.'

'Jesus H Christ,' Wells repeated when Krasin had left. He prowled round the drawing room like a boxer before a title fight. 'You can't trust those motherfuckers in Ukraine.'

Campbell rested an arm on the mantelpiece. 'Speaking as one from the Celtic fringe that feels Scotland hasn't benefited from North Sea Oil, I can understand what it feels like to live in a small country next to a big, powerful neighbour. On the other hand, Ukraine is none too small. I do believe it's well over twice the size of the United Kingdom, and we've got our own independent nuclear deterrent, so why shouldn't Ukraine?'

'Because, Jamie, after all that hype about the benefits of independence, their economy is in the shit bin. Unlike you Brits they've got no tradition of democracy. It's the classic scenario for their old fascist tendencies to come out on top.'

'Fascist?'

'Right. All Ukrainians are fascists under the skin. Who were the guards in the Nazi concentration camps? Ukrainians. Listen to me, Jamie, we need a strong Russia to keep those motherfuckers under control.' Wells looked at his wristwatch. 'I need to signal the Pentagon. We're going to have to squeeze the balls of those Ukrainians until they honour their pledge to give up all nuclear weapons stationed on their soil.'

'But Ron, we've only got Colonel Krasin's word for this.'

Wells paused at the door. 'Jamie, you're new around here. Let me tell you that Kolya and his people earned our trust during the '91 coup attempt.'

'I never realized my drawing room had quite that effect on people,' Sir Digby Everett said to Campbell when he returned to the ballroom. 'First Colonel Krasin leaves almost as soon as he arrives, and then Colonel Wells disappears as though he's seen a ghost. You didn't see a ghost in there, did you, Jamie?'

'We need to talk, Ambassador.'

'I thought that might be the case. We'll meet you outside the door.' Everett beamed at the Italian Defence Attaché and eased his way over to Lady Everett. 'Boys' talk, I'm afraid, Eleanor. Will you hold the fort?'

'Richard's by the drinks table, as usual,' said Lady Everett without altering her smile.

'Bless you.' Sir Digby Everett dispensed cheerful greetings as he wandered through the crowd. He arrived at the drinks table where a middle-aged man in a grey suit, who bore a passing resemblance to Prince Charles, was trying to chat up the wife of the Swedish Defence Attaché. 'Do forgive me, Mrs Lundquist,' Everett said, 'I'm afraid there's someone who insists on talking with Richard.'

'Now?' asked Richard Abercrombie as they moved away.

'Afraid so.'

Campbell was waiting outside the door. Abercrombie punched the code in the electronic lock and led them into a room within a room. Electronic impulses were beamed through the void between the inner and outer walls, ceilings and floors to jam any listening devices.

The three men sat round the conference table, and Campbell repeated the conversation almost word for word.

'Well, Richard,' Everett asked, 'what do you make of all this?'

'I don't like the look of this one, Ambassador,' Abercrombie said. 'Several politicians in Kiev have been demanding that Ukraine keeps the nuclear weapons stationed on its soil as long as Russia retains its nuclear weapons. We were told that all tactical nuclear warheads have been shipped to Russia for dismantling and that all strategic nuclear weapons in Ukraine are controlled by Moscow, so I've always regarded these demands as political posturing.'

'And now?'

'With relations between Russia and Ukraine on a knife edge, we are looking at a major international crisis.'

'What do you think London should do?'

'I agree with Wells. The West must prevent Ukraine backpedalling on its pledge to become a nuclear-free state. I'd say that NATO needs to put pressure on Ukraine before the situation gets out of control, starting with the threat of economic sanctions.'

'Jamie?'

'I'm new on the scene, Ambassador. I haven't got Richard's detailed knowledge of the situation out here.'

'No,' said Everett, 'but you can give us the viewpoint of an informed outsider.'

'I did put the Ukrainian case to Colonel Wells, but he wasn't having any of it.'

'That's hardly surprising,' Abercrombie said. 'Ever since the formation of the Commonwealth of Independent States, the Ukrainians have made agreements and then found excuses to renege when it suits them. Now it could suit them to be a nuclear power. We've simply got to be tough with these people, it's the only language they understand.'

Everett stretched back in his chair and closed his eyes. Campbell thought he had dozed off until Everett's deep voice ruminated, 'Russians have always taken a different view of Ukraine and Belarus than they have of their other colonies, you know. Many Russians don't regard them as colonies at all, but simply provinces of Russia.'

'Ambassador,' said Abercrombie, 'it's the Ukrainians, not the Russians, who are making the moves here. And damned dangerous moves at that, wouldn't you say, Jamie?'

'Those 130 SS-19s are each armed with six 550-kiloton warheads,' Campbell said. 'Put bluntly, every one of those 130 missiles packs the punch of 250 Hiroshimas.'

Still with his eyes closed, Everett said, 'Are we sure there aren't Russians in the military who are seeking an excuse to re-establish their historic suzerainty over Ukraine?'

An edge of frustration crept into Abercrombie's voice. 'With respect, Ambassador, however Russians may have viewed their Slav neighbours in the past, may I suggest that our task now is to deal with the immediate political realities. And that means preventing these missiles falling into the wrong hands before it's too late.'

Everett nodded as though in agreement, but said, 'Mind you, we seem to be placing a great deal of credence in this Krasin chappie. I do believe he was the fellow from whom Jamie's predecessor got the idea that a revived UPA was working with the IRA. I'm not sure I entirely trust Colonel Krasin.'

'Whether we trust him or not, Ambassador,' said Campbell, 'the fact is the Americans trust him.'

'Ah yes, the Americans. Very trusting people. Admirable quality, of course, but one does tend to get one's fingers burned if one is too trusting, especially of the military. I'm thinking of their being rather too ready to trust the likes of General Batista, General Pinochet, General Noriega, General Samoza, Major Daubesan, General Lon Nol, and a few other military gentlemen.' He nodded, this time to himself. 'On the whole, I think the Americans are in danger of jumping in too quickly on this one without looking where they're going.'

Abercrombie shot a despairing glance at Campbell. 'I think, Ambassador,' said Abercrombie, 'that we mustn't keep Jamie from preparing his report for London.'

'Of course, my dear fellow. But I do hope, Jamie, that you won't take it amiss if I pen my own thoughts to the Foreign Secretary. I don't believe London should do anything precipitate until we are certain that (a) Colonel Krasin's report is true; (b) the Ukrainians are able to bypass these blocking mechanisms and fire these missiles; and (c) they're crazy enough to be prepared to use them.' He turned to Abercrombie. 'What do you think, Richard?'

'Quite frankly, Ambassador,' said Abercrombie, 'I think the disputes between Russia and Ukraine could turn into a Yugoslavia with nukes.'

THIRTY TWO

It was only the second time since he had given Christine Lesyn the letter from Marchenkov's widow that Stepaniak had dared to walk home from work.

It was irrational, he knew, but he felt secure inside a packed, rush hour trolley bus where the smells of body-heated leather coats, wet artificial fur, plastic waterproofs, cheap scent, and unbathed human sweat suffocated the smell of fear.

On three days he hadn't gone into work at all. The morning after he'd given Lesyn the letter he rolled out of the sagging bed in his Uritskogo Street apartment, went to urinate, collected a bottle of vodka from the fridge, took the phone off the hook, and burrowed himself once more in the protective warmth of his bedclothes. The following day he ignored the persistent ringing of the doorbell. The pounding in his head was like a hammering on the door. But that was impossible: no one could reach the door without unlocking the steel grille that guarded the corridor. The hammering stopped. In the quiet he heard the scraping of a key in a lock. The vodka and his fear were playing tricks in his mind. He pulled the sheet, blankets, and the goatskin bedcover over his head.

Two sets of footsteps sounded on the linoleum. The bedroom door creaked open. His heart beat rapidly and sweat poured from his body. The only prayers he knew were invocations to Uncle Lenin.

Suddenly the sheet was pulled away from his clutching hands and he heard a throaty chuckle. 'He's here.'

He squinted in the bright light. Dressed in tweed jacket and grey trousers, Roman Bondar was drawing back the curtains.

Maria came into the room. She nearly choked on the pungent odour of sweated alcohol. 'Taras, what's wrong?'

'I had a dose of flu and a high temperature,' Stepaniak lied.

'And you took the traditional remedy.' Roman Bondar chuckled as he picked up three empty vodka bottles from the floor.

Maria's small face was white. 'We were desperately worried. Nobody knew where you were, and the operator said your phone was out of order. Daddy went and got Uncle Vasyl's spare keys.'

'Thanks,' Stepaniak mumbled.

Maria felt his moist brow. 'I'll make you some hot rose-hip.'

'I feel better now.'

'It's black coffee he needs,' Bondar said.

Showered, shaved, and dressed, Stepaniak found Maria and her father waiting for him in the kitchen.

'I don't know why Sonya put up that damned grille,' Roman Bondar complained. 'It makes this place feel like a prison.'

'You know perfectly well, Daddy,' Maria said as she poured coffee into three cups on the small, formica table. 'These apartments aren't safe any longer.'

Bondar shook his head. He ran his hand through his mane of white hair and loosened his tie. 'That was good thinking on your part, Taras,' he said. 'We're getting much better publicity from Christine's article than if I'd simply raised the matter in Parliament. America and Britain have responded by coming out in support of a big programme of economic assistance from the IMF to help us get on our feet.'

Maria smiled proudly. 'I told you we could rely on Taras.'

Bondar rubbed his hands together. 'Now all we have to do is find this Russian colonel.'

The third day that Stepaniak didn't turn up for work was the day after the television evening news reported that Valeria Marchenkova had poisoned her two sons and then poisoned herself, leaving a note to say they had nothing to live for after her husband's death. Maria phoned him: she was overcome with guilt about publicizing Valeria's letter; she begged him to be careful and not to take risks when searching for the Russian colonel.

Careful! What could he do? He was certain that Krasin was responsible for Marchenkova's death. He thought about running away, but that would be an admission of guilt. And where could he go? The GRU had agents in every country, and Krasin was a man who would never rest until a treacherous agent was punished. He thought about phoning Petrosyan, but what could he say? The weather's turned cold again and, by the way, that article was nothing to do with me?

Stepaniak spent the day at home, but he felt trapped in this top-floor apartment. The next day he went into work by trolley bus. It was safer among crowds.

Stepaniak's fragile courage was shaken later that week. When he arrived at work on Thursday, he found a note from Maria on his desk saying that her father had suffered a heart attack and was in hospital. Was Krasin responsible for this as well?

Stepaniak had nowhere to hide; he had no alternative but to continue his daily routine. At the weekend he went to see Roman Bondar in hospital. Petrosyan still hadn't contacted him. By Wednesday of the following week he braved himself to walk home from Rukh. He had the irrational fear that every car in the slow moving, rush hour traffic was following him, but no car stopped and nobody was waiting for him in the unlighted lobby of the apartment block.

It was very cold this Thursday evening. It had been very cold in his youth – one winter the temperature hadn't risen above minus twenty-five for a month – but he remembered that as a bright, bracing cold. This was a grey cold that chilled the bones. He comforted himself with the thought that if Petrosyan suspected he'd leaked Marchenkova's letter he would surely have picked him up by now. Nevertheless he walked on the left-hand side of the road so that he could watch the oncoming traffic.

He was walking downhill towards the River Lybid when he found the pavement blocked by temporary barriers sealing off works on one of the city's many leaking water mains. He crossed the road and continued downhill. The pavement led across the unfrozen sluggish green River Lybid, which was warmed by effluent from the smoke-belching electricity generating station. After crossing the river the pavement fell into shadow where it passed beneath the railway bridge. A hand grabbed his shoulder. An unshaven face, rubicund with alcohol, breathed over him. 'A contribution for the love of God to buy some food.' The old man held out his other hand. Stepaniak pulled himself free and walked on quickly up Uritskogo Street. His apartment block was in sight, higher up the hill on the other side of the road. He turned to see if it was safe to cross. A black Volga stopped and the passenger door opened.

'Another meeting of the literary circle?' Stepaniak joked nervously.

Petrosyan said nothing and made a U-turn to drive back towards Victory Square.

Stepaniak tried desperately to think of something to say. In the end he said, 'What do you want me to do now that Lesyn has blown the UPA?'

Petrosyan stared ahead and drove unhurriedly towards Podol. Stepaniak had found Petrosyan's chuckles unnerving; Petrosyan's silences made his blood run cold.

They made slow progress up Frunze Street. On the left he saw the four floodlight pylons and the east stand of the Spartak stadium. He had swum in the large pool inside the stadium complex when his local Komsomol spent a two-week summer camp on Trukhanov Island, across the River Dnieper from Podol. After swimming he took the prettiest girl to the wooded slopes behind the stadium and made love for the first time. How had that initiation into pleasure degenerated into a final act of self-loathing with Christine Lesyn?

Just after Shevchenko Square, the Poleskie Bus Station marked the end of civilization. Beyond stretched the highway through the darkening forest. Petrosyan switched on the Volga's headlights. He still hadn't spoken a word.

The Volga turned off the highway. Its headlights signalled the guard to open the green gate in the green fence, and the car bumped along the narrow road through the Myzhgyra dacha compound until it reached the two-storey stone house by the lake.

Without speaking, Petrosyan left the car and walked up to the door. Stepaniak was seized by a wild impulse to run for his life. Instead, he followed Petrosyan like a lamb to the slaughter.

Krasin was seated behind a walnut desk in a wood-panelled study, his bald-topped head bent over a map of Ukraine. He didn't rise to greet Stepaniak. Petrosyan moved an upright chair in front of the desk for Stepaniak to sit on. Stepaniak heard the scraping of a chair on the parquet. He glanced round. Petrosyan was sitting behind him. Underneath his own chair was an old rug. It was all arranged for the classic *rasstrel*, the shot fired up through the base of the skull when the condemned man's attention is distracted. The old rug would soak up most of the mess.

Krasin leaned back in the leather executive chair and stroked his chin with a pencil while his grey eyes observed Stepaniak's reactions. Stepaniak strained to prevent himself urinating in his pants. Finally, Krasin said, 'Lesyn's article was a serious blow.'

The dryness in Stepaniak's throat made his voice hoarse. 'I agree.'

'Lieutenant Colonel Petrosyan thinks that you've gone native. Lieutenant Colonel Petrosyan says that you've been seeing a lot of Bondar's daughter.'

'But you ordered me to use Maria to get close to Roman Bondar,' Stepaniak pleaded.

'Lieutenant Colonel Petrosyan thinks that you colluded with Maria Bondar in the article.'

'That's not true!' Stepaniak protested. 'When I went to see Lesyn to tell her the identity of Taras Borovets, she showed me the letter from Marchenkova. There was nothing I could do.'

Petrosyan's voice from behind said, 'You could have eliminated her.'

Krasin doodled with the pencil on a desk pad while not taking his eyes from Stepaniak. 'Wet jobs aren't Major Stepaniak's style. Seduction and disinformation are more his line.'

'You could have told me and I would have seen to it,' the voice from behind said.

Stepaniak turned round. 'It was too late. She'd already filed her story, which included the letter from Marchenkova.'

From in front Krasin said, 'Poor Marchenkova. An overdose of pyridostigmine was not the wisest choice for a suicide. I understand it causes particularly painful contractions of the gut and stomach muscles, together with involuntary defecation and urination, before death relieves the agony several hours later. Such a fate, unfortunately, seems to befall those who break their promises and betray their country. I suppose our Buddhist friends would call it karma.'

A warm wetness spread to Stepaniak's inner thighs. He put his hands on his lap to cover the telltale damp patch of urine.

'Lieutenant Colonel Petrosyan thinks that you broke your promise and betrayed your country,' Krasin mused.

'No, it's not true!' Stepaniak twisted round. Petrosyan had his gun hand inside his jacket. Stepaniak was sick with the knowledge that he would gladly have put Roman Bondar, and even Maria, on this chair in his place.

'No,' Krasin said. 'I told him that I didn't think it was true. But then Lieutenant Colonel Petrosyan thinks that I am too trusting. So I said to him, Major Stepaniak will be eager to prove he is not a traitor. Am I right?'

Stepaniak seized the lifeline. 'Yes, sir.'

'Good,' Krasin said as if that were the end of the matter. 'Lesyn's article has removed the knights we had operating behind our opponent's line of pawns. What do we do now, Major Stepaniak?'

The release of tension set his body trembling. He gripped his knees. 'We . . . er . . . we change our strategy.'

'Specifically, we turn the position to our advantage. How do you suggest we do that, Major?'

Stepaniak was too confused to think of the answer Krasin wanted to hear. 'I'm not sure, sir.'

'Tut, tut. What did we say before? Put yourself in the enemy's shoes. Lesyn's article has convinced him that we are trying to destabilize his country with the objective of re-establishing control over it. So what does he do?'

'Increase his defences.'

'Good. With what?'

'With the Ukrainian Army he's building up.'

Krasin shook his head. 'Armies consist of men. The problem with men these days is that you're never sure where their loyalties lie. Wouldn't you agree, Colonel?' No sound came from behind Stepaniak. Krasin returned his attention to Stepaniak. 'What alternative does he have?'

'Political support? From the European Community and NATO?'

Krasin's laugh was mirthless. 'Political support is as fickle as the loyalty of former Soviet officers. No, his best defence is that non-human means which deterred NATO from invading the Warsaw Pact countries for forty years.'

Stepaniak shifted in his chair. 'The bomb?'

'Precisely. If Ukraine has nuclear weapons, then Russia will be deterred from making claims on its territory even if, say, the people of Donbas vote to rejoin Russia.'

Stepaniak didn't know where this was leading or how he was supposed to prove his loyalty, but a sinking feeling in his stomach told him to expect the worst.

'It will not be surprising, therefore,' Krasin continued as though analysing a counterattack to a classic chess gambit, 'when a battalion of the Strategic Rocket Forces announces that it pledges its allegiance and its weapons to the defence of Ukraine.'

'But the Ukrainian Government agreed that all strategic nuclear weapons in Ukraine remain under Moscow's control until they can be dismantled,' Stepaniak said.

'Precisely. These troops no more trust the Ukrainian Government than they trust Russian command of strategic nuclear weapons. They do not pledge their allegiance to the Ukrainian Government, but to the Ukrainian Parliament. And here, my dear Major Stepaniak, is where you prove that loyalty of which Lieutenant Colonel Petrosyan is so distrustful.'

Stepaniak's throat was too dry to speak. He nodded.

Krasin rested his elbows on the desk and made a steeple with his fingers. He stared at Stepaniak over the top of the steeple. 'Christine Lesyn should find no difficulty accepting the announcement by these troops, especially when she's been prepared by you beforehand. You are to impress upon her that, whatever Roman Bondar has said publicly about removing all nuclear weapons from Ukraine, he believes Ukraine should only do so when Russia gives up all its nuclear weapons.'

A chink of light opened. Stepaniak saw a way to avoid involving Bondar. 'Roman Bondar is in hospital,' he said. 'He had a heart attack last week.'

Krasin raised his eyebrows. 'Lieutenant Colonel Petrosyan is very assiduous. He has informed me of this fact. It makes your task, Major Stepaniak, very much easier.'

'Too easy,' said Petrosyan's voice from behind. 'It's hardly a test of loyalty.'

Krasin broke the steeple and held out his hands as though helpless. 'You see what I mean, Major? However, do not fear. You shall have another opportunity to prove your loyalty. When troops move in to secure these missiles and several other installations, you will issue a statement in Bondar's name, on behalf of Rukh, calling upon the Ukrainian Army to fight to the death against the combined forces of Russia and NATO.'

Stepaniak's voice was several notes higher than usual. 'NATO? Will they be sending troops?'

Krasin's brow furrowed. 'Your statement must convince people that NATO, led by the Americans, is taking military measures to enforce the Ukrainian commitment to operational control by Moscow of all strategic nuclear weapons in Ukraine.'

'But it would be a massacre. The Ukrainian Army is no match for the Russian Army, let alone Russia plus NATO.'

Krasin sighed. 'Major Stepaniak, you seem very slow this evening. I trust that most regimental commanders of the Ukrainian Army will reach that conclusion rather more quickly. We are relying on your quixotic statement in Roman Bondar's name to produce that response. I don't think you will let us down, do you, Lieutenant Colonel Petrosyan?'

No response came from behind.

'When will this happen?' Stepaniak asked.

'When a battalion commander of the Strategic Rocket Forces telephones the Ukrainian Television Centre with his pledge of allegiance. Our paratroopers won't be far behind. I should prepare the ground with Christine Lesyn as soon as possible and have your statement ready to issue the moment the action begins.'

'Why do I have to use Bondar's name?' Stepaniak asked.

Krasin looked past him to Petrosyan. 'I think you should tell us why you must, Major Stepaniak.'

Stepaniak could hear the breathing of the man behind him. He tried to clear his head of fear in order to think. 'Because the statement must come from a credible leader,' Stepaniak said.

'More precisely, from the only man capable of uniting a panic-stricken country, provided he can use his influence with Western leaders. But your statement in his name will remove that influence. There, you see, think things through for yourself, Major.' Krasin smiled for the first time that evening. 'May I trust you, Major Stepaniak?'

Krasin knew him better than he knew himself. Stepaniak heard his voice giving the only answer of which he was capable. 'Yes.'

THIRTY THREE

'I trusted you, at least, to bring me some vodka,' Roman Bondar said to Stepaniak.

Maria adjusted the pillows that propped up Bondar in his hospital bed. 'Taras would have me to answer to if he did,' she said.

Roman Bondar had aged in these last few days. The spirit was still there: the blue eyes shone undimmed, but from sockets sunken and dark, while the once robust, weatherbeaten face hung slackly with a deathly pallor. Shorn of his white mane he must have looked like this in the Siberian prison camps, Stepaniak thought. It was easy to imagine. Stitch a rectangle of cloth stamped with a number onto the breast pocket of the red-and-white striped pyjamas and you had a prison uniform. The tubular metal bedstead was standard Soviet issue, and the ward of twenty-four tightly packed beds might have been a camp barracks, even to the concrete that showed through in large patches where the pale green plaster had peeled and flaked away. But Prisoner Bondar had spent most Siberian winters of his fifteen-year sentence in a punishment cell, usually an unheated wooden hut with a plank for a bed, and Prisoner Bondar hadn't had a loving daughter to fluff his pillows and tenderly stroke his large hands.

'Women!' Bondar said as though embarrassed, but the deep affection between father and daughter touched Stepaniak. It was an unselfish, reassuring emotion that Stepaniak hadn't experienced until he had met Maria and her family. His own father had been a hard, mean man who thought his son gutless, while his mother suffocated him with demands for the love she never received from her husband. Stepaniak had mourned neither. He would mourn Roman Bondar.

'Then *you* must smuggle some in, Father, in the guise of holy water,' Bondar announced.

Father Tanyuk was small, with a completely bald head and, unlike other priests Stepaniak had met, possessed of a self-effacing humour. He glanced to his left and his wide smile revealed a mouthful of gold fillings. 'But I would have to answer to Katrusia.'

'That's loyalty for you!' Bondar boomed. 'For ten years I looked after this man in the Perm camps, and this is how he repays me.'

Kateryna Bondar, her hair still in an untidy bun but dressed now in her white hospital coat, stockings, and flat shoes, walked down the ward towards Bondar's bed. She rubbed her hands together. 'What's this disturbance?'

'I've been betrayed by my friends,' Bondar complained. 'The sooner I'm out of here the better.'

'You're going nowhere for another three weeks,' Kateryna said. 'You're to have a complete rest, you're to take all your medication, and you're to keep strictly to the diet. In here, at least, my word is law.'

Bondar affected an attitude of humility. 'Yes, Doctor.'

Kateryna lifted her eyes to heaven – Stepaniak saw where Maria's gesture of frustration came from – and turned to talk to Father Tanyuk and Maria.

Stepaniak looked round the shabby ward, at the visiting families who brought flowers when the patients needed sterilized needles and fresh fruit, and tried to understand why Bondar hadn't used his influence to obtain privileged treatment. Bondar caught his eye. 'Tell me, Taras, do you think this gang of terrorists posing as the UPA was simply a renegade group of OMON troopers acting on their own initiative?'

Stepaniak gazed down at the grey blankets on the bed, made from woollen waste like the uniforms of the new Ukrainian Army. Was Roman Bondar deliberately using words like 'trust' and 'betray', or am I becoming paranoid? he wondered. 'Lieutenant Colonel Petrosyan is convinced they are,' he said. 'I've no reason to think otherwise.'

Bondar nodded. 'It's a shame that Petrosyan's had no success in identifying these people.'

'I agree. But he's working flat out on the case.'

Bondar tried to regain eye contact. 'The only thing the Interior Ministry was good for was its bureaucracy. Wouldn't you have thought that it had records of all the OMON troopers who operated in Ukraine?'

'Petrosyan did say something about Interior Ministry records being incomplete.'

Bondar raised his eyebrows. 'But not KGB records. Petrosyan needn't have left his own building to find the names and last known addresses of all former OMON troopers.'

Stepaniak sat down on the edge of the narrow bed; that way he could avoid those piercing blue eyes. 'Perhaps they've gone into hiding in Russia.'

'That would be the intelligent thing to do. But the Black Berets weren't especially noted for their intelligence. Wouldn't you say, Taras, that there's an intelligent mind behind all this?'

'I . . . I hadn't thought.'

Bondar nodded. 'Lying here, I've had nothing to do but think. Do you know what conclusion I've reached, Taras?'

Stepaniak's mouth was dry once more. No more inquisitions, please. 'I don't know.'

'It seems to me,' Bondar said, 'that if I wanted to destabilize Ukraine, I would do three things. First, I'd weaken the Army by fomenting distrust between officers of Russian and Ukrainian origins. Second, I'd provoke ethnic conflict between Russian and Ukrainian communities in the country. Third, I'd carry out the first two measures in such a way as to reinforce in the West the old Soviet propaganda about Ukrainian fascism and terrorism.'

Stepaniak picked at a loose thread on the blanket and said nothing.

'What kind of mind would think up a plan like that, Taras?'

'An evil one,' Stepaniak said with conviction.

'An evil one, yes, but also one that is well versed in such campaigns, wouldn't you say, Taras?'

Stepaniak focused on the red carnations that Maria had put in a vase on top of the small bedside cabinet. 'Probably. I wouldn't know.'

Kateryna and Maria were laughing at some remark of Father

Tanyuk's. Bondar beckoned Stepaniak to come closer. 'Have you got any cigarettes?'

'No,' Stepaniak said, 'but I've got some cheroots.'

'Put them under the pillow while Katrusia's not looking,' Bondar whispered.

As Stepaniak leaned over to secrete his packet of cheroots, Bondar said, 'What do you think of Lieutenant Colonel Petrosyan?'

Stepaniak hesitated. Petrosyan, he had decided, was a sadist. 'Petrosyan seems a conscientious officer. Les Koval said that he's on our side.'

'Lieutenant Colonel Petrosyan of the KGB,' said Bondar, 'expressed his private support for Rukh's objectives back in July '91 – before the coup attempt – and offered his help, on condition that he remained anonymous. He told us he was sympathetic to our demand that Ukraine should have its own army, and he gave us information when we organized the first congress of the Ukrainian Officers' Union. That's why Les and I trusted him. While I've been lying here I've been thinking about the help he gave us, the advance warnings of KGB plans to disrupt our meetings, and so on. Do you know what conclusion I've reached, Taras?'

Why did he always have to phrase questions like that? Stepaniak shook his head.

Bondar leaned back on his pillow. 'Petrosyan didn't tell us anything we couldn't have worked out for ourselves if we hadn't been so naïve and surprised that the information was coming from a senior KGB officer.'

Stepaniak dared not remain passive and simply agree with everything Bondar said, that would be too suspicious. 'You can also interpret the facts to conclude that Petrosyan is genuine.'

'Ah yes. You're quite right to suggest that I'm becoming paranoid. Did you ever have any dealings with the KGB, Taras?'

'Only the Third Chief Directorate officer in my regiment.' Stepaniak bit his tongue. Most soldiers would have referred to the political officer or the counterintelligence officer, but not to a specific KGB directorate.

Bondar's eyes sought him out. 'Ah yes. You were in the Army when you defected to the West?'

'We were stationed at Zossen-Wünsdorf in the German

Democratic Republic,' Stepaniak said, 'and I was sent to deliver documents to the Allies in West Berlin.' Stop it! Stop it! All this authenticating detail to try and convince. Someone like Roman Bondar was bound to see through it.

Bondar was silent for a while. Then he said, 'Tell me, Taras, do you think I should trust Lieutenant Colonel Petrosyan?'

'I . . .'

'Romko!' Kateryna's voice was low but firm. 'No drink *and* no politics.'

'This is worse than Perm-36,' Bondar complained.

'Daddy! Don't joke about things like that!'

'Marusia, Marusia,' said Father Tanyuk, 'you either joke about Perm-36 or you become bitter and twisted. Let the old man have his joke.'

'Old man! Listen to me . . .'

'No,' Kateryna said. 'You listen to me. Visiting time has ended. You've had enough excitement for one day.'

'May I have a word with my daughter before she leaves? May I do that, please, Doctor?'

Kateryna couldn't maintain her stern expression in the face of the big man's mock humility. 'Five minutes, and that's all.'

As Kateryna accompanied Stepaniak and Father Tanyuk out of the ward, Stepaniak asked, 'How ill is he, Kateryna?'

'Romko's as strong as an ox,' said Father Tanyuk.

'I wouldn't like to see the ox with his heart,' Kateryna said quietly. 'If he follows the regime we've given him, he should recover and be able to resume a more or less normal life. But any big shock or stress could trigger another attack, and if that happens . . .' She sighed. 'If that happens, he'll be needing you, Father, not me.'

While Father Tanyuk stayed to visit other Catholic patients in the hospital, Stepaniak took Maria back to her parents' apartment. 'Take care, Maria,' Stepaniak said as she opened the apartment door.

'Come on in,' Maria said.

He hesitated on the threshold.

She took off her hat, coat, and boots. 'For heaven's sake, why are you so shy all of a sudden? Daddy thinks I'm old enough not to need a chaperon any longer, while Mother thinks I'm too old to be in any danger.' She looked at him. 'Taras, that was meant to be a joke.'

He came inside and took off his fur hat and parka. It wasn't the apartment he expected the Chairman of the Parliamentary Commission for Foreign Affairs to have. Situated in the unfashionable part of the fashionable Pechersk district, the modest two-bedroom apartment might have been the home of a middle-ranking apparatchik who had faithfully served the oppressive Shcherbitsky regime in Ukraine and who now professed that he had been a closet nationalist all his life. But the nationalist memorabilia displayed in the living room had not been hastily assembled after the Communist Party was banned in 1991. Alongside the icons, pictures of Greek-rite Ukrainian Catholic metropolitans, and family portraits, Stepaniak recognized the photograph he'd first seen in the *Sunday Telegraph* of Roman Bondar leading a banned procession of Ukrainian Catholics through the streets of Lviv in 1989, and another of Bondar being arrested by OMON troops while he was addressing a meeting of the Ukrainian Helsinki Union in Ivan Franko Park. Having now tasted freedom, Ukrainians would not be so passive when Krasin's annexation of east Ukraine took place. And Stepaniak knew who would be at the head of the barricades. 'I need a drink,' he said.

'If a drink will take that death mask off your face, then go ahead.'

'Your father's very ill, Maria,' Stepaniak snapped. 'Don't joke about things like that.'

She looked at him. 'As Father Tanyuk said, you either joke about something like that or you become bitter and twisted. I'm trying to be as brave as Daddy.' She ran into his arms. 'Hold me, Taras.'

He put his arms round her. Her hair smelled so soft, so gentle. Her body shuddered as she tried to suppress the sobbing. The warm yielding body pressed into his. His penis began to stiffen. Then another emotion overwhelmed him. It was like the affection between Maria and her father, but much more powerful. He tried to fight it, but he knew he hadn't the strength to take Maria's trust and love and then betray her and her father. He tightened his grip so that her head was buried in his chest and she couldn't see his face. 'Maria,' he said into her hair, 'we must protect your father. We must find a way of insulating him from shock. Something is going to happen that will shatter his world.'

She tried to look up at him but he held her head tight to his chest. 'Russian troops are preparing to annex east Ukraine,' he said.

She struggled free. 'We must stop them, we must . . .'

'We can't,' he said hopelessly.

'What do you mean, *can't*?'

He went to the kitchen, took a bottle of vodka from the fridge, and poured himself a large drink. She was standing in the middle of the living room, her large eyes opened wide in disbelief. Before she could say anything, he spelled it out. 'Strategic Rocket Force troops will announce that they've pledged their allegiance and their nuclear missiles to the Ukrainian Parliament. Shortly after that, Russian troops will move in. The West will support the action in order to safeguard the intercontinental ballistic missiles.' He slumped onto the couch.

'Daddy will . . .'

'No! You mustn't tell him. The stress would kill him.'

'Then *you* must do something. Tell the West, warn them now.'

He shook his head. 'It's no good, Maria. I don't know when, I don't know where, I don't know how.'

'But you must try.'

How could she understand what they were up against? 'Maria, believe me, the only thing we can do is to isolate your father from all this until he's completely recovered.'

'Taras, my father would want you to stop it, not protect him from it!'

'Maria, can't you see, it's hopeless. If I say that regiments of the Russian Army are planning to annex east Ukraine, nobody will listen to me without proof. The Russian Government knows nothing about it.' He took a large swallow of vodka. 'In the unlikely event that anyone does listen to me, the people behind the plan will have those missile troops make the announcement straight away, and then the West will be *telling* the Russian Army to move in and safeguard the missiles.' He poured himself another large drink. 'I'll have achieved nothing except my own death.'

'*Your* death?'

His knuckles whitened as he gripped the glass. 'Do you know how long General Marchenkov took to die? Do you know what poison was used to kill his widow and his sons?'

'Then don't let them die in vain,' she pleaded.

'There's nothing I can do to stop it.'

She knelt on the floor in front of the couch so that she could look into his eyes. 'Taras, my father spent fifteen years in the labour camps because he wouldn't give in to people like these. The reason he's in hospital now is because he continues with the struggle. Are you telling me that you won't lift a finger and tell Chrystia all you know so that she can get it published in the West?'

'You mean Christine? She'd only publish it if she thought it would help get her a job in the West. I've no evidence to back the story, so she won't touch it.'

'No, Taras, she's changed. Chrystia's decided to stay in Ukraine and help us.'

'And a leopard changes its spots,' Stepaniak said bitterly. 'Maria, you can't be so innocent. You can't believe her after all she's done to you.'

'When did you last see Chrystia?'

'When I gave her Marchenkova's letter.'

'Before then I don't think I would have believed her. But she came to see me after she'd written the article that exposed the UPA as agents of the Russian military. She had the courage to admit that she'd been used by them to discredit Rukh.'

He said nothing.

'Chrystia also said that you'd been used by them,' Maria said quietly. 'Is it true, Taras, or have you been part of them from the start?'

He turned away from those large luminous eyes.

She bit her lip. 'Before I left the hospital, my father said that he thought you were working for the KGB.' She reached up with both hands and turned his head round to face her. 'But I told him it wasn't true. That's right, isn't it, Taras?'

He could stand it no longer. He jumped to his feet. 'I am not your father! I am not a fucking saint. Most people in this world are shits. Me? I'm like most people.'

She was still on her knees. Her voice was empty. 'You are working for them.'

He said nothing.

'You told me your father was a Ukrainian nationalist.' She sounded betrayed, not angry.

'My father was as much a Ukrainian nationalist as I am. But in those days ambition didn't mean living in the West, it meant joining the Party, working for the KGB, and marrying a Russian general's daughter.'

'Do you believe in communism?'

'Of course not.'

'What do you believe in, Taras?'

When Krasin had asked him that question, he'd replied patriotism, but only because that was what Krasin wanted to hear. Beliefs in Motherland, Lenin, or God were props for people not smart enough to think for themselves. Since his schoolboy eyes had been opened to the real world, he'd only ever believed in looking after Number One. And now Maria had exposed the worthlessness of that belief. Her love had forced him to betray his own selfishness, leaving him with nothing – nothing to protect himself against Krasin. Images of what lay in store for him turned fear into anger at the one who had disarmed him and now asked him to walk into the lion's den. 'What right have you to ask a question like that? Do you think you're God?' He jabbed a finger at the icon of Christ Pantocrator, modelled on the mosaic in Saint Sophia's Cathedral. 'Why not ask *him* to save your precious country? Don't ask a mere mortal like me. I'm already risking my life telling you this so that you can protect your father from the shock. Don't ask me to sign my own death warrant.'

She rose from her knees. 'And all this time you pretended to share our dreams, our beliefs.'

'You're fooling yourself. Grow up, Maria. You *wanted* me to be like your father. You *wanted* me to share his beliefs.'

'What do *you* want, Taras?'

He turned away and stared out of the window. He couldn't

bear to see the hurt in her eyes. Her voice conveyed no recrimination, just a quiet determination. 'Will anything change your mind? Will anything persuade you to tell Chrystia all you know?'

He continued staring out of the window. A young couple walked down the street wheeling a pram as though they had a future.

'Answer me, Taras.'

He turned round. Her eyes looked down, her long dress and her underwear lay at her feet. Disguised until now by shapeless clothes, her white nymph-like body aroused his lust, from the high, proud breasts, the flat stomach, the shapely legs, to the tuft of golden down hiding that part of her he thought would always be denied him.

'This is the only thing you've ever wanted from me, isn't it? If you have it, will you make that telephone call?'

A tremor ran through her body. He could convince himself it was a quiver of passion. She looked at him while her empty voice continued. 'Why do you hesitate? You've used me every other way, don't you want to complete your conquest?' Her eyes left him and welled with tears. 'Or am I not attractive enough for that?'

Attractive? Her nakedness surpassed even the fantasies he'd conjured as he had caressed and excited Christine's willing body: it was always the image of an open mouthed, quivering Maria that kept alive the part of him that penetrated deep into the warm, wet, eager embrace of Christine's womanhood. And now the fantasy had come alive.

His voice rose from a hoarse whisper to a scream. 'No. No! NO!'

Tears spilled over and ran down her cheeks and onto her breasts.

He tore himself from the room and stumbled out of the apartment, leaving behind the rabbitskin hat she'd given him.

THIRTY FOUR

The empty vodka bottle lay on the living room floor of the Uritskogo Street apartment. Stepaniak saw with the clarity possessed by the sober. He opened the French window and stepped into the cold. Next to him on the narrow balcony lay Toli's toboggan. Nine storeys below, the icy path beckoned. Within seconds he could be there. He had nowhere else to go. He had defiled the only woman who had ever offered him love instead of sex. Without laying a finger on her, he had desecrated Maria in a more vicious and unforgivable way than those KGB officers when she was fourteen: he had violated not her body but her faith, her trust, and her love. He couldn't now tell Lesyn that Roman Bondar supported the seizing of nuclear missiles, he couldn't telephone the Ukrainian Television Centre when the invasion began and say that Roman Bondar called upon the Ukrainian Army to fight to the death against the combined forces of Russia and NATO. But this 'disloyalty' to Krasin would seal his fate. Far better to take one painless step over the flimsy guard rail than suffer whatever agonizing death Krasin would exact.

He summoned up the courage for this escape into . . . into where? It was better if he didn't look down. Above, the sky was a cobalt blue. Ahead, against a horizontal red band of sunset, the identical tall rectangular apartment blocks that lined Uritskogo Street were silhouetted black, save for golden points of lighted windows. Like two lines of giant dominoes they climbed uphill in a gentle curve. On the horizon the valley between the dominoes glowed a deeper red, the centre of a vast furnace setting the night on fire. Is this what a nuclear explosion looks like?

The image of Maria's white sacrificial body which the vodka

had failed to drown was replaced by young Toli, his face rapt by Stepaniak's lies and his thyroid riddled with cancer. This image remained even after the sun slipped below the earth and the furnace faded into the blackness of night.

THIRTY FIVE

'You must do what you believe to be right,' Father Tanyuk's kindly voice said.

'I don't want a moral lecture,' Stepaniak snapped. 'I don't believe in anything, can't you understand?'

Tanyuk scratched his bald head and then put his hands back inside his dressing gown pockets. It was cold inside the priest's bedsitter. Above the sofa-bed on which Tanyuk sat, the face of the crucified Christ stared down at Stepaniak. 'I'm sorry, Taras. Most people who come to me in the middle of the night tend to want moral guidance.'

'I needed to talk to somebody, to see if there was something I could do to prevent the invasion.' Stepaniak stood up. 'Don't tell anyone what I've said. I came to you because priests are supposed never to reveal what they're told in confidence.'

'In confession,' Tanyuk corrected him. 'For what it's worth, I agree that informing the West without any proof would achieve nothing except, as you say, your own death. And from what you tell me of this Colonel Krasin, that would be a particularly painful death.'

'If that's all you've got to say . . .'

'But,' Tanyuk interrupted, 'it seems to me that if you do want to do something positive then you should try and obtain proof.'

'How can I?' He started towards the door.

'I'm only a priest. We need somebody who knows about these things. I'm thinking of a believer who can be relied upon to keep his word if we ask him not to divulge what we tell him.'

Stepaniak stopped at the door. 'Who?'

'Yaroslav Melnik.'

'No.'

'Why not?'

Melnik had suspected him from the beginning; Stepaniak's success with Maria had inflamed that suspicion into a determination to expose Stepaniak's duplicity and then . . . Stepaniak didn't want to think what form his vengeance would take. 'He's jealous of me, Father.'

'Are you sure it's not the other way round?' Tanyuk asked. 'Taras, if you genuinely want to do something practical to prevent this invasion, then you haven't got much choice nor, I suspect, much time.'

An hour later Yaroslav Melnik was sitting at the small formica-topped table in the priest's kitchen, which resembled Stepaniak's in Uritskogo Street except that here, instead of Mickey Mouse transfers stuck onto cracked tiles and laminated cupboards, Father Tanyuk had tried to give some colour to the soulless room by hanging icons and taping gaudy posters of saints.

Father Tanyuk wrapped a towel round the handle of the enamel kettle and poured hot water into three mugs containing instant coffee powder. 'I'm afraid I've no milk or sugar.'

Stepaniak offered Melnik one of his cheroots. Melnik ignored him and took a cigarette from his own packet, struck a match, and held the flame to the cigarette while he inhaled. He exhaled through clenched teeth, still holding the lighted match which he let burn down to the thumb and forefinger that held it. He didn't flinch. When he spoke his words were addressed to the priest, but the unconcealed hatred in his eyes was directed at Stepaniak. 'I've given my word, Father, but after hearing what he's had to say, I wish to God I hadn't.'

'Now, now,' Tanyuk chided. 'Taras wouldn't have told you anything unless I'd assured him that you would keep your word.'

'You can rely on me to keep my promise, but what about him? Can we trust him? How do we know that what he's telling us now isn't some lie to divert us?'

The priest took a cigarette from Melnik's packet and lit it from the gas oven. 'I'm not sure you have any alternative, Yaro.' Out of habit from his labour camp years he took a small puff and breathed in air with the smoke in order to make the cigarette last longer. 'If I'm any judge of character, I'd say Taras is being honest. Maybe for the first time, but facing up to past dishonesty isn't easy. I don't think we should make it any harder for him.'

Stepaniak watched while Melnik wiped the back of his hand across his walrus moustache where it had become wet from the coffee. This ignorant sod couldn't help him.

'Get me some paper, Father,' Melnik said. He took a pencil from the back pocket of his jeans, licked the lead, and when Tanyuk had put a sheet of paper on the table he began writing a list. 'First, the "where". There are only two strategic missile centres in Ukraine, one at Derezhnya and one at Pervomaysk. We have some members of the Union of Ukrainian Officers at Derezhnya but none at Pervomaysk.'

'Could the ones at Derezhnya find out if it's their base that will declare allegiance to the Ukrainian Parliament?' Tanyuk asked.

Melnik inhaled cigarette smoke and blew out a long, grey stream. 'I doubt it. The commanders would keep known Ukrainian sympathizers in the dark.'

'Can you make an informed guess?' Stepaniak asked.

'Derezhnya only has the older SS-19 missiles. In addition to SS-19s Pervomaysk has a majority of the former Soviet Union's silo-based SS-24s, the most modern, which the Russian military wants to keep, despite the START2 treaty. The base commander at Pervomaysk is a bastard: he sympathized with the coup attempt in '91 and should be in jail along with the rest, except that Moscow prefers reliable hardliners in charge of its nuclear missiles outside Russia. He'd cooperate with any plot to move Russian troops into Ukraine.' He took another drag on his cigarette. 'I'd put my money on Pervomaysk.'

'This isn't a game of roulette,' Stepaniak muttered.

'Then we can be pretty sure who will make the telephone call pledging allegiance?' Father Tanyuk asked.

Melnik shook his head. 'It obviously can't be the base commander, nobody would believe him. It's got to be one of the battalion commanders.'

'That's what I was told to expect,' Stepaniak said.

'This brings us to the problem of "how",' Melnik continued. He drew another column on the sheet. 'Each missile centre isn't a centre at all, it's a missile field stretching over a vast area. Somewhere like the Pervomaysk field will comprise eight to ten rocket complexes, and each rocket complex will control a battalion of missiles: between six and ten missiles in silos at least four hundred metres apart. Each missile battalion is operated by four shifts, three shifts per day with one shift in reserve. Each shift consists of ten officers and twelve troopers divided into four teams: an information reception and processing team, a targeting team, a mechanical and electrical engineering team, and a launch team. They work in separate bunkers and they're all essential to operate the missiles. That means a minimum of one shift would have to declare allegiance to Ukraine and, more likely, all four shifts, giving us around ninety "defectors". Then there's the matter of the guards who are supposed to patrol the trenches surrounding each rocket complex.'

'Just hold it there,' Stepaniak said. 'These details are classified top secret. You talked about not trusting me. I think you should explain how you know so much.'

Melnik's moustache curled back in a smirk. 'Didn't Father Tanyuk tell you? I was a major in the Strategic Rocket Forces.'

'Where?' Stepaniak challenged.

'At Drovyanaya, south of Chita, about 175 kilometres from the Mongolian border. But all Soviet Strategic Rocket Centres operate on precisely the same principles. It's part of the Soviet mentality.'

'And when did you suddenly decide to give up your prestigious military position and come and work for peanuts in a ramshackle organization?'

Melnik glared at him. 'When I was taken to see a nuclear test explosion at Semipalatinsk. It was the same time as Chernobyl.'

'Please,' Father Tanyuk said, 'this isn't getting us anywhere.'

Melnik wrote down another item in the 'how' column. 'It's not enough for these ninety rocket troops and their guards physically to take over the missiles. In theory there are three safety measures. First, no nuclear missile can be fired without feeding in codes transmitted from Moscow. Second, we were told that, in the event of unauthorized activity at one rocket complex, its battalion of missiles can be taken over by another rocket complex. Third, we were told that Moscow can also override directly.'

'You don't sound convinced,' Father Tanyuk said.

Melnik lit a new cigarette from the stub of his old one. 'The American security system is based on technology, the Soviet system is based on mistrust. The Soviets relied heavily on organizational safeguards, one of which is disinformation so that no one except the high command knows the true state of nuclear capability and security.' He suddenly thumped his fist on the table. 'That's what's been troubling me, Father! I doubt that the missiles are as secure as the military has told the Americans, but the fact is that the West has bought all the assurances that Moscow put out after the coup attempt.' He stared at Stepaniak. 'His story doesn't wash, Father. There's got to be something more than SRF troops seizing the missiles if they're to panic the West into thinking they can actually fire them.' He stood up. 'I think he should tell us all he knows.'

'Taras?' Father Tanyuk asked.

'I don't know anything more,' Stepaniak insisted.

'Are you sure?'

Stepaniak nodded. 'But I wouldn't put anything past Krasin.'

'I believe him,' Father Tanyuk said.

Melnik put his hands on the table and leaned threateningly over Stepaniak. 'Even if we take his word, Father, we still need to find out "how". We also need to know "when".'

'Any suggestions?' Tanyuk asked.

Melnik pursed his lips. 'We could lure Petrosyan to a meeting and then make him talk.'

'No violence,' Tanyuk said.

Melnik shrugged. 'You won't be involved, Father.'

'Save your macho show, Melnik,' Stepaniak said. 'I'm sure Petrosyan knows no more than I do. He's only a pawn, like me. Well, maybe he's a bishop, but the only one who does know the whole game plan is the chess master, Krasin.'

'And who is the only one who can reach Krasin?' Melnik asked pointedly.

'Leave me out of this,' Stepaniak said.

'Scared?'

'It's not my fight. I've done enough by telling you all I know.'

'You are scared. And meanwhile your chessmaster friend is planning to play around with a few nuclear missiles in Ukraine before cutting our country in two.'

Father Tanyuk looked at Stepaniak. Outside, the sky had lightened. Dawn would break soon over a free Ukraine. But free for how long? 'Taras,' Tanyuk said, 'can't you trap Krasin into giving you the evidence we need to take to the West without having to meet him face to face?'

'How?'

'Phone him. Tell him you're concerned that the statement you're putting out in Bondar's name will lack credibility because the Americans believe the missiles can't be fired without codes from Moscow. Yaro can record the conversation.'

Stepaniak looked at Melnik.

'No problem. I can be back here within an hour with a machine that wires into the phone.'

Perhaps this was the way out for him, a way to stop the invasion without putting himself in danger. If it worked Krasin would be in a Russian jail before he could get to him. Stepaniak swallowed. 'I'll try it.'

Stepaniak, seated on the one chair in the priest's bedsitting room, felt Melnik's eyes boring into his back. He stared at the red telephone on the small table and at the black wire leading from the telephone to a cassette recorder on the floor.

Stepaniak cleared his throat. His clammy hands picked up the telephone and dialled the Moscow contact number. When the operator answered he gave his codeword. 'This is Eliot. I want to speak to Leskov.'

A voice answered. It wasn't Krasin's. Stepaniak repeated his request.

'Leskov isn't here. He's in Kiev.'

Stepaniak felt sick. The 'when' must be very soon. 'It's urgent. I need to get his approval for a poem he commissioned. Can you give me his number?'

'Eliot, you say? Hold on.' After what seemed like hours the

voice came back on the phone. 'I'm authorized to give you a number in an emergency.'

Stepaniak wrote down the Kiev number. He turned round. Melnik and Tanyuk were watching him. He took a deep breath, picked up the handset again, and dialled.

'Yes?' The voice was Krasin's.

'Eliot here. I've been working on the poem you asked me to write. Parts of it don't sound authentic. I'm worried it won't produce the response we want. Can I explain?'

'Certainly. Come round to my place at ten tonight. You know where I am.' The line went dead.

Stepaniak's trembling hand had difficulty putting the handset back on the cradle of the telephone.

'It looks as though Krasin's down here to supervise the final details,' Melnik said. 'We'll have to wire you up for sound.'

'No!' Stepaniak rasped. 'It's no good. It won't work.'

'You needn't be in there more than half an hour,' Melnik said. 'Tell him you're concerned about credibility and have him check the wording of your Bondar statement. Say just enough for him to incriminate himself and then leave.'

Stepaniak searched for any excuse. 'He'd spot a tape recorder a mile away.'

Melnik shook his head. 'We'll use a miniaturized radio microphone and we'll be nearby in a car with the receiver, ready to back you up if things go wrong. But they won't. It's perfectly straightforward.'

'Have you got the equipment?'

'Not yet,' Melnik said, putting on his coat, 'but we've lots of contacts in the military and the security service. There's nothing you can't buy these days with dollars. I'll be back before six, Father.'

The priest sat down on the bed. He was still in his dressing gown. 'Yaro may be brash, but he means well.'

'Sure,' Stepaniak said. 'It just happens to be my hide that he's putting on the line, not his own.'

'That's true,' said the priest. 'But it is his country, and his people, that are also on the line, as you put it. How many innocent people will be killed if the invasion plan goes ahead?'

'Listen, Father, I don't want any moral blackmail, right? You haven't met Krasin, you haven't seen him at work. I can't face him. I just can't face him.'

'I'll make some more coffee. If you want to shave, use my razor in the bathroom.'

Stepaniak moved the chair so that the crucified Christ wasn't watching him. The telephone rang. Stepaniak picked up the handset. He recognized the voice. He didn't speak, but put his hand over the mouthpiece and called out, 'Telephone, Father.'

Tanyuk picked up the phone. 'Marusia.'

Stepaniak sat there, desperately trying to listen to the conversation. The one thing he hadn't confided to the priest was Maria's offering herself to him if he would try and stop Krasin's plan.

Tanyuk put the phone down.

'Did she mention me, Father?'

Tanyuk nodded. 'She asked me if I was going to see Romko again today at three. She said you wouldn't be there.'

THIRTY SIX

The headlights of oncoming cars periodically illuminated Stepaniak's face before passing by and letting it submerge in the dark anonymity of Vasyl Ladenyuk's Moskvich which he'd parked by the side of the road. The miniaturized radio microphone was small and inconspicuous – if he wasn't searched. Melnik said that it transmitted over a long range, but it needed to be within two metres of the source to pick up sounds clearly.

From previous experience of bungled operations Stepaniak hadn't wanted anyone else involved, but Melnik insisted. They needed a car for him and a back-up vehicle for the receiver and recorder. Maria already knew about Krasin's plan and she could borrow her uncle's car. Les Koval would need to know and he had a van. Stepaniak was glad now that Melnik had brought in Maria. That last haunting image of her, with nothing left but her body to offer, was partly expunged by the revival of hope in her eyes, the full kiss on his lips, and the whispered 'Thank you, Taras. May God protect you.' It gave him more courage than the hand gun in the shoulder holster which Melnik had strapped onto him. 'Purely for emergencies,' Melnik said. 'It'll give us time to get to you in the unlikely event that something goes wrong.'

'And if Krasin spots it?'

Melnik's moustache pulled back in a grin. 'Tell him that you always carry it in case Rukh discovers you're working for him.'

Stepaniak was still undecided whether to remove the shoulder holster and gun that felt like a ton weight. He looked at his watch. He'd run out of time. 'Testing, one, two, three,' he said. He looked in his rear view mirror. Way back down Minsk Prospekt the headlights of a stationary van flashed three times. Stepaniak turned the key in the ignition and drove slowly back onto the highway through the forest.

This time the guard at Myzhgyra did ask for identification. It seemed for ever before the guard put down the phone in his booth and opened the green gate. A full moon shone through the snow-laden boughs of the pines and spruces, casting shadows onto the rutted road. When he reached the clearing in front of the frozen lake Stepaniak stopped. Six cars were parked in a line outside the dacha, each with telltale black number plates. Stepaniak made a U-turn and parked the Moskvich on the edge of the road, leaving the key in the ignition ready for an emergency exit.

The burly man who opened the door was dressed in jeans, but the navy blue hoops on the vest revealed by the open leather jacket suggested the military. 'Wait here,' he said without ceremony, after leading Stepaniak to a small room for storing skates, skis, a variety of quilted jackets, fur coats, and white camouflage smocks used for hunting in the snow. And a locked rack of rifles. Stepaniak felt like the prey. How soon before the hunter came in pursuit? He coughed so that Melnik and the others would know the transmitter was still working. Knots had fallen out from the old pine panelling that lined the walls, providing ready-made peepholes. There was no heating in the room, but a bead of sweat ran from his hairline down onto his eyebrow and trickled into his eye. He rubbed it away with the back of his hand. His skin beneath the shoulder holster was clammy. Melnik had said he should be in and out within half an hour. He'd already been in this room twenty-seven minutes.

'Leskov will see you now,' said the man who had opened the front door. Stepaniak followed him down a short corridor. Krasin stood half in and half out of the study, talking to men grouped round a table. Behind them coloured pins were stuck into a large wall map of western Russia and Ukraine. Krasin turned round. 'Sorry to keep you waiting.'

Stepaniak followed Krasin into the living room and sat, as instructed, in one chair in front of the log fire while Krasin took the other chair. All Stepaniak had to do was induce Krasin to talk about his plan with sufficient details and names to incriminate himself, and then get out.

Krasin, dressed in black polo neck sweater and black trousers, examined Stepaniak. 'Aren't you hot in front of the fire? Take off your jacket.'

The weight of the gun in his shoulder holster had increased to two tons. 'I'm fine, thanks, Colonel. The reason I wanted to see you is that . . .'

'Two cups,' said Krasin to his aide, who had brought in a tray holding a coffee percolator and one cup and saucer.

'I'm worried that the statement I'm giving in Bondar's name will lack credibility,' Stepaniak said when the aide had gone.

Krasin nodded and sipped his coffee.

'It occurred to me,' Stepaniak persisted, 'that, because those missiles can't be fired without codes sent from Moscow, the West won't believe there's any serious threat if a battalion of SRF troops declares allegiance to Ukraine. Certainly not a big enough threat for NATO to send troops in.' Again Krasin made no response. 'Please tell me what I should do,' Stepaniak prompted, trying to disguise the edge of desperation creeping into his voice.

Krasin paused reflectively. 'I think,' he said finally, 'that you should drink up your coffee.' His lips curled back in a smile. 'You're going on a long journey.'

Stepaniak's heart sank. 'Where?'

'To where all your questions will be answered.'

THIRTY SEVEN

'They're going to kill him!' Maria shouted. 'Drive in there. Stop them.'

'Don't panic,' Koval replied.

Maria turned round from the front passenger seat of the van. 'Father, tell him!'

'Rushing in at this stage might be the worst thing we could do, Marusia,' Father Tanyuk said.

Melnik looked up from the recording equipment. 'Let's wait until Stepaniak calls for help.'

Stepaniak suppressed the urge to scream for help as he followed the leather jacketed man out of the dacha. He heard Krasin's footsteps crunch the frozen snow behind him. At every step he tried to decide if and when he should take out his gun. To his left the line of shiny black cars faced impenetrable black trees; to his right the white beach shelved to the frozen white lake. Some disturbance – a gust of wind? – sent a large grey owl flapping slowly and silently into the night. The frosted branches of a spruce by the beach were left shivering in the moonlight. When his parents rowed at his grandfather's dacha, he used to escape to the tree by the Pechenezh Reservoir where the yellow eyes of 'his' grey owl would stare unblinkingly at him from concentric dark rings on its flat face. His owl was unafraid.

Krasin's aide opened the rear passenger door of one of the black Volgas and nodded to Stepaniak. Stepaniak looked in vain for the owl before climbing in the car. The other rear passenger door opened and Krasin got in.

'Where are we going?' Stepaniak asked again.

Krasin smiled. 'I told you. To where all your questions will be answered. Right, Sergeant.'

Stepaniak looked at the muscular neck of the leather jacketed man, who switched off the interior light, reversed the Volga out of its parking space, and drove up the narrow road past Ladenyuk's Moskvich. After leaving Myzhgyra they crossed the highway and turned left, back towards Kiev.

If they'd wanted to kill him, surely they would have done it at the dacha, or in the grounds, Stepaniak reasoned. If he could prompt Krasin to talk now, he might be able to jump out when the car stopped at traffic lights in town. But all Krasin would say was, 'We've a long journey. I'm getting some sleep and I advise you to do the same.' Krasin took off his padded ski jacket, folded it to make a pillow, leaned back in his seat, and was asleep within seconds.

They sped past the Spartak stadium on Frunze Street. Stepaniak looked out of the rear window. The headlights of Koval's van dwindled to pinpricks. Ahead, the street lighting cast a weak blue sheen over the neoclassical buildings on Kiev's Red Square. At least half a dozen roads led away from the square.

Maria's voice was strained. 'Can you see them?'

'No,' said Koval. 'But they were heading towards Red Square.'

'Where will they go from there?' Father Tanyuk asked.

Koval put his foot down, but the van wouldn't go any faster. He slowed when they reached the square, trying to guess which direction Krasin's car had taken. He drove round, while Maria frantically peered down the exits from the square.

From behind, the receiver crackled into life:

You wouldn't believe there's a fuel shortage. Don't you think it's criminal to floodlight Saint Andrew's Church?

Floodlighting any church is a waste of money as far as I'm concerned.

Go slowly over the cobbles, or you'll wake the colonel.

Koval lit a cigarette in relief. 'They're going up the Andreyevsky Descent.'

*

By the time the van had climbed the cobbled hill leading to the baroque, blue, white and gilt, green domed Saint Andrew's Church, fear gripped Stepaniak's stomach. The bull necked sergeant was driving down Vladimirskaya Street; further down the street stood the headquarters of the National Security Service. Were they meeting up with Petrosyan, or did Krasin intend to use the NSB 'persuaders'?

'There's another one,' Stepaniak said hoarsely. 'I bet the floodlights on Saint Sophia's Monastery use enough power to light a whole housing estate.' The sergeant made no reply. Lights shone from a dozen windows of the menacing granite NSB headquarters. It passed them by on the left. Where the hell were they going? He must think up some other way of telling Koval the route.

The taillights of the black sedan disappeared behind the metro station on Leo Tolstoy Street. 'The Volga's turned into Chervonoarmeyskaya Street,' said Maria.

Koval grimaced. 'It looks like our friend Krasin meant what he said about a long journey.' Two lines of weak street lamps stretched ahead into the night as the road headed south from the city centre. Heavier traffic slowed the Volga through this part of Chervonoarmeyskaya, past stone apartment houses built at the end of the century in neo-baroque and art nouveau styles, and modern concrete-and-glass blocks with their ground floor clothes shops and bookshops.

'Have we got enough petrol?' Maria asked.

Koval looked at the gauge. 'A quarter of a tank. Let's hope it's enough.'

'What do you mean, Les, *hope*?'

'We just keep going until the petrol runs out,' Koval said. 'There's nothing else we can do.'

Maria tried to suppress the hysteria that threatened to overwhelm her. 'There must be *something* we can do.'

They stopped a dozen cars behind the Volga, at the traffic lights on the junction with Ivana Fedorova Street.

'I know where we can get petrol,' Melnik said from behind.

'At half past eleven at night?' Koval asked.

'At any time for enough dollars,' Melnik said.

'But . . .'

'I've got enough dollars,' Melnik said.

The traffic lights switched to green. Many of the cars in front turned right towards the concrete towers of the massive Zheleznodorozhny housing estate. The Volga drove straight on, past the twin spired towers of the neo-Gothic Saint Nicholas's Catholic Church. Koval had to accelerate to keep the Volga in sight. 'Where's your petrol source?'

'We need to turn back towards town.'

'But we'll lose them!' Maria said.

'If we run out of petrol we'll lose them anyway,' Melnik said.

'Let's stay with them until we know which road out of Kiev they're taking,' said Koval, 'then we'll cut back and fill up the tank.'

'Isn't that a risk?' Father Tanyuk asked.

'Got a better idea, Father?'

Koval slowed as a mustard coloured militia Volga, siren wailing and red and blue lamps flashing, overtook them and blocked his view of the black Volga. When the militia car turned off Chervonoarmeyskaya, the black Volga had disappeared.

'Did anyone see which way they went?' Maria shouted.

'Shit!' said Koval.

Stepaniak prayed that the militia car behind would stop them for speeding, but it screeched into the road opposite the floodlit concave façade of the Ukraine Palace of Culture, leaving in its wake one car and an army lorry; of Koval's van there was no trace. Moscow Square was critical. Four routes led out of the square: east to cross the Dnieper by the new South Bridge and continue along the high-speed road to Borispol Airport or beyond to the Russian border; south-east for the government dacha compound at Koncha-Zaspa or beyond to God knows where; south to Odessa; or west to Zhulyani Airport, and he could see no purpose in going further west than that. If they were going to catch a plane, he was on his own.

They passed the gloomy Central Bus Terminal in Moscow Square and took the exit signposted for the southbound M20 to Odessa. The Volga sped down the near-empty Sorokaletya

Oktyabrya Prospekt. Stepaniak had to find some means of slowing down the car and telling Koval the route. Ahead he spotted a lighted window with a sign above. 'Can we stop at the Yaroslavna Café?' he said. 'I need a leak.'

The sergeant said nothing.

'That coffee's gone straight to my bladder,' Stepaniak said.

The Yaroslavna Café disappeared into the distance behind them.

'Pull in by the park,' Krasin said, without moving from his sleeping position.

Had Krasin been feigning sleep all this time?

The sergeant pulled into the kerb after the junction with Goloseyevskaya Square. 'I'll join you,' Krasin said.

The two men crossed the wide road and entered Goloseyevsky Park by the side gate on a street that led from the square. The café and the lavatories by the frozen boating lake were locked. Krasin shrugged and began urinating on the snow. The steaming yellow stream curved down, turning the snow a straw colour. Still it came, melting a crater in the discoloured snow that widened and filled with bubbling liquid like some Icelandic hot spring. Stepaniak moved away and urinated against one of the oak trees that bordered the lake, hoping to disguise how pathetic was his excuse for stopping the car. He stood with his back to Krasin long after he'd emptied himself. With a forced laugh he zipped up his jeans. 'Shit, it's cold enough to freeze the prick off a polar bear. I trust it'll get warmer as we head south.' Expressionless, Krasin waited for him. There was no opportunity to give Koval more specific directions. He prayed it was enough for Koval to take the correct exit from Moscow Square.

THIRTY EIGHT

Only one clue betrayed the awesome potential for destruction that lay hidden in the dark forest ahead. Illuminated by the car's headlights, the red-and-white hooped pole barring their path might have been protecting a railway crossing. To the left of the pole the grey guard box opened to reveal a youth dressed in the militia's unintimidating grey artificial fur hat and greatcoat with red flashings. Even the white lettering on the red octagonal sign to the right of the pole – STOP in English, not Russian – wasn't ominous. It was the klaxon on top of the guard box that hinted at something sinister beyond.

The young soldier who was dressed in militia uniform bent down towards the opened rear passenger window. Krasin said, 'Colonel Leskov, Major Stepaniak, and driver.'

The guard went to his box, used a yellow telephone to make a call, and returned with a clipboard. 'Please sign here, sir.'

Krasin signed, looked at his watch, and entered '03:49' under the column 'Time In'. Stepaniak tried to estimate how far behind Maria and the others were. He had to believe that they had followed the Volga south down the M20 and then taken the eastbound exit at Krivoye Ozero. The alternative was too terrible to contemplate.

The guard raised the pole and the Volga entered a Forbidden Zone.

The headlights picked out a straight, snow covered road tunnelling through black trees. They passed several side roads before they came to a pair of gates made of tubular steel surrounding a solid steel panel with a red star at its centre. At the left-hand side a huge noticeboard, heedless of the changes that had swept the world in '91, was headed by Lenin's resolute face and proclaimed: *Soldiers of the USSR be proud to do your duty for the defence of the socialist Motherland!* The noticeboard at the right-hand side urged members of the Strategic Rocket Forces to be vigilant *for you are the missile shield of the Motherland!*

The soldier who came out of the guard house also wore a nylon fur hat, but with an enamel badge of a red star within a golden wreath pinned to the front. A Kalashnikov assault rifle was slung over the shoulder of his khaki greatcoat. He too made a telephone check and asked Krasin to sign the time of entry before he opened the gates and let the Volga through. It was a short drive to the small parade ground that loomed ghostly in the moonlight: a silver rectangle surrounded by sleeping single-storey buildings whose one lighted window shone like a watching eye. The Volga stopped in the wedge of light from the window. Heavy curtains were drawn, casting darkness over the car. The door by the window opened, flooding the car once more with light. A burly, uniformed man, whose epaulettes bore a colonel's three stars between two red lines, walked down the steps from the verandah to the car. He opened the rear passenger door. 'Welcome, Kolya,' the colonel said. 'You caught me by surprise.' He grinned. 'You're one minute early.'

'Good to see you again, Vanya,' Krasin replied as he climbed out of the car.

A log fire blazed in a plain, cast iron hearth, warming a room that passed for luxurious compared with most regimental headquarters. Photographs on the white wall included one of Gorbachev from the days when his portrait showed no birthmark on his forehead. When Stepaniak had passed that red-and-white hooped pole into the forest, he'd entered a time capsule.

'Colonel Muratov,' Krasin said, 'I'd like you to meet Major Stepaniak.'

Ivan Vasilievich Muratov was in his early forties. His flat features and slit eyes suggested Yakut or Buryat ancestry, and gave him a suspicious squint when he looked at Stepaniak. 'Welcome, Major.'

'It's a privilege to meet you, Colonel,' said Stepaniak. 'I hope I'm able to put out a convincing statement in Bondar's name.'

Muratov's brow creased into a frown and he looked pointedly towards the corner of the room. A fresh-faced youth stood stiffly to attention, Kalashnikov sloped across his breast, in front of a large red flag emblazoned with a gold star and regimental insignia. Change the youth's uniform for blue trousers and white shirt with red scarf, and remove the bullets from the long curved ammunition clip of the Kalashnikov, and he might have been Young Pioneer Stepaniak standing guard in Victory Square. Clearly the troops weren't privy to the plot, and there was no chance of an incriminating conversation here.

An aide brought in a flask of coffee. Muratov's expression changed to a smirk. 'A late supper or an early breakfast. Help yourself,' he said, indicating a table laden with food.

Stepaniak waited until Krasin had selected what he wanted and Muratov had filled his plate with eggs, several slices of sausage and fatty ham, plus bread and butter. The nerves that knotted Stepaniak's stomach robbed him of appetite, but he took two eggs and some black bread and butter. When Muratov poured out a vodka for himself, Stepaniak followed his example rather than that of Krasin who drank mineral water. He was about to crack his eggshell when Muratov jabbed the handle of a teaspoon through the shell of an egg and sucked out its raw contents. Stepaniak felt sick and looked for somewhere to get rid of the eggs on his plate.

Stepaniak dallied over the meal to give Koval as much time as possible to drive within range of the radio mike – if the back-up van had followed him – but as soon as Krasin finished his coffee Muratov looked at his watch. 'We should be making a move.' Muratov put on his greatcoat and his flat officer's hat, and ushered them outside where a UAZ jeep waited.

From the rear passenger bench that he shared with Krasin, Stepaniak peered between Muratov's large hat and the driver's head to try and memorize the route in case he needed to make a quick escape, but in the dark the side roads leading from the main road appeared identical. The four-wheel-drive UAZ bumped down one of these ice-covered side roads until its headlights lit up a tubular steel gate with cross struts supporting a red star. On either side a high wire fence topped by three rows of barbed wire stretched into the darkness. Once the guard recognized Muratov's jeep, he opened the gate and the UAZ drove on down a well marked road through the forest. Stepaniak sneaked a look at his watch. *If* Koval had followed the Volga, he should be in range now. Stepaniak had to make contact at the risk of clumsily breaking the silence that Krasin and Muratov kept. 'I've never been to a missile site before, Colonel. Where are we heading now?'

Muratov turned round and said more than Stepaniak had dared hope. 'Missile Station Number 3. It's one of the original ones, built for the SS-19s.'

The UAZ stopped outside a small single-storey barracks. An eerie silence hung over the clearing beyond the barracks. Wire fences surrounded mounds that rose from the snow like barrows in a prehistoric burial site.

Five soldiers in combat uniform waited in the officers' recreation room. Only one object fixed to the mock-brick wall-papered wall was conventional: the identity chart consisting of head-and-shoulders photographs of members of the battalion. The usual charts showing insignia of rank from marshal down to sergeant, correct methods of saluting, and army hierarchies were missing, as were conventional portraits of government leaders. In their place, blue-and-yellow flags and Ukrainian tridents adorned the walls together with two other portraits. Stepaniak looked at the inscription under one of them: *Roman Shukhevych, Supreme Commander of the UPA, 1943–1950*. He didn't need to read the name under the second one. Stepaniak gazed at the broad face and unruly white hair of Roman Bondar, willing the photograph to tell him where Maria was.

'I thought you'd appreciate that touch,' Muratov said to him before introducing Krasin to the officers. 'This is Lieutenant Colonel Hurenko, the battalion commander, who will make the announcement from the command bunker.' The tall, blond Ukrainian officer possessed the firm grip and unsmiling stare of either a fanatic or a determined careerist. 'Major Lavrenyuk commands the launch detachment yellow shift, Major Mironov the blue shift, Major Dalgat the black shift, who are on reserve this week, and Major Silakov commands the battalion guard.

Gentlemen,' Muratov said, 'it's my pleasure to introduce Colonel Leskov, who will give you the detailed briefing.'

The announcement must be close, Stepaniak thought. The poor bastards aren't being told Krasin's real name. I wonder what else he'll lie about.

'At ease, gentlemen,' Krasin said. 'First, on behalf of General Churbanov, I want to thank you for the mission you are about to fulfil. When you undertook your training, I'm sure you never envisaged such a mission. But you were selected for the élite force of the Army because of your fitness, your intelligence, your discipline, and your dedication to the Motherland. Now you have been selected as the élite of the élite to perform a task that will save the Motherland from disintegrating into scores of banana republics and restore pride to the Army that is her shield. No greater honour could be bestowed on you. Your names will go down in history alongside the defenders of Leningrad and the liberators of Ukraine from fascism in the Great Patriotic War.'

Stepaniak saw pride and resolution on their faces. Krasin could sell ice cubes to the Chukchi in the middle of winter.

Krasin turned to Hurenko. 'What is your state of preparation, Colonel?'

Hurenko's back stiffened. 'Sir, the battalion knows that its senior officers have agreed to take the oath of allegiance to Ukraine. Most of the guards are Ukrainian conscripts and are fully behind the decision. The other officers will follow our lead, if only for the sake of their jobs.'

'Good,' said Krasin. He faced the officers, legs apart, hands clasped behind his back. His deep voice radiated confidence. 'When Lieutenant Colonel Hurenko telephones the Ukrainian Television Centre to inform the world that you have pledged your allegiance and your missiles to the Ukrainian Parliament, this will produce a period of confusion. Colonel Muratov will telephone, ostensibly to reason with you. You will reject all his overtures, his requests for meetings, and his threats. This will prolong the confusion. The General Staff has already informed NATO and the Ukrainian Ministry of Defence about routine exercises being undertaken by certain Army divisions. At Defection plus five minutes these routine exercises will become Operation Snowstorm. At Defection plus one hour twenty-five minutes, men and BMDs* of the 106th Guards Airborne Division will parachute in and attack this base. Air defence systems in Ukraine are either under our control or else we have loyal officers in place who will disrupt any attempt to impede the attack. The attack will be swift and decisive. After token resistance by the guards, Lieutenant Colonel Hurenko will announce your surrender. The Spetsnaz battalion that leads the assault will take you prisoner, and within a further two and a half hours a Halo helicopter will land and take you to Russia, apparently for court martial. In practice you will be flown on from Tula and accommodated in rather agreeable circumstances at Khabarovsk in the Far Eastern Military District. After the situation has stabilized the President will announce an amnesty for the sake of Russo-Ukrainian relations. Any questions, gentlemen?'

Stepaniak touched the miniaturized radio mike underneath his shirt and prayed that it was working – and that Melnik was close enough to record all this.

'What time will the announcement be made, sir?' asked Mironov.

'For operational reasons you will only be informed immediately before it happens.'

'What about our resistance, sir?' asked Silakov. 'How do we avoid casualties?'

Krasin looked him straight in the eye. 'I will not lie to you, Major Silakov. We cannot avoid token casualties. Just before he makes the announcement, Lieutenant Colonel Hurenko will authorize the guards to be issued with one magazine each of 7.62-calibre bullets for their Kalashnikov AK-MSs, and order them to take up their positions in the guard routes. The Spetsnaz battalion, however, will be armed with 5.45 tumbler bullets for their AKS-74s. The battle will be short and one-sided. It is your responsibility, Major, to ensure that all officers are kept well out of the firing line, and only a few conscripts need be taken out before Lieutenant Colonel Hurenko signals your surrender.'

* *Bronevaya Mashina Desantnaya*, an armoured vehicle designed to be dropped from an aircraft.

Krasin turned to Stepaniak. 'This is Major Stepaniak who is operating undercover as a Rukh press officer. He will issue the Rukh statement welcoming your action, thereby discrediting the Ukrainian nationalists in the eyes of the West.'

'How certain are you the plan will succeed, sir?' Hurenko asked.

'With your dedication, I am absolutely certain,' Krasin concluded.

If only Stepaniak were certain that Maria was outside the base and that Melnik's equipment was recording all this.

Maria peered out of the van's front window. 'He's coming here.'

The soldier in militia uniform put down the yellow telephone in his guard box next to the red-and-white hooped pole and walked towards them.

'Turn off the receiver,' Koval said. Melnik reluctantly switched the machine off.

The guard undid the flap of the holster strapped to the belt round his greatcoat.

'Be careful,' Maria whispered.

'I've got a gun,' Melnik said.

Koval wound down his window.

The guard was close enough to show cheeks that needed shaving only once a week when he stopped and pulled a Makarov from his holster. Widening his stance and bending slightly at the knees as he'd been taught, he took a two-handed grip on the gun and pointed it through the window. 'Stop or I shoot!'

Koval leaned out of the window. 'We are stopped, that's the problem.'

'What are you doing here?' the young guard demanded.

'I wish I knew,' said Koval. 'We're supposed to be on stage for an all-night gig in Kirovograd, but we're lost.'

'You're a rock group?' the guard asked.

'Maria and the Freedom Fighters,' said Koval. 'This is our lead singer.' Maria smiled at him.

The guard put his gun back in his holster and fastened down the flap. 'Pleased to meet you,' he said. 'My name's Mikhail. I play the guitar, but not very well.'

'Good to meet you, Mikhail,' said Koval, stretching his arm through the opened window to shake the guard's hand. 'How the hell do I get to Kirovograd?'

'Drive back down this road until you meet the main road, turn left and carry straight on. Kirovograd is signposted. It's about 140 kilometres from here.'

'Thanks, Mikhail. Keep on practising.'

'Before you go . . .'

'Yes?'

The guard glanced round. 'Do you have a cigarette?'

Koval reached inside the glove compartment, took out a packet of Stolichny, and handed it to the guard. 'Keep them.'

As Koval reversed and turned, the guard waved. 'Peace!'

Stepaniak followed Hurenko, Muratov and Krasin from the battalion barracks. Muratov led them along a narrow concrete path with white-painted borders that had been cleared of snow and ice. 'Don't step off the path,' he smirked. 'There may be mines out there.' By now Stepaniak didn't know whether there were mines or whether the warning was yet more disinformation.

The path led to another tubular steel gate in a wire mesh fence topped by strands of barbed wire. Hurenko unlocked the gate and locked it again behind them. They continued along the path until they came to a snow-covered mound. Stepaniak stepped back onto a ventilation grid so that Hurenko could reach a yellow tin box fixed to the camouflage-painted front of the bunker. Hurenko took a telephone handset from the box and said, 'Lieutenant Colonel Hurenko here. I'm coming down with Colonel Muratov and two visitors.'

Hurenko turned the red wheel at the centre of the bunker door and pulled the door open. 'The command bunker, gentlemen.' And not a lock in sight, Stepaniak thought, apart from the gate, and a wire cutter would open the mesh fence on either side of the gate within seconds. It didn't need a Spetsnaz battalion, only a boy scout troop, to effect entry.

To Stepaniak's eyes the missile control room was something out of a 1950s American science fiction movie, but in institutional green and grey instead of black and white. Steel cabinets and giant consoles that used valves instead of microchips lined most of the walls. The two control panels, one in the centre of the room and the other at the far end, employed heavy switches and buttons. An LCD digital screen, like the one at the paediatric hospital updating appointments, was positioned above each control panel. Even the telephones by the panels would have been less conspicuous in a museum than in a nuclear missile control room. Stepaniak saw nothing resembling a modern computer: electromagnetic rather than electronic technology ruled here. Could this room, and others like it, really obliterate Western civilization?

A wiry, crew cut man rose from the seat behind the central console and saluted. 'Major Nikolayev is in charge of the Red Shift launch detachment,' Hurenko said, 'and Lieutenant Kovshov is Second Launch Officer.' An eager young man stood to attention beside his console, in front of the red battalion flag with its gold star and gold lettering, that provided the only colour amid the drabness.

Krasin repeated his briefing to the two officers and added, 'Shortly after Lieutenant Colonel Hurenko makes the telephone call to the Ukrainian Television Centre from here, the power supply to your control panels will be cut. Don't be alarmed. Just follow Lieutenant Colonel Hurenko's instructions.'

Hurenko stayed in the bunker. When Stepaniak emerged into the cold night air, a grey wash was beginning to permeate the eastern sky. If Koval had followed them, he must surely be in range. Stepaniak took a chance. 'Colonel, your briefing hasn't answered my question: why should the West be panicked into supporting our action when Moscow controls the unblocking and launch codes to fire these missiles?'

Krasin turned to him. Blanched by moonlight, the gaunt face below the bald-topped dome head appeared ghoulish. 'It's not only the West that believes a sequence of codes generated from Moscow has to appear on each of those screens down there before Nikolayev's ten missiles can be fired. Everybody except Hurenko in the Missile Battalion believes it too. But your analysis is quite correct. It will need more than a telephone call from Hurenko to terrify NATO into supporting an invasion of Ukraine.'

'What will?'

Krasin bared his teeth in a smile that sent shivers down Stepaniak's spine. 'Follow Colonel Muratov. We'll show you.'

THIRTY NINE

It was cold in the van with the engine switched off. Melnik rubbed his hands together. The operation had succeeded: Krasin's words had reached the van parked off the approach road to the missile field and were trapped on magnetic tape. Melnik switched off the recorder. 'OK, Les, let's go,' he said. 'Full speed for Kiev.'

'Wait!' Maria was aghast. 'What about Taras?'

'He's an experienced undercover agent,' Melnik said. 'He can look after himself.'

Don't worry, Stepaniak had said, winking at Maria, nothing can go wrong. But she knew how frightened he was, and so she hugged him, kissed him on the lips, and whispered, Thank you, Taras. May God protect you. She wished she'd said more. Yaro repeated his assurance that Taras wouldn't be in there more than half an hour. That was over seven hours ago. 'But we promised him! Yaro, you promised to be close by, ready to help if anything went wrong.'

'Marusia, my Marusia,' Melnik soothed. 'Things have changed.'

'I'm not your Marusia! You gave Taras your word.'

'For God's sake, grow up,' Melnik snapped. 'Once the invasion starts, Ukraine will stand no chance of stopping it. Think of all your father has worked and suffered for. Think of over thirty million Ukrainians back under the Russian yoke. This is the first realistic chance in its history that Ukraine has had to become an independent nation. Are you prepared to risk all that for one man who's spent his whole life betraying the trust of Ukrainians?'

'Taras has changed,' Maria said.

'What do you want us to do? Charge in there and commit suicide? Then who will warn the West about the planned invasion?'

'We gave him our word,' Maria persisted. 'He only went to see Krasin because he trusted our word.'

'We're wasting time,' Melnik said. 'Les, do you want me to take a turn at driving?'

Father Tanyuk reached over and took the keys out of the ignition. 'Yaro,' he said, 'stop and think what you're doing.'

'I know exactly what I'm doing, Father. I'm trying to save the Ukrainian nation.'

'Do you want to become like the rulers you despised? Do you want to build a state based on deceit, just like the Soviet state? Give your word and then break it because you decide it's in the national interest?'

Irritation edged Melnik's voice. 'Father, put things into perspective. The interests of the nation are more important than the interests of one person.'

'Yaro, a nation is nothing if it isn't a people bonded by trust. Break that bond and you have no nation, whatever language its people have in common.'

Koval took back the keys from the priest. 'I'm not interested in philosophy or morals, Father. But we still don't know how and when Krasin plans to trigger the invasion. I vote we wait until we find that out before leaving. If Taras can get to us by then, that solves all our problems.'

The fear began in his groin. It rose up his spine and it drained the strength from his legs as he trudged behind Muratov and in front of Krasin along a narrow path. They came to one of the guard trenches that snaked around the launch complex, where panicking young conscripts would be butchered by salvoes of 5.45s fired by battle-hardened Spetsnaz paratroopers. With a shudder Stepaniak recalled that day on the military academy firing range: the recoil from an AKS-74 that he was using threw the gun off target and a 5.45 tumbler bullet hit a fellow trainee near the elbow; it ripped off his arm and he died through loss of blood. Stepaniak paused and looked down at the concrete-block lining of the guard trench. Soon it would be running with the blood of young boys. And not only the young conscripts. Krasin would not allow any of this battalion to remain alive as potential witnesses against him. Nor would he let Stepaniak live. If Maria and the others were out there, they'd surely recorded all the evidence they needed and they'd be waiting for him. If they weren't . . . If they weren't, he must find a way of telling the West what Krasin and his co-conspirators planned. With only two men near him this was his best opportunity to escape. The fear turned his arms and his legs to jelly. He forced himself to imagine Marchenkov's torture. A fate like that awaited him if he failed to take any action. He had nothing to lose, but he did have a chance now to prevent the invasion and save his own life.

He sneezed. He took out a large handkerchief and blew his nose with his left hand while slipping his right hand inside his jacket. He pulled the gun from its shoulder holster. 'That's far enough, Muratov,' he said, pointing the semiautomatic pistol at Krasin's chest. He released the safety lever and pulled back the bolt.

'Both of you, raise your hands and make no noise.' He stepped back off the path. 'Muratov, down here, next to Krasin.' He kept his gun on Krasin.

'The mines!' Muratov shouted.

Stepaniak stopped. 'Pull a stunt like that again and I'll blow your head off.'

Muratov raised his hands and walked back down the path towards Krasin. Krasin hadn't moved, not even to raise his hands.

'You heard me, raise your hands above your head,' Stepaniak ordered. 'Now, with your right hand, both of you slowly remove your guns.'

Krasin laughed. 'You've been watching too many movies. I don't carry a gun.'

'Neither do I,' Muratov said.

Stepaniak thought that Muratov was probably telling the truth. He never knew when Krasin was telling the truth. 'This is what we're going to do. We're going to act naturally. We're going to walk back to the jeep, Muratov in front, Krasin next, and me behind with this gun in my pocket pointing at Krasin's back.

We're going to get in the jeep and drive to the Volga. Krasin will drive the jeep and then the Volga. You, Muratov, will be in the front passenger seat. We'll leave the missile field and you, Muratov, will clear us through all the gates. Any attempt from either of you to give the game away and I'll shoot. Now, start walking.'

Krasin still hadn't moved.

'I said walk!'

Krasin said nothing, but he stared at Stepaniak. Muratov stopped and watched them both.

'Do you want me to shoot you?' Stepaniak prayed it wouldn't come to that. One shot would bring the guards running.

Still Krasin said nothing. Then, moving slowly and purposefully, he walked towards Stepaniak, fixing him with those grey eyes.

Stepaniak put up his left hand and changed to a two-handed grip to prevent the gun trembling. 'Stop or I'll shoot!'

Krasin stopped within a metre of him. Slowly he raised his hands, pulling up the bottom of his black polo neck sweater to reveal his bare torso. With his right hand he tapped his heart. 'Here.' Then he tapped the centre of his forehead. 'Or here.'

Stepaniak's heart pounded. He tried to avoid the fearless eyes that stared into him.

With a sudden feint to his right, Krasin chopped the edge of his left hand down on Stepaniak's right wrist. Stepaniak screamed with pain and the gun clattered onto the concrete path. Krasin put his foot on it, and then bent down and picked it up. He pushed back the safety lever and tossed the gun to Muratov.

'God, you took a risk,' Muratov said.

'Not really,' Krasin replied. 'Let me tell you about friend Stepaniak. Give him a cardboard target and he's a reasonable marksman. Give him a real live target and he hasn't the balls to shoot in cold blood. He was graded unsuitable for wet jobs. Fortunately for him he could put his balls to other uses and his grandfather was a general, so he wasn't thrown out of the service.'

'I'll call the guards.'

Krasin looked at his watch. 'Don't. We haven't got time.'

'Shall I shoot him now?'

Krasin smiled. 'No. I've got another use for Stepaniak. Tear off the braid from your hat.'

Muratov frowned, but removed his hat and ripped away the double row of gold cord. Krasin grabbed Stepaniak's right wrist, which was badly bruised if not broken, and twisted it. 'Hold your wrists together,' he ordered.

Sobbing with pain and humiliation, Stepaniak held out his wrists while Krasin tied them together with the gold cord.

'We've lost time, march.'

'That's it,' said Melnik. 'There's nothing we can do for him now. Let's go.'

Maria stifled a scream. 'No!'

'We still haven't found out how and when,' Koval said.

FORTY

They stood above a manhole cover. Nearby, a larger and more elaborately secured steel cover had been cleared of snow. Its camouflage paint was intended to blend with the grass when viewed by surveillance satellite; now it stood out darkly against the twilight winter landscape.

Muratov raised the manhole cover. 'You go down first, Vanya,' Krasin said. 'You next, Stepaniak. I'll follow.'

With his wrists tied together in front of him, Stepaniak needed to sit down in the snow, swing his legs over and down into the manhole, and roll sideways to grab the top rung of the metal ladder. Pain shot through him when his right wrist took his weight. Gingerly he stepped down four rungs; he could go no further without releasing his grip on the top rung. He glanced down. The circle of light was terrifyingly small. He pushed his back hard against the rounded wall of the vertical tunnel to wedge himself while his bound hands reluctantly released their grip on the top rung and grabbed for the security of the third rung down. He lost count of the number of times he repeated this agonizing operation, not daring to look down again until his groping left foot touched concrete and his throbbing wrists dropped limply in front of him.

He blinked in the unreal fluorescent light. Faded notices warning against hazards, from inflammable fuels to radioactivity, curled on three concrete-block walls of a maintenance bay. In place of the fourth wall, a short passage led to the lower part of a huge white cylinder that ended in a flared exhaust nozzle. Two men in blue coveralls with identity tags on their chests looked up from a workbench; one held a screwdriver, the other had a cigarette dangling from his lips.

'This is an intruder,' Muratov said. 'He needn't concern you.'

Muratov's flat, expressionless face frightened Stepaniak. He backed away and put up his bound hands to protect his head, but Muratov's fist sank into his solar plexus, doubling him up in pain. He staggered back into the wall and his protesting legs gave up the struggle. He slithered down the wall until his bottom hit the hard concrete floor. Like a marionette whose strings had been cut, he slumped there, lacking the will to move, hoping that if he stayed still they wouldn't inflict any more pain on him.

Krasin jumped down the last two rungs and joined Muratov, who had returned his attention to the men in coveralls. 'This is Colonel Leskov who is in overall command of the operation. Colonel, permit me to introduce you to Senior Engineer Chestnoy and Senior Engineer Smolyakov from the Dnepropetrovsk Missile Development and Production Centre. The troops think that they're here on routine maintenance.'

Krasin glared at Smolyakov, who removed the cigarette, threw it on the concrete floor, and ground it out with the heel of his boot. 'Haven't you completed the job yet?'

'The missile's been retargeted and it's in a launch-ready configuration,' Chestnoy said defensively.

'The bypass?'

Chestnoy pointed his screwdriver at a large metal box fixed to one wall. Its cover had been removed, and wires in plastic sleeves of different colours fanned out from junctions and terminals before converging into three thick cables and one thin one. The thin cable and a thick one joined other cables and flexible pipes trailing down the passage to the missile. Another cable disappeared into a pipe projecting from the wall. The third, and newest, cable led to a console on the workbench. 'We've wired up this console to the junction box and to the missile. Pull this green lever' – as he did so a row of green indicator lights flashed on – 'and all the launch systems are powered up directly through here, cutting out the consoles in the command bunker and bypassing the blocking mechanisms.' He flipped the switch back and the lights went out. 'If you pull this red lever when the lights are on, the missile launches. It's crude, but it serves its purpose.'

'What about the warheads?'

'The warheads will arm automatically when the independent re-entry vehicles separate from the missile and attain a critical descent velocity.'

'Flight time to target?'

'Just as I told Vladimir Kirillovich Sedykh, approximately eighteen minutes.'

'Good,' said Krasin, rubbing his hands together, 'we're ready to go.'

'Not quite,' Chestnoy said. 'We've still to complete wiring up the console to the explosive bolts on the hatch.'

Krasin frowned. 'How long will that take?'

Chestnoy shrugged. 'Half an hour, an hour at most.'

'Are you certain?'

'More certain than my wage packet.'

'You needn't worry about your wage packet after this operation. You'll be set up for life.'

Stepaniak knew what that meant for these poor devils.

'What are we going to do with him?' Muratov asked, nodding in the direction of Stepaniak, crumpled into a foetal position by a wall.

Stepaniak's right wrist was swelling and the cord bit deeper and deeper, causing excruciating pain.

'We're going to take him back to the battalion HQ and release him.'

'Release the bastard!'

Krasin smiled. 'And when the gutless little rat runs for freedom, we'll use him for target practice with an AKS-74. I'll phone his statement through to the Ukrainian Television Centre from your office. In the panic they won't know it isn't him speaking. After the Spetsnaz overrun the battalion and find his body, it will prove Bondar's complicity in the nuclear missile seizure.'

It was his body they were talking about. Krasin intended to use his dead body to destroy Roman Bondar's good name. He was beneath Krasin's contempt. And why not? He'd led an utterly worthless life. He'd failed at the one decent thing he'd tried to do. If only . . . There were too many 'if onlys'. Was Maria in the van listening to this humiliation? Did she, too, despise his cowardice? If only he'd told her what he felt for her before he drove off in Vasyl's car she might not think so badly of him. No. That was typically selfish, just like his mother, always wanting to be loved, never giving love. What had he ever given Maria? If only . . . If only he'd possessed a fraction of her selflessness, her faith, her courage. But it was too late now. The only good to come out of this would be Krasin's words recorded on tape that Maria could use to prevent the invasion – *if* Koval had followed him to Pervomaysk.

Krasin looked at his watch. '05:37. Right,' he said to the two engineers, 'you will launch the missile at 07:05.'

'We were told 07:05 tomorrow,' Smolyakov protested. He appealed to Muratov. 'That's right, isn't it, Colonel?'

'Launch has been brought forward,' Krasin said. 'Blame him.' He turned to Stepaniak. 'Do you think I swallowed all that concern of yours about Bondar's statement lacking credibility? You deduced correctly that a defection of an SRF battalion wasn't enough to panic the West into supporting Operation Snowstorm, but you were rather too anxious to find out what else we planned. Now you know.' His lips pulled back from his teeth in that intimidating smile Stepaniak had first seen at GRU headquarters. 'Hurenko will demonstrate that Ukraine is able and willing to go nuclear to defend its territorial claims by firing a missile at a target in Russia.'

All Stepaniak could do was shake his head and say, 'You're insane.'

Krasin's smile froze. He stabbed his index finger at Stepaniak's hunched body.'*You* are directly responsible for the detonation of six nuclear warheads. By tomorrow the commander of the Zemlya Frantsa Iosifa anti-missile attack station would have been given a confidential briefing on the trajectory of the missile; he would have shot it down over the Barents Sea. Thanks to you, we've only enough time to bring forward Operation Snowstorm by twenty-four hours.'

A muscle in Muratov's left cheek twitched. His eyes signalled Krasin to follow him out of earshot of Stepaniak and the engineers. 'Kolya, can't you delay long enough to brief the anti-missile station?'

Krasin shook his head. 'We don't know who Stepaniak has betrayed us to. The stakes are too high. We daren't risk any delay.'

'Not even to ensure the missile is shot down?'

'Don't worry, the target's a small island in the Arctic Ocean and there won't be much collateral damage, but the timing of Operation Snowstorm is vital. It must begin while Ukrainian soldiers are having breakfast and the American President is asleep.'

'Go! For Christ's sake, go!' Melnik shouted.

'Go where?' Koval asked.

'We've got to contact the American President. Drive to the nearest village!' Melnik yelled.

'Do you think you can just walk into a peasant's shack, pick up a telephone, and tell the American President that a Russian colonel is about to launch a nuclear missile from Ukraine at Russian territory. We've got to get a connection to Kiev. We've got to authenticate the tape recording, we've got . . .'

'How long will it take us to get to Kirovograd?' Father Tanyuk asked.

Koval's voice was dead. 'We've an hour and a quarter before the missile is fired. We haven't time to contact anyone who matters, still less convince them. And once that missile is fired and the Russian invasion has started, it'll be too late.'

Maria said quietly, 'Taras knows that.'

One engineer was unspooling brown cable while his colleague led the free end towards the tunnel.

Stepaniak was back on the balcony, watching the sunset emit a fiery red glow between the apartment blocks that lined Uritskogo Street. He saw Maria's sacrificial white body and Toli's cancer-ridden thyroid.

He pushed himself to his feet and shouted, 'If you can hear me, Marusia, this is for you – and for Toli! Tell your God not to blink.' He pulled the green lever on the console.

Krasin spun round. He was less than ten metres away. His eyes fixed Stepaniak as he tensed himself to spring. This time Stepaniak held his stare. He even smiled as his bound hands pulled the red lever next to the row of glowing green lights.

For a moment nothing happened. Four men froze, as though part of a tableau, gazing down the passage with expressions ranging from disbelief to fear. Stepaniak watched with the relief of one who has shed the burden of a lifetime.

The white cylinder rumbled and clouds of dense white smoke shot from the exhaust nozzle, billowing out and up the passage to fill the maintenance bay with a white mist. The cylinder roared and a dazzling white tongue leapt from the nozzle, so bright that it shone through the mist. The flame-belching cylinder rose slowly until its nose cone hit the closed silo hatch. It juddered violently and burst apart into an expanding ball of fire.

Maria grabbed the arm of the priest. The deafening explosion from the loudspeaker behind them cut to silence. A finger of fire leapt from the forest, and then an explosion, like the loudspeaker's but muffled and reverberating, shook the van.

Maria's ashen face turned to the priest, tears streaming from her eyes. His eyes were closed and his lips were moving. 'Remember Your servant, Taras, O Lord, because of Your goodness, and forgive all the sins he committed in life, for no one is sinless but You. Grant him, O Lord, rest among the saints, where there is no pain, no sorrow, no mourning, but only life without end.'

'Amen,' she whispered.

EPILOGUE

Missile explodes at Ukrainian nuclear base

Russian President says all nuclear weapons to be dismantled

By Jonathan Smythe in Moscow **and Chrystia Lesyna** in Kiev

A nuclear catastrophe was narrowly averted yesterday when a multiple-warheaded missile exploded in its silo at a former Soviet missile base in Ukraine.

Three Russian army officers and two civilian engineers are believed to have died in the blast which ripped through the underground installation, but the SS-19 intercontinental ballistic missile's six nuclear warheads did not detonate and were recovered intact.

"We can only thank God that a greater tragedy did not take place," said the Russian President. The President has accepted the resignation of General Yuri Churbanov, who had overall responsibility for nuclear weapons of the former Soviet Army. Other resignations from the top ranks of the Army and the defence industry are believed to be imminent, according to sources in Moscow and Kiev.

The Russian President said the missile was accidentally fired during routine maintenance procedures at the Pervomaysk missile field, hidden in a forest 160 miles south of the Ukrainian capital of Kiev. The nuclear warheads did not detonate because the missile exploded before the automatic warhead arming process was completed. Soviet military leaders had previously assured the West there was no danger of a missile being fired by accident or falling into the wrong hands because of a complex "fail-safe" procedure similar to that in the United States which requires presidential authorization for launch.

Immediately following the accident the Russian President issued a decree ordering all nuclear weapons of the former Soviet Union, including those based in Russia, to be taken off alert status prior to being dismantled. In a statement broadcast simultaneously on Russian and Ukrainian television, he said he had taken the decision because the accident revealed the enormous risks of keeping such weapons of mass destruction. Russia and the other former Soviet republics no longer faced any threat from the West and had no disputes with each other that could not be settled by negotiation, he said.

He invited the Presidents of Ukraine and Kazakhstan each to nominate one third of the members of a special commission who will oversee the destruction of the vast nuclear arsenal of the former Soviet Union. He also invited them to put aside once and for all the enmities between their peoples that were based on past injustices and join him in working for a worldwide ban on all nuclear weapons. "Let us now work together for the future, to save the planet for our children and our children's children."

A State Department spokesman in Washington said last night the accident had "confirmed our worst fears". He welcomed the Russian President's disarmament statement, but declined to say if the United States would take reciprocal measures. Senior intelligence sources in both Britain and the United States have warned for some time of the potential danger of nuclear weapons in the former Soviet republics falling into the wrong hands or being used by one republic to threaten another in the bitter quarrels that have arisen since the collapse of the USSR.

In Kiev last night, Maria Bondar, daughter of the ailing Ukrainian nationalist leader Roman Bondar, said she was at Pervomaysk at the time of the explosion. After ascertaining its cause, she spoke on the telephone to the Russian President. She fully endorsed his subsequent statement and called upon the Ukrainian President to work with the Russian President for peace between their two nations. "Let this be the memorial to those who died in this tragedy," she said.